## Oh, God help me, I'm lost to her.

Derek crushed his body against hers, squeezing his eyes shut and trying to sort out his emotions. He could feel the beating of her heart, could feel his own. He grasped a fistful of her flowing hair and gently pulled her head back so he could look down into her face.

Cassandra, intoxicated by the love-potion, was eager, clutching him with unbridled passion. He picked her up and she wrapped her legs around his waist. Derek took her mouth again, his palms molding her hips. He collapsed on the bed with her, his loins burning with need, his heart thundering.

"I shouldn't be doing this, not now," he breathed out hoarsely. "You're going to hate me in the morning."

"No, I could never hate you, not when you make me feel like this."

She was untouched, pure, he knew that for sure now, and he was glad. He wanted to be the first; he wanted to be the only man to have her.

# *White Rose*

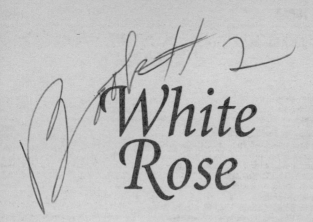

# White Rose

*by*

## Linda Ladd

A TOPAZ BOOK

**TOPAZ**
Published by the Penguin Group
Penguin Books USA Inc., 375 Hudson Street,
New York, New York 10014, U.S.A.
Penguin Books Ltd, 27 Wrights Lane,
London W8 5TZ, England
Penguin Books Australia Ltd, Ringwood,
Victoria, Australia
Penguin Books Canada Ltd, 10 Alcorn Avenue,
Toronto, Ontario, Canada M4V 3B2
Penguin Books (N.Z.) Ltd, 182–190 Wairau Road,
Auckland 10, New Zealand

Penguin Books Ltd, Registered Offices:
Harmondsworth, Middlesex, England

First published by Topaz, an imprint of Dutton Signet,
a division of Penguin Books USA Inc.

First Printing, June, 1994
10  9  8  7  6  5  4  3  2  1

 Topaz is a trademark of New American Library,
a division of Penguin Books USA Inc.

Printed in the United States of America

*White Rose* is dedicated to Audrey LaFehr—an editor to die for. Thanks for being so nice.

And to Nancy (Killer at the Net) Baker and Ann Mary (Never Miss a Shot) Gilbert—a doubles team to reckon with.

And to my good friends, Linda Lang Bartell and Judith E. French—two fantastic writers who stand by me through thick and thin.

And to another terrific writer, my good buddy and sidekick, Lori Copeland, for showing me the ropes and making me laugh.

# Chapter 1

Cold rain drummed rhythmically atop the tin roof of the Sheldon Brothers Mercantile Store, but from where Derek Courtland crouched in the shadows of the alley running alongside its dark display window, he was barely aware of the spattering drops soaking his broad shoulders. Luckily, the black cavalry hat pulled low over his brow and the navy-blue military overcoat that his Yankee jailors had given to him when he had been transferred from a federal prison ship in New York Harbor to the Old Penitentiary in Washington, D.C., kept him both warm and dry.

But the bad weather was the least of his problems. At the moment his sole concern was the rowdy tavern just across the street from his hiding place.

Male patrons had been arriving alone and in groups since before nightfall. Now, as the tinny chords of a player piano jangled out into the quiet night, a multitude of shadows flitted across the two elaborately etched plate-glass windows flanking the front entrance.

Courtland's intense black eyes sharpened as a man lurched through the swinging doors and staggered across the street toward him. Pressing his back against the brick wall, he watched the drunk weave past the mouth of the alley, then stumble off down the planked sidewalk. An off-key, whistled rendition of "Yankee Doodle Dandy" pierced the pattering drizzle until the inebriated man turned the corner and disappeared from view.

Returning his full attention to the boisterous tavern, Courtland narrowed his eyes and strained to read the ornately lettered red sign that creaked in the wind above the front door. Unable to make out the name of the saloon in the darkness, he inched up behind a barrel set at the corner of the building to catch the rainwater gushing down the roof gutters. From his new vantage point, he could see the flower painted on the swaying board. A white rose. Thank God. After searching all night, he had finally found his rendezvous point.

His Confederate contact, a young woman named Cassandra Delaney, was supposed to meet him inside the White Rose Tavern, and he just hoped to the devil she hadn't gotten cold feet and fled the place. For nearly twenty-four hours he had been on the move without food or rest, and he was exhausted from lack of sleep. Worse than that, every bluebelly north of Richmond was out scouring the countryside for him. He was damn lucky to have evaded recapture for as long as he had.

Frowning blackly, he stared at the bustling saloon. The Delaney woman had better have one hell of a good plan to get him out of the United States and back aboard his ship. He was a seaman, not a soldier, and he had been stranded on land too long this time. He hungered incessantly for the clean, salty tang of the sea and the gentle sway of the *Mamu*'s decks beneath his feet.

Nervously fingering the butt of the ivory-handled derringer stuck in his belt, he considered his next move. Although his long coat would conceal his weapon, he didn't like the idea of blithely traipsing into a crowded public taproom. Hell, he was a wanted man, and his Australian accent would give him away the first time he opened his mouth.

Swamped with frustration, he clenched his teeth and rubbed the thick black stubble covering his chin and jaw. Why the devil had he allowed himself to get involved in such a dangerous predicament in the first place? Even more annoying was the fact that Cassandra Delaney had engineered his escape using his younger sister, Lily, as his primary accomplice.

Now Lily was missing and had been since they had been forced to separate when they had run into a federal roadblock the previous night. His only hope was that she and Kapi and Rigi, the young aboriginal twins she had brought with her from their home in Melbourne, had already found their way to the White Rose. The youngsters were born hunters and trackers with an uncanny sense of direction. Surely they would have no trouble leading Lily into Fredericksburg.

Dammit, he thought furiously, he should never have gotten mixed up in the bloody American rebellion in the first place. But if he hadn't run the *Mamu* through the Union blockade so many times during the past two years, he wouldn't have the tidy little fortune awaiting him in a Nassau bank. His life had been on a steady keel, free and easy, until the unlucky day that Lily had decided to come to the United States to find him. Unfortunately, she had run smack-dab into a federal agent named Harte Delaney who had used her as bait to lure Derek into a Yankee trap.

Derek shook all thoughts of his initial capture out of his mind. Right now he had to concentrate on finding Lily and getting them both the hell out of the United States and back to Melbourne where they belonged.

Fortifying his resolve, he heaved a deep breath and pulled his collar up to shield his face. He stepped down off the board-planked sidewalk, his tall black boots sinking ankle deep in the filthy mire clogging the unpaved street. Glancing up and down the dark storefronts, he was encouraged that nothing was stirring except the shadow figures moving across the blazing windows of the White Rose.

Swinging saloon doors marked the portal, and he stopped in front of them, realizing the place was even more packed with people than he had first thought. *A drunken crowd just might work to my advantage, though,* he thought, *because men swilling whiskey and fondling women won't be quite so apt to notice a stranger.*

Entering the place was damn risky, but there was a foolproof way he could find out what awaited him inside. He closed his fingers tightly over the top of the swinging door and waited for the strange sixth sense that he had inherited from his grandmother to trigger a warning of impending disaster. No prickle of foreboding swept down his spine, but he was cautious enough to keep his right hand near his gun as he pushed through the saloon doors. He stepped inside, then froze in his footsteps.

At least a dozen Yankee soldiers leaned indolently against the polished mahogany bar. Dressed in their dark blue uniforms adorned with shiny brass buttons, they were well armed with federal-issue Colt revolvers. While he watched, they clinked beer mugs and shouted a toast to their president, a man by the name of Abraham Lincoln. To his relief, no one paid heed to his arrival, and it didn't take him long to realize why. Six scantily attired young women were dancing wildly on a dais at the far end of the room. Extraordinarily well endowed, the girls were displaying enough naked leg and bosom to entice any red-blooded man's undivided attention, including his own.

As they pranced and cavorted and flapped their frilly white petticoats, Derek recognized the dance as a rather provincial version of the French cancan.

He had seen the genuine production on several occasions when he had set the crew of the *Mamu* loose in the streets of Paris, and while the buxom American young ladies onstage were bouncing and gyrating and giving the performance their best effort, they couldn't compare to the lovely, long-legged Parisiennes.

However, the soldiers remained enthralled enough with the energetic show for Derek to make his way unseen toward a less crowded spot near the door. Three scarred-up chairs surrounded a green-baize-topped table, and he eased down in the one that kept his back to the wall.

Nerves knotted tight with tension, he slowly scanned the jam-packed room. According to Lily, Cassandra Delaney was a staunch southern patriot who had been spying on her own brother, Harte Delaney, for the duration of the fighting. Though he was well accustomed to the American Civil War and the evil deeds spawned on both sides, Derek did not envy the man such a treacherous sister.

Now he wasn't so sure of her prowess as a secret agent, either. Meeting him in a public place overflowing with enemy soldiers wasn't exactly a brilliant idea. He had met her once under even more bizarre circumstances when she had waltzed into his prison cell wearing a fake beard and the baggy attire of a male undertaker. She had shoved a loaded derringer into his hands, then blithely informed him that she was going to spring him from jail. She had shown guts, and her disguise had been good enough that all he could hope to recognize again were her eyes. In the flickering candlelight of the prison they had glinted pure silvery blue, a beautiful shade that was unique enough for him to identify without trouble.

Derek's hand tightened around his pistol as a young boy shuffled toward his table. Big-boned and sandy-haired, the youth looked about seventeen— too young to cause Derek much concern. When he spoke, he avoided eye contact.

"Want a drink, mister? Or maybe some vittles?"

"Beer's good enough."

While the boy ambled off, Derek studied the people in the room. Onstage, the girls whipped their skirts over their heads then pivoted to reveal shapely, pantalet-clad bottoms. The audience roared with raucous hoots and shrill catcalls. At the far end of the bar a narrow staircase rose to the second floor, and Derek's eyes settled on the balustraded upper balcony. He hoped to God that Lily and the boys were already up there, safe and sound and waiting for him.

Lily should never have been involved in his jailbreak, and she wouldn't have been if he had kept in closer contact with his family during the last few years. Had Derek known about his father's death and returned to Australia, Lily wouldn't have come to America searching for him and he wouldn't be slinking through enemy territory with half of General Grant's army out gunning for him.

As his gaze circuited the room for the third time, he watched a saloon girl grab the arm of a Yankee

wearing sergeant stripes on his sleeve and entice
him up the stairs with a flirtatious smile. The man
trotted along in her wake, his ruddy, bewhiskered
jowls wreathed with an eager grin. The White Rose
offered more than whiskey and poker to weary soldiers. Hell, no wonder the place did such a boom-
ing business.

When the piano finally twanged its last discordant
notes, the cancan dancers skipped nimbly down the
stage steps and melted into the crowd of wildly
cheering admirers. Derek examined them closely,
hoping to detect some mannerism that might identify Cassandra Delaney. There was nothing remotely
familiar about any of them.

An excited commotion brought his attention back
to the bar, and he found most of the Yankees watching a woman who had appeared at the top of the
stairs. Derek stared at the beautiful redhead with
the same awe the other men were exhibiting. Her
hair wasn't just red—it was the warm, gleaming
color of flames reflected in polished copper. Pearl-
studded hairpins and black satin ribbons held her
thick, luxurious coils atop her head, and curling ten-
drils framed her face and wisped gently around her
slender nape. She wore a tight-fitting turquoise silk
gown cinched snugly around her tiny waist and
caught up with black bows to reveal long shapely
legs provocatively encased in black lace stockings.

As she started down the steps trailing a slender
hand along the banister, Derek's eyes riveted on the
low-plunging, scalloped bodice where a glimpse of

creamy flesh tantalized his imagination. The gown would tempt a monk to carnal sin, and the hard stirrings in Derek's loins indicated that he was not immune. He couldn't take his eyes off the fiery-haired beauty.

When she stopped at the bottom of the steps, she ignored the interest she had incited among the patrons. When her wandering gaze found Derek's unwavering stare, their eyes burned together for one white-hot instant before she glanced away. A moment later she began to wend her way across the crowded floor to him. The closer she came, the better she looked, and the more Derek hoped the gorgeous woman would turn out to be Cassandra Delaney. When she reached his table, she smiled down at him out of golden-lashed, silver-blue eyes.

"Want some company, stranger?"

As she spoke, she traced a long, scarlet-painted nail down through the thick black beard covering his cheek. When her fingertip parted his lower lip, pure, unadulterated, raw lust jolted alive and exploded through his blood like a ball of fire.

"You betcha," he muttered hoarsely, thinking Cassandra Delaney had certainly perfected the art of enticing men. Forcibly dragging his admiring eyes away from her beautiful face and flawless ivory skin, he glanced warily toward the bar. The woman caressing his mouth could make a man forget his left from his right. Derek could not let himself be thus affected—not unless he wanted to end up dangling from a Yankee noose.

Unfortunately, just as he propped up his first line of defense against her feminine charms, Cassandra Delaney decided to slide slowly onto his lap and lock bare white arms around his neck. She smiled into his eyes, her soft curves pressing intimately against his chest. Enveloped by the sweet essence of gardenias, his masculine response surged to perilous highs. Damnation, he had been locked up away from women way too long.

"You better kiss me, Courtland."

Her whisper was husky, breathed hotly against his earlobe. Derek wasted no time obliging her. Her red lips were every bit as soft and desirable as everything else about her, and he held her tightly, his fist snarled in her hair as he enjoyed the first woman he had touched since before Harte Delaney had thrown him into prison.

"That's enough," she murmured a moment later, tearing her mouth from his exploring lips. She pushed against his chest, but Derek had ideas of his own. She tasted too good, smelled too good, felt too good.

"Where's Lily?" he whispered, finding her lips again, then the soft, fragrant side of her slender throat. She didn't resist his advances and Derek pressed his mouth to the angle of her jaw.

"The Yankees got her this morning, a few miles north of here—"

Her low words set his muscles tense with dread, and Cassandra quickly leaned back and slid her fingers into the thick black waves at his temples. She smiled seductively, but her eyes were serious.

"Smile at me, and quit looking so upset. Lily's all right. They've taken her back to Washington, and Harte will take care of her once she gets there. My brother's crazy in love with her, in case you don't know."

Derek did know. And Lily was in love with him, too, despite the fact that the handsome Union officer had used her innocence to lure Derek into a trap. Cassandra moistened her full lips with the tip of her tongue, and Derek struggled for self-control.

"You're damn good at this sort of thing, darlin'," he mumbled thickly as she writhed temptingly in his arms.

"Just do exactly what I say and you'll get out of here in one piece. Now pretend you're in a hurry to get me alone upstairs."

Derek felt like laughing. "No pretense necessary, ma'am."

He thrust back his chair and stood, clamping her slender body close against his unarmed side. Well aware of the dozens of male eyes charting their progress, he pulled her toward the steps, in no way faking his eagerness to get upstairs. Cassandra was clinging to his arm and smiling up at him so suggestively that his pulse leaped and he endeavored to recall every detail Lily had mentioned about Cassandra Delaney.

If he remembered correctly, his sister had told him that the Delaney family was both wealthy and socially prominent. Cassandra's father had been heir to a shipping dynasty up north somewhere—Rhode Island, maybe. Her mother had been just as aristocratic, a blueblood from the state of Virginia. A very patrician set of forebears indeed but on opposite sides of this damnable war between the states. And with that kind of background, just where the devil had Cassandra Delaney learned to play the role of a whore so well?

# Chapter 2

More than pleased to bid farewell to the Yankee menace enjoying themselves in the taproom, Derek followed the enticing sway of Cassandra Delaney's slim hips along the second-floor banister. Midway down a different, dimly lit corridor, she retrieved a key hidden in her bodice, unlocked a door, and quickly motioned for him to precede her.

As Cassandra secured the lock behind them, Derek surveyed his surroundings with some surprise. The large bedchamber was furnished sparingly but with considerable elegance. The elaborately carved walnut four-poster bed and matching wardrobe appeared more suited to the royal governor's mansion in Melbourne than the upper floor of a tavern. An oval mirror, ornately framed in gold and draped with flowing forest-green brocade, hung above a marble-topped dressing table positioned between two tall, lace-curtained windows.

Derek walked across the room and lifted a panel of the frilled ivory lace, relieved to see both windows opened onto a balcony that overlooked the front street. He always made a habit of checking for an escape hatch, just in case something went wrong.

"Where the devil have you been?"

Shocked by the fury in Cassandra's voice, not to mention her use of profanity, Derek swung around and found his lovely companion's face flushed with rage.

"You should have been here *last* night!" she went on angrily, the flirtatious manner she had exhibited so charmingly downstairs dropping from her like an iron anchor off a frayed rope. "Now we've got Yankees patrolling every major road within fifty miles of here!"

Derek had always found women irresistible when roweled up and scratching mad, and at the moment, with her anger-pinkened face and sparkling azure eyes, Cassandra Delaney was beautiful beyond compare. Her chest was heaving beneath the flimsy silk of her plunging décolletage in a way he could not help but notice. When she saw his interest, she snatched up a black silk scarf from the bedpost and slung it around her shoulders, effectively denying him the delectable view.

"Quit staring at me like I'm some prize filly you're bidding on!" she snapped, her finely arched golden brows dipping into a hostile slant. "You're acting as if you've never laid eyes on a female before!"

Derek grinned because her observation wasn't far off the mark. "If you'll remember, Miss Delaney, I've had the misfortune of being locked up in solitary confinement for the last four months. Women do look damn good to me right now, and forgive me for saying so, but I find it a bit hard to ignore how fine you look in that particular gown. And the way you were rubbing that luscious little body of yours all over me a few minutes ago didn't help in the least."

Like a crimson tide sweeping in over a white beach, a slow wave of color rose beneath her creamy skin until her finely sculptured cheekbones burned with a deep rosy hue.

"Don't ever make the mistake of thinking I'm a loose woman, Captain Courtland. The only reason I degraded myself by donning this lewd costume was to save your neck. And I must say it's completely incomprehensible to me how you managed to lose Lily and get half the Union army on your tail when all you had to do was simply drive a wagon down here from Washington."

A spark of irritation flickered alive inside Derek. "Pardon me, *madam*"—he emphasized the word to annoy her and fully succeeded, judging by the way her full, scarlet-painted lips compressed into a thin, tight line—"maybe if you'd thought to alert us about the military checkpoints set up along the road you told us to take, we could have avoided capture. But since you didn't warn us that they'd be searching every wagon that came by, we were caught by surprise. That's how I got separated from my sister and the boys, and that's why I didn't make it here until now."

His voice dripped scorn, and Cassandra glanced

away. She hauled in a deep, frustrated breath as she spoke, and Derek's eyes were drawn against his will to her full breasts.

"I'm just worried about getting you out of here alive. It's going to be a lot more difficult now, so we'll have to be very careful how we proceed. The first thing we have to do is get out of these clothes. I've got disguises for us."

Cassandra sat down in front of the mirror. She tugged pins and ribbons from her thick, coppery locks, and Derek watched with fascination as the silky waves sifted slowly down to cover her bare shoulders.

"There's really no need to worry about Lily, you know," she said quietly. She leaned forward slightly, her silver-blue eyes capturing his gaze in the looking glass. "One of my couriers saw her when she was under escort back to Washington. The Yankees were treating her well. She's probably already been remanded back into Harte's custody."

"Maybe, but I'll feel better when I know for sure."

Without answering him, Cassandra retrieved a silver hairbrush from her drawer and pulled it slowly through her shiny hair.

"What about Kapi and Rigi?" Derek asked then. "Were they captured with Lily?"

"No. My men got to them before the Yankees did. The twins have already been taken out of Virginia by a different route. We'll meet them in Nassau, because it's too dangerous for you and the boys to travel through the South together."

"How'd you know the *Mamu*'s in Nassau?" Derek demanded in surprise.

"Confederate agents keep track of the whereabouts of our blockade runners. After Harte took you into custody, your ship returned there to a cove near the Malmora Pub. So that's where I had the boys taken."

"I'm impressed with your thoroughness," he admitted, then frowned when he thought of his sister's plight. "What makes you think Harte's going to intercede for Lily? He's going to be mad as hell when he finds out she helped me escape."

Cassandra twisted around. She looked exasperated with his question. "Well, of course he won't like it, but he loves her so much that he'll never let anything bad happen to her." She shrugged a slender shoulder. "Lily didn't want to come with us anyway. She's probably glad she got caught so she can stay with Harte. If you ask me, you better quit fretting about Lily and concern yourself with your own problems. We've got a long way to go before you're safely on the deck of your ship."

Derek wasn't sure just what to make of Cassandra Delaney, but he had to admit that she had more guts and brains than most men he had known. "I guess I owe you a debt of gratitude," he remarked with begrudging respect, but even as he spoke, he could not stop his eyes from wandering over every inch of her desirable body. "And I must say I like you better as a saloon girl than as a bearded undertaker."

"I do what I have to do, Captain Courtland. Sometimes I like it, and sometimes I don't," she answered flatly, gathering her long wavy curls in one hand while she picked up a pink ribbon.

Derek caught her drift. "Look, lady, it was your idea to break me out of jail. Now you're acting annoyed with the bother."

Cassandra finished tying her hair back at the nape, then gazed steadfastly at his reflected image. "I'm not sorry I helped you escape, Captain. What I am sorry about is that one of my men got himself caught by the Yankees last night while he was out trying to find you. He's a good friend, and now he'll probably rot in some Yankee prison camp for the duration of the war. Sorry I'm not in a very good mood, but there is a war going on, you know."

Her eyes were somber, worried about her colleague, and Derek knew how it felt to languish in a cell. "I appreciate what your people are doing for me," he said apologetically.

Cassandra picked up a linen towel from the dressing table and began to wipe off the bright red lipstick outlining her mouth. "The important thing is to get you back to your ship so that—"

An urgent knock on the door interrupted her in midsentence. Cassandra shot to her feet in alarm, and Derek pulled his gun. She warned him to silence with an outstretched palm while three short raps ensued. Two more came seconds later, and Cassandra immediately moved to unlock the door.

"That's Harry. Something's gone wrong downstairs."

The blond-haired boy who had brought Derek's beer to him earlier that evening ducked quickly into the room.

"A Union patrol just rode in!" he whispered urgently. "They're downstairs. Courtland's the one they're after, but they don't know what he looks like. All they know is that he's somewhere in this county. Johnny offered up a round of free whiskeys to give me time to warn you. They'll be coming up here any minute."

"Stall them, Harry! Tell them I've got one of their officers in my room and he doesn't want anyone to know he's up here. You know what else to say! Hurry!"

Derek was already parting the curtains with his gun barrel. On the street below, he could see six or seven horses with federal saddles tied up at the hitching rail. Soldiers were tramping down the planked sidewalks in both directions. "Is there a back way out of here?"

"Yes, but the Yankees will have it covered by the time you get down there. You'll have to stay here and hope that Harry can keep them at bay—"

"Like hell I will. I'm not sitting around here like some rabbit in a bloody trap until they put a bullet between my eyes."

"When are you going to start trusting me?" she hissed furiously as she jerked open the doors of a tall wardrobe. "I'm telling you they won't bother you if they think you're a high-ranking Union officer."

Derek scowled, thinking her plan was as stupid as it was risky. "What the hell's going to make them believe I'm a Yankee?"

"This will."

Cassandra held up an immaculately tailored dark blue jacket. Two silver oak leaves decorated the gold braided epaulets.

"Where in the bloody hell did you come up with a Yankee major's uniform?"

Cassandra slung the coat over the bedpost where it could be seen from the doorway. "I stole it from my brother's closet the last time I visited his house."

Derek stared incredulously at her. "You don't have many scruples, do you?"

"Look, Courtland, we're smack-dab in the middle of a war, in case you've forgotten. Harte would do the same thing to me if he got the chance. You had better be glad I had the wherewithal to filch Harte's coat when I got the opportunity. My lack of"—she sarcastically emphasized the next word—"*scruples* just might save your hide this very night."

Frowning, Derek parted the curtains again and found more Yankees converging on the saloon.

"Get in the bed and be quick about it!" Cassandra ordered. "There's only one reason a man would bring me up here, and if we're not doing it when they come, they're going to wonder why."

"What do you mean? Are you suggesting what I think you—"

Derek's words faltered as she yanked open the buttons securing the front of her gown. His jaw dropped a notch when she stripped the garment the rest of the way off her shoulders, then wriggled completely out of it. She stepped away from the lace and silk pooling around her ankles, then scrambled atop the high tester bed wearing only her corset and pantalets. She jerked back the velvet bedspread.

"What are you waiting for?" she cried, her breasts heaving in her agitation. "Get your clothes off!"

Derek tore his eyes off her nearly naked body. "Forget it, lady. I'll be damned if I'll get captured with my pants down. I'll take my chances with this." He held up his gun.

"Oh, quit being an idiot and use your head! This is our only chance! Take off your coat and shirt! Do it, Courtland, before you get both of us killed!"

Derek hesitated until he heard deep voices outside in the hall. Cassandra's plan didn't have a chance in hell of working, but he had little choice now. He wrestled off his coat and kicked it under the bed, then dove under the bedspread. Cassandra Delaney came up on her knees and opened his shirt with one sharp jerk. His buttons flew all over the bed.

"Get it off!" she whispered fiercely. "They're right outside!"

Derek transferred his pistol to his other hand while Cassandra nearly ripped his shirt off his back. She stuffed it under the pillow. Derek grabbed her and pulled her on top of him.

"What are you doing?" she demanded breathlessly, pushing against his chest.

Derek covered her mouth with his palm. "Now you listen, for a change. Lovers don't sit side by side in bed like Methodist missionaries. Straddle me so I can hide my gun behind you."

"I hardly think that's necessary," she sputtered angrily.

"You're going to do it anyway," he muttered, gripping her waist tightly and holding her firmly in place.

"All right," Cassandra conceded quickly, "but I want you to know that I don't like this one little bit."

"This stupid idea was yours, not mine," he reminded her, holding his gun ready as he watched the door. "Just try to look as if you're enjoying yourself. I have a reputation to uphold."

"Yes, I'm sure you do." Cassandra settled herself gingerly atop his loins as if climbing on a particularly loathsome beast. With her knees hugging his narrow waist, she blushed with embarrassment and braced her open palms on his naked chest. "I want to assure you that I'm a respectable woman, Courtland, and that under normal circumstances I wouldn't be doing anything remotely resembling this."

"Too bad for me." He shifted her bodily to a more intimate spot. He ignored her gasp of outrage. "If they don't go for this, I'll probably have to shoot my way out, so just keep down and out of my way."

Sobered, Cassandra looked down at him, her unbound hair flowing over the muscles of his chest. Derek grasped a handful of the flowing silk as someone pounded a fist against the door. He pulled her down, and she began kissing him passionately as the door was thrust open. A man sniggered.

"All right, now, feller, you's gonna hafta get yersef out from under that purty little lady."

To Derek's relief, only one young soldier had been assigned to search the room. He could hear other men clomping past the door to check out the other chambers lining the hall. Derek sat up slowly, his finger on the trigger as Cassandra slid off his legs and sat on her knees beside him. Once the Yankee saw her, he stared in open-mouthed awe at the way her breasts nearly spilled over the top of her lacy undergarments. Derek took advantage of the man's distraction.

"What's the meaning of this intrusion, Private?" he demanded harshly, trying to mask his Australian accent.

The Yankee dragged his eyes off Cassandra and appeared shocked when he saw Derek, as if he had forgotten there was a man in bed with the ravishing redhead. Then he caught sight of the uniform draped on the bedpost. His young face first paled, then reflected pure horror.

"S-sorry, sir. The boy outside done tole me who you was, but I thought he was just funnin' with me. I don't mean to be disturbin' you, but we's lookin' for a Johnny Reb who got away from his guards up north of here."

"As you can plainly see, Private, I am here alone with this young lady." Without taking his eyes off the soldier at the threshold, Derek pulled Cassandra closer and pressed a kiss against her temple. Thank God the boy was young and green. Chances were he had never dealt with any officer higher than his own corporal.

"Yes, sir, I can see that, sir. Sorry to be botherin' you. My best regards to the general on the fine job he's doin', sir." He backed out the door to join his comrades in the corridor, but his eyes shifted back to Cassandra one last time before the door closed off his view.

Derek and Cassandra remained rigid with tension as they listened to loud voices and slamming doors until the Yankees finished their search and clomped away out of earshot.

"I told you the jacket would work," Cassandra whispered, disentangling herself from his tight grip.

Derek shifted to his side and brought her back tightly against him. "Not yet. He might come back for another look at you." He grinned, sliding his left hand into her silky tresses. "Tell me, what did he mean by the remark about the general?"

Cassandra relaxed slightly. "Harry told him you were on General Grant's staff and were"—she grinned mischievously—"the general's favorite son-in-law."

Derek laughed softly, admiring her daring cleverness. Now that they were out of imminent danger, however, all he could think about was how warm and soft she felt in his embrace. When she raised her incredible silvery blue eyes, his starved senses surged out of control. Still holding his gun, he tangled his fingers in her hair and kissed her long and hard, the way he had wanted to do since the first moment he had seen her.

She struggled against his hold, but Derek wasn't ready to let her go. He possessed her sweet mouth with greedy, eager hunger until he could finally force himself to stop. The moment he did, she was out of the bed, rubbing her lips with the back of her arm, her exquisite face mottled with rage.

"Don't you ever do that again, do you hear me? So help me, if you can't treat me with respect, you can find your own way out of here!"

Derek stared at her, appalled by the way she was trembling. He had made a big mistake manhandling her. He had to have her help, and Cassandra Delaney had meant what she'd said. But, God help him, he had never wanted a woman with the intensity that he wanted her. He'd pay an emperor's ransom to have her in his arms again, for one night or one hour or even one minute.

# Chapter 3

Her entire body trembling from Derek Courtland's mind-numbing kiss, Cassandra slipped
on a silk wrapper to cover her dishabille. She paced
a few shaky footsteps away from him while she regained her dignity. She *had* been insulted by his
behavior. She *had* meant every indignant word she
had uttered. Then why was her heart throbbing out
of control? Why was her face burning like fire?

Angry at herself, she took a deep breath. Her
overreaction to his masculinity was ridiculous. The
man was obviously used to taking whatever he
wanted, including any woman who struck his fancy.
She had known he was arrogant from the beginning,
of course. Any man so devastatingly good-looking
was bound to be. Naturally she had been around
other handsome, powerful men since the war had
started, had even duped many of them into revealing
secret information on northern troop movements.
Fortunately, though, none of them had ever affected
her like Derek Courtland did. He made her feel
out of control, which was both embarrassing and

humiliating. Suddenly she was glad her mission was to get him out of the country as soon as possible.

Peering cautiously out the window, she found that the last stragglers in the Union search party were cantering out of town, headed south toward the road to Richmond. Derek Courtland had been incredibly lucky that an inexperienced, easily bullied soldier had entered their room instead of a commissioned officer. They were safe for the moment but certainly needed to get out of town before another Yankee patrol rode in.

"Look, Miss Delaney," Courtland said in his deeply accented speech. "I'm sorry if I offended you. But like I said earlier, I'm only human, and I'm attracted as hell to you. I can't help it. It's your own fault for being so beautiful."

Cassandra turned to find him much too close for comfort. He gave a sheepish shrug, then grinned, his teeth astonishingly white against his unshaved black beard. He had donned his shirt again, but the front hung loose and unbuttoned, and she quickly glanced away from the tangle of dark hair across the molded muscles of his chest. Cold chills rose on her flesh, and she angrily rubbed her arms.

"The important thing is to get out of Fredericksburg before something else goes wrong," she said briskly, chagrined at how breathless she sounded.

When he smiled as if he knew exactly how irregular her heartbeat had been since he had shown up, she knelt down to retrieve a bundle of clothing from where she had hidden it underneath the bed. She had planned to have Derek pose as an invalid, with herself masquerading as his nurse. Now, though, she realized such a ruse would never work. He was too strong and openly virile for anyone to believe he was recovering from a serious illness. His size alone was so intimidating that no matter where they went, everyone would notice him, especially women.

Annoyed by the complications that were destroying her intricate escape plans, she frowned and studied him up and down with a critical eye. "Look at you, Courtland. I bet you've never been sick a day in your life, have you?"

Derek looked surprised, then quirked a dark brow. "Actually, I am rather fit." He presented his slow, engaging grin. "But I did suffer a bit of the croup when I was a lad, if that'll make you feel better."

"We are not playing a parlor game here, Captain," she reminded him in icy tones. "We could be shot crossing the Potomac. I daresay you wouldn't find that eventuality particularly amusing."

"Not particularly, I daresay." He grinned, unperturbed by her ire. "Didn't Lily and I already cross the Potomac River on our way down here?"

"Yes, but we're going to have to ford it again in order to get back into Maryland."

"Why the hell are we heading north when we're so close to Confederate lines?"

"Because every Yankee in Virginia knows you're in this vicinity and they'll all be expecting you to head south. Nobody will expect you to be stupid enough to turn around and go back into Yankee territory where you could be captured and hanged for treason."

"Yeah, and that sounds like a pretty damn good reason not to."

"Exactly, and that's why we're going to do it. I declare, Courtland, don't you have any experience at evading capture?"

"I always managed to maintain my freedom until the day your brother used my sister to get to me."

"Harte's a very good spy, I'll give him that much," Cassandra admitted, "but I am, too, maybe even better. So if you'll trust me and do exactly what I say, you'll be just fine."

Derek didn't look exactly convinced. "All right, as long as you don't ask me to get in bed with you again," he teased.

Cassandra shot him a scornful look. "Not in your lifetime, Captain Courtland."

"Fine. So where do we go from here?"

In truth, Cassandra wasn't quite sure how to proceed, now that her initial plan wouldn't work. Gazing at him, she strove to select the best course of action. If only he looked small and sickly, her job would be so much easier. "I suppose you'll have to pose as a Union officer again. Harte's uniform worked well enough tonight. You're about his size, aren't you? How tall are you?"

"Six-foot-three."

His long legs and muscular physique made him seem even taller. Furious at her continued preoccupation with his body, she riveted her concentration on the job at hand. "You'll be more believable with a wound of some sort. And that would explain why you're not off fighting with your unit."

Cassandra tapped a forefinger against her chin as she pondered the problem. "We'll have to do something about your accent, too. It really sounds quite absurd, you know, a lot more pronounced than Lily's is. I'm surprised that Yankee boy didn't suspect you right off." An idea suddenly occurred to her. "I know. We'll wrap a bandage around your neck and say you've been shot in the vocal cords."

Derek stared at her a moment, then barked a derogatory laugh. "If some Reb's bullet was that bloody true to aim, darlin', I wouldn't have much head left to worry about."

"Then we'll say someone stuck you in the neck with a bayonet," she snapped, the truth of his observation making her feel silly.

His black eyes glinted, and she knew he wanted to laugh at her again. "Pretty damned unlikely."

"Oh, what difference does it make? We'll wrap some around your head, too, to help disguise your appearance. And don't refer to us as rebels! We're Confederates and proud of it. All you have to remember is to keep your mouth shut and let me do the talking. I'm used to traveling in disguise, and I know what to say."

"And what part will you play in this grand design of yours, Miss Delaney?"

"I was going to be your nurse, but since you're so all-fired healthy-looking, I guess I'll have to be your wife."

"Now, that does sound like a good idea." His gaze slid slowly down over her body until she could almost feel the heat through her thin gown.

Cassandra's pulse jumped and accelerated alarmingly. Traveling alone with Derek Courtland was probably a mistake, but entrusting his safety to anyone else was out of the question. The *Mamu* was too important to the South.

Hardening her resolve to keep their relationship strictly business, she fetched Harte's blue coat and held it up for Derek to try on. He slipped his arms into the sleeves and shrugged it over his broad shoulders, and Cassandra marveled anew at his size. To her surprise the coat fit reasonably well, but Derek Courtland certainly seemed much more imposing to her than her brother ever had.

"Sit down and I'll fashion your bandages for you."

As Derek buttoned up the jacket, Cassandra hurriedly retrieved a roll of gauze and a pair of scissors from a basket inside her dressing table drawer. Unwinding a length of the thin white cloth, she moved to where he sat waiting on the foot of the bed. As she carefully wrapped it around his neck, his eyes intimately roamed every inch of her face and neck. Annoyed when the rude perusal continued unchecked, she gritted her teeth and contemplated jerking the gauze tight enough to make those black eyes of his bulge from their sockets.

"Please stop looking at me like that," she said tightly. She had put up with his disrespect for as long as she intended to.

"Like what?"

"You know exactly what I'm talking about."

"I just can't seem to take my eyes off you."

Cassandra picked up her sewing shears and held them poised in her hand. "Tell me, Captain, why do I get the distinct impression that you've repeated that rather unoriginal compliment to enough women to people North America?"

Derek laughed softly. "Ah, that may well be true, but there's a big difference this time. With you, I really mean it."

Cassandra looked at his handsome face, at his arrogant, self-confident smile. "You're wasting your time, Courtland. I'm not the least bit interested in you, except for getting you back to your ship."

"I wish I could say the same about you."

Enough was enough, Cassandra thought. She had to nip in the bud his pursuit of her, and she knew exactly how to do it.

"I think you should know that I'm spoken for, Captain. So you really are wasting all these crude efforts to seduce me."

"I'll be the judge of that," he murmured, hotly examining her lips. "Tell me, please, who's the lucky man?"

"No one you'd know," she murmured, making up the details of her nonexistent engagement as she went along. "We should have been married already, but for the war."

"What a shame," he replied with a smile that meant just the opposite. "Could your fiancé be young Harry from downstairs?"

Startled by such an absurd suggestion, Cassandra shook her head. "Of course not. Harry's just a boy."

"Who, then?"

The first name that occurred to her was one of Harte's fellow officers who had pursued her in Washington for the past two years. "If you must know, his name is Felix O'Henry. He's a Union officer."

"The poor mate's name is Felix?" Derek Courtland was rude enough to laugh. "Does he know that he's engaged to a spy who's the scourge of the Yankee army?"

"It wouldn't matter to him."

"He must be bloody understanding."

Cassandra ignored his sarcasm and picked up a small vial of stage blood she had hidden among the rolls of gauze. She unstoppered the lid and dotted a drop or two on the bandage just above the fancy gold braid decorating the front of his collar.

"What unfortunate Yankee did you drain this from, Cassie, luv?" Derek asked with another devilish grin. "Or did you steal that from your poor beleaguered brother, too, the last time you went home for a visit? While he was napping, perhaps?"

"Don't be ridiculous. It's from a theatrical company that furnishes a lot of my disguises. I also get things at the institution."

"And what institution would that be?"

"The Smithsonian, which happens to be the national institution of higher learning located in Washington. I work there."

"When you're not out spying or helping to break hardened convicts like me out of prison?"

"Precisely." Cassandra had to admit, albeit begrudgingly, that Derek Courtland did have a certain charm about him. No wonder his sister, Lily, adored him so much. Somehow she felt quite certain that a lot of other women worshiped him even more than Lily did. He probably had a woman or two, maybe even three, in every port he frequented, all of whom were no doubt counting the days until he sailed back into their beds. But she had more sense than to become involved with a man like him, no matter how attractive he was.

"Are you married, Captain Courtland?" she asked as nonchalantly as such a question could be.

"Please, call me Derek. After all, you're soon to be my wife."

"Are you evading my question, Captain?"

"I'm not wed, but then I've only just met you."

With increasing difficulty, Cassandra fought the effect of his slow smile and the way he constantly stared at her mouth. After wrapping a good bit of gauze around his forehead, she snipped the gauze near his right temple, knotted the ends, then stepped back to survey her handiwork. "I guess that will pass as a head wound. A cane might be a nice touch, too. You're to go by the name of David Carringer, and I'll be your wife, Constance. When we get to Baltimore, we'll try to get passage on the *Rachel Ann* out of Liverpool. Once we're out of the country, you can board the *Mamu* and resume your runs through the blockade."

"So that's why you're going to all this trouble to get me out?" He leaned against the bedpost and awaited her answer, and something in his eyes bothered Cassandra. The easy amusement was gone, replaced by—what? wariness?

"Of course, that's the reason we wanted you out of jail. Your work is of the utmost importance to our cause. You're a valuable asset to the South."

"I ran the blockade for the gold I was paid, and that's the only reason."

"I hardly think that's anything to brag about," she answered uncertainly, an inexplicable wave of disappointment flooding over her. Despite his brash arrogance, even she had admired the *Mamu*'s exploits against the federal gunboats.

"We can pay you."

"I'm not interested. It's too dangerous now."

"In gold."

"How much?"

"I've been authorized to offer you five hundred

dollars to take a cargo back into Wilmington. Plus fifty percent of the profit."

"I think we just might be able to do business after all, Miss Delaney."

Cassandra turned away, no longer worried about her reaction to Derek Courtland's charm. His blatant display of greed and lack of honor sickened her. She wanted nothing to do with such a man.

# Chapter 4

The rain pelted down, cold needles driven by the wind directly into the mare's face. When the horse stumbled in the mud, Derek tightened the reins and urged the animal onward through the darkness. The covered buggy was too lightweight for the rough terrain, and beside him, Cassandra held on tightly as the mare lurched forward out of the mire.

Derek squinted into the dark, foggy night, wondering where the hell they were. It seemed like they were out in the middle of nowhere, but at least the isolation and bad conditions would lessen the likelihood of running into Yankee patrols.

"There's a fork in the road ahead," came Cassandra's voice from where she sat huddled in the folds of her winter cloak. "That's where we'll turn toward the river."

Derek glanced at her, not yet sure she knew what she was doing. Little conversation had passed between them since she had told him what the South wanted in return for freeing him from his Yankee jail cell. Despite what he had told her, he had no intention of running the blockade again. The North had bottled up the southern coastline so tightly that an eel couldn't wriggle through their net of watchful gunboats. He wasn't about to endanger the *Mamu* or his crew, not for Cassandra Delaney, the Confederate States of America, or anyone else.

He had little choice at the moment but to agree with just about anything she suggested, as reckless as most of her ideas were. He had to trust her to get him out of the United States.

"Here it is." Cassandra leaned forward and peered through the dense ground fog.

"Are we close to the Potomac now?"

"No. We have to ford this creek in order to reach Manassas Junction. There, we can catch the Orange and Alexandria train into Baltimore."

Derek twisted to look at her. "Are you suggesting that we just climb aboard a Yankee train and enjoy the ride?"

"Exactly," she answered with blithe unconcern.

Sorry he had asked, Derek jerked the reins to one side and guided the laboring horse onto a weed-choked, deeply rutted path. Moments later he began to hear the murmur of rushing water. He reined the mare to a standstill.

"Okay, now what?"

"Shhh."

Not used to taking orders from anybody, especially not from some harebrained woman, be she beautiful or not, Derek forced himself to hold his tongue. He just hoped to God she was as good at this as she claimed to be. For several minutes there was only the mingled sounds of rain, wind, and the gurgling river. He pulled his gun when a man's voice rose guardedly out of the night.

"White Rose?"

"Here." Before Cassandra's reply had faded, a figure materialized out of the misty gloom on her side of the carriage.

"Is everything all right, Robert?" she asked softly.

"Yes," he answered as he lifted her to the ground. "What happened? You were supposed to be here last night."

"Courtland got himself in trouble outside Fredericksburg."

"What about the girl?"

"They got Lily, but my brother will intercede for her when he finds out what happened."

Derek climbed out and was surprised when the man immediately stretched out his arm for a handshake. "It's a great honor to meet you, Captain. My sister and her family have been bottled up in Charleston for over a year now. She's mentioned your ship by name in her letters. You've done a great service for the Confederacy."

"I understand they closed in around Charleston a couple of months ago," Derek answered, shaking the man's hand.

"That's right, but Margaret and the children headed down to my uncle's plantation in South Carolina. I pray to God they made it there safely."

"Let's go, Courtland," Cassandra ordered brusquely,

already moving off toward the bank. "If we don't reach the depot early enough, we'll have to hide out in the woods until morning. That's too risky."

Derek hardly thought that to be as reckless as boarding a train back into enemy territory, but he had to trust her judgment. As Robert assisted Cassandra into the bow of a small rowboat, Derek took his place in the stern. As soon as Robert pushed them off from the bank, he picked up the oars and dipped them into the water. Despite the miserable weather, it felt wonderful to be free.

Cassandra huddled deeper into her hooded cape while he bent his back to the rowing. The bob and sway of the water beneath the hull felt good after so long away from the sea, and he pulled harder on the oars, eager for Cassandra to lead him wherever she would, as long as he ended up back on the *Mamu*.

"There's the signal," Cassandra whispered from in front of him. "See, the lantern blinking there among the trees. There's a beach there. Head for it."

Derek changed course slightly and propelled the light skiff across the rain-swollen stream. Apparently Cassandra Delaney headed an extensive, well-trained network of Confederate spies. Despite the brashness of her plans, she just might get him off American soil alive, after all.

The minute the boat scraped in the sand on the far side of the creek, a man Cassandra called Jed led them without a word to a farm wagon waiting in a thicket of trees. He melted away into the darkness before Derek knew he was gone.

"Jed's a man of few words, I take it," he murmured, helping Cassandra aboard, then climbing in after her.

"Take a lesson from him, Courtland. Voices travel over water."

"Yes ma'am," he muttered sourly.

Within ten minutes, they had reached the road that led to Manassas.

"Stop here, and we'll walk the rest of the way to the depot. There won't be many passengers around the waiting room this late, but if there is anyone, I'll do the talking."

Thankful he had a gun tucked in his belt, Derek walked alongside her through the darkness, feeling rather like a particularly plump lamb being led to slaughter. He half expected to see a wanted poster with his face on it tacked to the wall. Inside the depot building, several gas lamps were burning, and he could see the stationmaster where he sat behind his desk. No one else was in evidence.

"I guess we had better go inside," Cassandra muttered, chafing her hands together. "It'll look suspicious if we loiter about out here in the cold." She peered up at him, her vivid blue eyes searching his face. "Do you think you can carry this off?"

"It's a damned foolish idea," he muttered under his breath.

"What?"

"Nothing. Let's just get this over with."

Cassandra shook her head in exasperation. "Would you quit worrying? I've done a lot of things riskier than this."

"I believe that."

"Just keep your mouth shut and remember you're weak and wounded."

"The only thing I'm weak from is the lack of food."

"Your stomach is certainly the least of your problems, Captain. Remember, let me do the talking," she finished as she turned the doorknob and preceded him into the warmth of Manassas Junction Station.

Just inside the door Cassandra was pleased as pie to find no other travelers awaiting the train. The stationmaster had looked up when the bell on the door jingled, then stood and moved around his desk to where a Franklin stove was glowing red-hot.

"Evenin', folks. I'm the stationmaster here. Name's Harvey Kenyon." The little man's eyes went at once to Derek's bandages. Thank goodness the lighting was none too bright, Cassandra thought.

"How do you do, Mr. Kenyon. I am Mrs. David Carringer, and I'm afraid I'll have to speak for my husband. As you see, he's been wounded."

"Damned filthy Rebs," the man muttered vehemently, then faltered in apology. "Forgive my language, ma'am."

"You are only reflecting my own opinion, sir, I assure you. That's why I've come all this way to bring my David home to Baltimore, where he can rest and recover his voice." She gave Derek a pitying look, wishing he would touch his throat as if he were in pain. He looked tense and edgy, as if any moment he would pull a gun and shoot the place up. "Is there a northbound train due through here tonight?"

"Not until morning, I'm afraid, ma'am."

Cassandra put the back of her hand to her forehead, feigning extreme fatigue. "Oh, dear, I'm just so exhausted. We've been traveling by stagecoach for three days and nights."

As Cassandra had hoped, the man appeared shocked and concerned. He didn't seem to be overly intelligent, either, which boded well for them. He hastened to lead them to a leather couch near the stove.

"Major, is there anything I might get you that would make you more comfortable? I make it a practice to show my gratitude to the brave heroes fighting for the preservation of our blessed Union."

Cassandra looked warily at Derek. He had stood silently beside her listening, as she had instructed him to. But now he was nodding at Mr. Kenyon and patting his belly.

"Why, I believe the major's trying to tell me he's hungry, ma'am. Could that be the case?"

Cassandra bit her lip and affected a look of acute embarrassment. "I'm afraid we've been slightly short of coin, sir. You see, I had to use our savings to pay for the operation that saved David's vocal cords."

She withdrew a handkerchief from her sleeve and dabbed at an imaginary tear.

"My dear lady, don't you worry yourself for one little minute about paying me for your supper. I have a pot of beef stew warming on the stove, and my wife sent along a whole loaf of fresh-baked bread and a plate of blackberry cobbler this evening when I came to work. I would be rightly honored if you'd accept my hospitality."

Derek barely suppressed a groan.

"You're too kind," Cassandra murmured demurely with downcast eyes. "I suppose David can swallow bits of stew if I cut them into small pieces."

"Sit down now, please, both of you, and I'll fix you up a plate in a jiffy."

"You should have been onstage," Derek murmured very low as the stationmaster moved away. "That performance was first-rate."

"I told you that I knew what I was doing," she whispered back, glancing at Mr. Kenyon, who was dipping up their supper. When he came back carrying a tray, she smiled gratefully at him.

"Here you are, Major, nice and hot," Kenyon said, placing the bowls of the steaming stew in their hands. "I have a spot of whiskey in my desk, too. It'd help the food go down, I'd wager."

Derek nodded—a bit too eagerly, Cassandra thought—and she glared a warning at him as the stationmaster hustled off to fetch his bottle. Derek spooned up a few hasty bites while the man's back was turned, and Cassandra snatched the bowl out of his hands.

"You can't wolf your food down like that, or he'll know. Remember, you've just had an operation."

"I haven't eaten in two days, dammit," Derek ground out under his breath. "Give me back that stew."

They both looked up, faces wreathed with innocent smiles, as Mr. Kenyon arrived and handed a glass of whiskey to Derek. Derek nodded his thanks, then tossed it down in one deep draught.

"Darling, please, be more circumspect," Cassandra begged sweetly, narrowing her eyes with a dire warning. "You'll hurt your throat."

Derek held the glass out for a refill. As Mr. Kenyon obliged, Cassandra gazed gratefully up at him.

"You're certainly the answer to our prayers, Mr. Kenyon."

The stationmaster beamed with pleasure, just the way Cassandra knew he would. Men were extraordinarily easy to manipulate, she thought happily, until her attention was diverted by the faraway wail of a train whistle.

Mr. Kenyon frowned and scratched his graying pate. "What the tarnation? There ain't no express due in till morning 'round eight o'clock." He looked at Cassandra, an expression of understanding dawning in his watery blue eyes. "I guess the Lord is truly watchin' over your poor husband, Mrs. Carringer. I'll flag the engineer to a stop so you can be on your way home without delay. God do work in mysterious ways, don't He, ma'am?"

"Oh, yes, He does. I was just telling my husband that very thing a few hours ago when he hovered on the very brink of despair."

As Kenyon moved away again, a smug smile settled across Cassandra's face. "You see, Courtland, I do know my business. Maybe now you'll appreciate my talents and stop your constant whining."

"I'll appreciate your talents once we're safely in Baltimore, and that's a long way away."

"Suit yourself, Captain, but I believe my continued successes only prove that Providence must truly rest on the side of the Confederacy."

Just as she finished her spiel, her face flushed with patriotic fervor, Mr. Kenyon rushed back through the door, a wide smile stretched across his ruddy face. "Why, Mrs. Carringer, there truly must be an angel lookin' over your shoulder. Just guess what kinda special train this here is?"

Cassandra smiled graciously. "Why, I can't imagine, Mr. Kenyon. What kind is it?"

"It's a Union hospital train carrying our wounded up to Washington. There's a doctor on board and when I told him about the major, he said he'd come take a look-see at the major's throat and make sure it's healin' up all right. Ain't this the darndest thing?" He smiled and shook his head as he returned to his office.

"Yes, quite the darndest thing," Cassandra managed through a hard swallow, her face turning an even whiter shade of porcelain. Out of the corner of her eye, she saw Derek stop wolfing his food and place his hand inside his coat where he kept his gun. Pretending to embrace him in joy, she whispered sharply, "Don't you dare do something stupid with that gun. I'll think of a way to keep the doctor away from you. Just follow my lead in everything I say."

"You had better think of something damn quick," Derek mumbled, his eyes glued to the door behind her. "Here comes the doctor."

# Chapter 5

As a blue-coated soldier entered the depot and strode purposefully toward them, Derek's forefinger itched where it rested on the trigger. The Yankee doctor was short of stature and slightly built with neatly cut reddish blond hair. He wore long curly sideburns and had lieutenant's bars decorating his shoulders.

"Oh, my Lord, no." Cassandra moaned under her breath as if she had seen an apparition.

Derek eyed her expectantly as the Union doctor halted in his tracks several feet away.

"Cassie? Can that really be you?"

*Oh, God, we're dead now.* Derek groaned inwardly. *So much for Cassandra's talents and the Providence of God.* Now he would probably have to shoot his way out of the depot. He braced himself for Cassandra's solution to their dilemma. She wasted no time bursting into hysterical tears.

"Oh, Stephen, I can't believe it. I sat here praying for God to send an angel to help us, and then you just walked through that door."

*Oh, brother,* Derek thought, marveling at the genuine-looking tears wetting Cassandra's cheeks.

"You poor darling, what's wrong?" the poor Yankee chump said, draping a comforting arm around Cassandra's shaking shoulders. Cassandra did quite a bit more dabbing and sniffling before she loudly blew her nose and finally got hold of her emotions. Derek waited in tense dread, deathly afraid to hear what she would come up with next.

"It's poor David. My heart's just breaking to watch him suffer so."

"David? Who's he?" Stephen looked confused, but he couldn't be any more so than Derek was.

"Yes, he's sustained the most terrible head injury." Her voice broke with a pitiful-sounding sob. "He'll never be the same, Stephen. He can't speak or hear a word anyone says. It's his brain, you see—it's been damaged irreparably."

*Oh, Lord, she is completely out of her mind now,* Derek thought furiously as Stephen turned astonished eyes on his face. Derek tried to look as dull and dim-witted as possible until the doctor returned his regard to Cassandra.

"Cassie, I'm so dreadfully sorry. But who is this man? Surely you're not traveling alone with him?"

Cassandra looked extremely uncomfortable with his question, which made Derek want to squirm in his chair.

"He's my husband, Stephen. I'm sorry you had to find out this way."

Derek looked back at Stephen. The poor man's

face literally fell, as if his bones had melted and lost their shape. He looked so green and awful for a moment that Derek thought he was going to be sick right in front of their eyes.

"But Cassie," he said thickly, "I thought that you and I . . . that after the war you were going to—" his voice failed him.

*The bloke's in love with her,* Derek realized as Stephen forced down a couple of convulsive swallows while Cassandra looked suitably bereft.

"I guess I just don't understand," the doctor tried then. "I saw Harte just last week at the War Department, and he never mentioned a word about your marriage."

Cassandra had the decency to look ashamed. "I met David in a hospital where I was nursing our wounded soldiers. It all happened very fast and we were married at once because he had to return to his unit in Tennessee. He hadn't been gone a week when he was hit by an artillery shell."

Her voice choked, and Derek thought it was a good time for her to be rendered speechless, since her story sounded fishy as hell. Fortunately, Stephen was too upset to pick up on the weaker points of her performance.

"I'm sorry about your husband," Stephen murmured. He kept glancing at Derek, and Derek kept trying to feign a brain-damaged expression.

"Are you absolutely certain that his prognosis is really so dire?" Stephen was asking Cassandra. "He seems alert and strong, though he does have a peculiar vacuous look in his eyes. Perhaps he could see a doctor who specializes in cranial traumas. There should be any number of such physicians in New York or Boston."

"That's where we're headed at this very moment," she lied blithely, her composure under stress eliciting a burst of admiration in Derek's heart. "We've heard of a Dr. Livingstone practicing in Baltimore. Are you familiar with him, Stephen?"

*Probably not,* Derek decided, *since she had no doubt just made the man up.*

"Why, no, I'm not, which is surprising since I am well acquainted with most of the surgeons practicing there."

"He's British," Cassandra countered without blinking an eye. "I believe he only just arrived in the country a few months ago. He'll be returning to London soon. That's why I'm so desperate to get David up to see him. Do you have any idea when the next train to Baltimore will come through here?"

"No, but you'll ride with me on the hospital train, of course. I'll be disembarking in Washington, but there's no reason the two of you can't journey on to Baltimore. I'll arrange everything, my dear, so don't you worry your pretty little head." Stephen had clearly recovered from his shock, no doubt thinking that the injured husband might soon make a widow of Cassandra. "Come, let's help poor David find his way aboard the train. I have a private compartment that I'll be pleased to give up so the two of you will not be disturbed. He can walk, can't he?"

"Yes, but we'll have to lead him, the poor, simple-minded darling."

*Poor, simple-minded darling?* Derek thought, clamping his jaw furiously as Cassandra solicitously took hold of his right arm. Stephen took a very firm grip on his other side. He turned Derek's head around with his hands until Derek was forced to look directly into his mild brown eyes.

"I don't know if you can understand what I'm saying," he uttered in slow, succinct syllables, "but I want you to know we all appreciate the tremendous sacrifice you've made for everyone who believes in the United States of America."

This was the most godawful, nightmarish predicament he had ever found himself embroiled in, Derek thought, trying to look confused. He was entrapped in an absurd drama with a crazy woman, whose brain was obviously affected a lot worse than his would ever be.

"Come along, my poor darling David," she was crooning up into his face. Tears shone in her eyes, and to his disbelief, one even dripped dramatically off her long eyelashes. She dabbed it away and smiled tremulously up at Stephen. "Stephen's going to be our guardian angel. We have to be very, very grateful to him."

*Like hell,* Derek thought as the doctor left to open the door. He grabbed Cassandra's arm. "Are you mad, Cassandra?"

"No, you are, so you'd better start acting like it."

"There's no way in hell I'm getting on a train full of Yankee soldiers."

"Oh, my darling, you mustn't be difficult," she said loud enough for Stephen to hear, "or Stephen will have to sedate you. Stephen, please, won't you come back and help me get David aboard? Sometimes he just doesn't understand what's best for him. I'm afraid he's a bit lame, too. He was thrown from his horse during the heat of the battle when a shell hit near him and he was left for dead. He's very lucky that an old farm woman with Union loyalties found him and managed to get him to the field hospital."

She really *was* crazy. And he was trapped like a rat in the maze she was fabricating.

To his chagrin, Stephen believed every word that came out of her lying lips. The doctor took an even firmer grip on his arm. Cassandra had his right arm in a viselike hold that she hardly seemed capable of. Forced to be led along like a damned idiot by two people who barely reached his shoulder, Derek cursed the woman thoroughly as she related more absurd details of his war wounds. Good God, she was adept at lying, and she must have nerves of steel to climb so nonchalantly aboard a train filled to capacity with armed Yankees.

As Stephen assisted her onto the iron platform at the rear of the steaming train, Cassandra swept her full skirt to one side, unable to believe how well things were working out. She laughed inside. Who could ever have imagined that she would run into an old beau, a man who had doted on her for years and could pave her way all the way to Baltimore? If Derek would quit looking so keen-witted, she was confident everything would work out just fine.

"Darling, you really must try to relax," she chided gently, ignoring the furious look she saw when he turned his black eyes on her. "Everything's going to be fine, I promise you."

"That's right, Major," Stephen said soothingly, patting Derek's shoulder. "Cassie, I have morphine in my satchel if you think it would calm him for the duration of the trip."

The look Derek gave her could have brought down a charging elephant, and Cassandra quickly shook her head. "I really don't think that's necessary, David. He's just very tired and cranky. We've been traveling all day."

"Most of the men are sleeping," Stephen whispered softly as he led them through a passenger car which had been converted into draped berths for transporting casualties.

Thank goodness they had boarded in the middle of the night, Cassandra thought. Perhaps Derek's delay in reaching the White Rose had been a blessing in disguise.

"Here's my compartment," Stephen announced. "It's rather cramped, I'm afraid, but at least it will afford you some comfort."

Cassandra helped Derek inside and steered him immediately to the draped bed. She shoved him down onto the bunk as Stephen lingered at the door, and she wished Derek would quit being so uncooperative. For the first time he actually did what she wanted him to and stretched out on top of the mattress. She made a show of tucking a blanket around his legs, then gave him a fierce frown designed to keep him quiet.

Turning, she presented Stephen with her most charming smile. "He'll sleep now, I think, Stephen. I can't tell you how grateful we both are for your kindness."

"I am just glad I could be of help," he replied softly, helping her off with her cloak. He hung her cape on a peg while Cassandra seated herself on a small chair near the bed. Now all she had to do was exchange pleasantries with him until they reached Washington, where he would get off the train.

"I do hope you've been well, Stephen," she remarked as he pulled a stool near her. "I've often asked Harte about you."

Stephen's face assumed such a melancholy expression that Cassandra was immediately alert to danger. He leaned very close to her and spoke in low, agonized distress. "Cassie, I know this isn't the time or the place, with your poor maimed husband so ill, but I must tell you what's in my heart."

"Oh, no, Stephen, please. David's lying right here."

"He can't hear us. You said yourself that he's asleep." A loud phony snore came from the bed.

Cassandra glanced at Derek and saw that his eyes

were closed. He was listening to every word they said, she knew, and probably enjoying her discomfort. What's more, she had a bad feeling that Stephen was about to embark on an intimate tête-à-tête. His next words proved her right.

"I love you, Cassie. I always have. You must have sensed how I felt about you."

She had known, of course, that he had found her attractive, but it hadn't occurred to her that he actually loved her. She fought to gather her thoughts, lowering her lashes to hide her anxiety.

"Stephen, you mustn't talk this way. I'm a married woman now."

Stephen's face crumpled, and for one terrible moment Cassandra thought he was going to cry. Instead, he stood and paced a few steps away.

"I keep remembering the last time I saw you— when I visited you in Dr. Henry's apartment at the Smithsonian."

He had boldly stolen a kiss that day, Cassandra recalled. She hoped he wouldn't mention it with Derek Courtland lying there and listening to every word he said.

"I fell hopelessly in love with you that day, Cassie. You're so beautiful and sweet and honest."

At his last words, Derek stirred restlessly on the cot, and Cassandra knew why.

"When you allowed me to kiss you and hold you that day, I knew I had to have you as my wife. I was going to ask Harte for your hand in marriage as soon as the war was over."

Cassandra rose, afraid to hear more. "I'm very flattered, Stephen, any woman would be to have the affections of a wonderful man like you. But I cannot bring myself to dishonor my dear husband by listening to such talk of what might have been. If you'll forgive me, I think I'll go lie down next to him. I'm really quite exhausted myself."

When she climbed in the bed and swept the privacy curtains together, Derek was lying with his palms laced behind his head. He grinned mockingly at her.

Sitting on her knees, she put her fingers to her lips and signaled him to be quiet. When she heard Stephen leave the compartment, she exhaled and sagged with relief.

"He's gone now, but keep your voice down. He could come back at any moment."

"That was quite a revealing conversation. First Felix, and now poor Stephen. Tell me, Cassie, darlin', just how many Yankees are in love with you?"

"My job depends on being friendly to Yankee officers. Stephen's really a very nice man. I'm sorry he has to be hurt." She settled herself in the opposite corner beside his boots. "On the other hand, we're safe and sound on our way to Baltimore. Now do you believe me when I say I know what I'm doing?"

"I think you're damn lucky to still be alive, as reckless as you are."

Cassandra ignored his criticism. She shoved his

booted feet aside and curled up with a pillow against the wall. She turned her back on him.

"I don't know about you, but I intend to get some sleep while we can."

Eyes closed, she lay still and tried to ignore his closeness, but she was much more troubled by the feel of the long length of him touching her back than any fear of disclosure to the Yankees. *I am so silly when it comes to him,* she thought furiously, then her exhaustion caught up with her. She slept so deeply that even Derek Courtland's handsome face did not haunt her dreams.

# Chapter 6

Woven deep into the shimmering fabric of his dreams, Derek heard a bell, dinging insistently the way a fire alarm would. A sudden lurch brought him upright in bed. Wide awake, he remembered boarding the Yankee train. He realized the ringing was that of a station bell, and his eyes darted around the compartment in search of Cassandra Delaney. He was alone. Where the hell had she gone?

Carefully he raised the window shade an inch and immediately caught sight of Cassandra's trim figure among the people crowding the platform. She strolled along, arm in arm with Stephen. Derek quickly sought out the depot sign. Washington, District of Columbia. After all the grief and hardship he had gone through to make it to Fredericksburg, Cassandra had promptly delivered him back where he had started from.

Stretchers lined the platform where the wounded were being carried off the train. He could see a convoy of military ambulances lined up at the far end of the platform. Nurses in white gowns and head scarves moved among the sick, and pedestrians, a good many in Union blue uniforms, scurried around the busy landing. He began to sweat as the locomotive gathered steam and the departing whistle blew a warning.

Several more minutes passed before Cassandra reappeared again, crossing to the train, laughing up into the face of a young man who carried a round silver tray. She was leading him around as if he wore a ring in his nose, but Derek wasn't surprised. She obviously had that effect on most men she encountered.

Not long after, she swept with rustling skirts into the compartment toting the tray with her. Derek looked up and down the outside corridor, then shut the door. He scowled angrily at her. "Why the hell did you go off and leave me here alone? You should have at least awakened me so I'd be on guard."

Cassandra gave him a surprised look as she lowered the heavy tray onto the bed. "What's the matter with you? I was only gone for a few minutes. I got some breakfast for you, and I found out what happened to Lily."

His sister's name shook away all Derek's other thoughts. "Where is she? Is she all right?"

"Yes. They took her to the prison for interrogation, but that's all I could find out. But you don't need to worry because Harte can, and will, pull the necessary strings to get her out. He probably already has."

"Well, I am worried. If I wasn't so sure Harte was an honorable man, I'd get off this train and go get her."

Cassandra's delicate blond brows drew together in a small frown. "And you'd end up dead or sharing a cell with her." She snatched off the white napkin covering the food, and Derek was shocked to find an onyx-handled six-shooter and black leather holster wrapped in a gun belt. He wasted no time claiming the weapon. He weighted it in his hand, pleased to have a decent gun again. Derringers were for women.

"Where'd you get this?"

"As I've told you countless times, Courtland, I know what I'm doing. I have my agents working every depot from Virginia to Boston so I'll know who's going where and with whom. The boy who prepared this tray was one of my best."

"Isn't he a bit young to be an agent?"

"He's fourteen. Most men older than that are already in the army. Now do you want breakfast or not?"

Derek's stomach growled. He nodded, and Cassandra removed another napkin and unveiled a plate of fried potatoes and scrambled eggs.

As he began to eat, she picked up one of the mugs of hot coffee and sipped the rich brew. "Stephen said they'll unload most of the wounded here, then go on to Baltimore. We've already said our good-bye and he's on his way to the Douglas Hospital. After you eat your fill, lie back and relax. I'm going forward now and see if I can help care for the men who're staying aboard."

Derek stopped eating, his fork poised near his mouth. "You're going to nurse the Yankees."

"They bleed just like anyone else. If I can be of some comfort to them, I will." She set down her cup. "And if I overhear anything that will help our side, more's the better. I am not completely heartless, Captain."

Derek shook his head as she swept out to nurse her foes. He had never met anyone quite like Cassandra Delaney. She had no fear, that was for damn certain, but slowly and surely she was getting him back to his ship. He just hoped her luck held out that long.

Nearly five hours later, the locomotive chugged into the Baltimore station. Cassandra leaned close to the window, keeping her eyes peeled for any sign of Georgia. As relieved as she was to have made the journey so quickly, she knew Derek Courtland was not out of harm's way. She wouldn't be able to relax until they were on board the *Rachel Ann* and out to sea.

"Who are you looking for? More men to put under your spell?"

Derek had asked his question from where he leaned against the pillows. Now that he had gotten some food and rest, he looked more handsome than ever, even with that sarcastic grin on his face. If he had such a devastating effect on Cassandra, Georgia would surely never be able to keep her hands off him.

"No, it's a woman," she answered finally. "She runs things for me here in Baltimore."

"What woman?"

"What difference does it make? She's good at her job. That's all you should care about."

Cassandra turned back to the window just as Georgia rounded the corner of the platform. Tall and slim with dark eyes and auburn hair, Georgia was very pretty. Cassandra wondered if Derek would find her attractive. She didn't have to guess about Georgia's opinion of Derek. Georgia loved men, any shape or size, and Derek had more than enough of both to entice any woman.

"Come on. She's waiting for us. She's going to provide us with new identities and papers on the way to the docks."

"I trust I won't have to be a simpleminded dolt this time?"

"That's up to you. Now keep quiet until we're inside the carriage or someone might pick up your accent. The North's got agents crawling all over the railway stations watching for suspicious-acting passengers."

"Tell me in advance, Cassie darlin'," Derek asked, strapping on the gun belt, "do you have any jilted fiancés running around in Baltimore? I want to be prepared this time, in case I'm challenged to a duel or something."

"I wasn't engaged to Stephen. I can't help it if he fell in love with me."

Derek surprised her by giving a soft laugh. "Ah, but how many other men fall into that category, luv? A dozen? Two dozen?"

Cassandra frowned. "I'm sure the number of women you've had would make a paltry sum out of the number of men who have courted me."

"You flatter me, darlin'," he murmured back, spinning the cylinder to make sure the revolver was fully loaded.

Cassandra led the way onto the railed platform at the rear of the car, thankful that they encountered no one en route who might have questioned them. There were Union soldiers everywhere—waiting in line at the ticket window, lounging on baggage wagons while they waited for their transports—but a large crowd would help conceal their arrival.

Outside the train, she took Derek's arm and moved quickly among the bustling travelers toward where Georgia was standing under the eaves dressed in the white robes and flowing wimple of a Sister of Mercy. When Cassandra finally made her way there, she embraced her old friend as if she hadn't seen her three days ago in Washington.

"Good gracious, what a fine-looking man," Georgia whispered as they hugged each other. "I nearly swallowed my tongue when I saw that beautiful face of his, not to mention—"

"Just leave him be, Georgia. We won't have time for any dalliances between the two of you, though

I'm sure he'd enjoy it immensely. Have you made the arrangements for us to board the ship?"

"Yes. They weigh anchor at high tide, and that's anytime now. Thank God you came when you did. We're to go directly to the docks. I've got everything you'll need here." She raised the worn blue carpetbag she was carrying in her right hand.

"Sister Georgia, please allow me to introduce my husband, Major David Carringer," Cassandra said for the benefit of a Yankee sergeant standing nearby. She patted Derek's arm in a show of affection. "He's been wounded in the throat, so I'm afraid he isn't able to speak."

"Words aren't necessary, as handsome as you are," Georgia whispered to Derek, gazing at him boldly with frank admiration.

Derek quickly covered his shock, then cocked a speculative brow. He bent down close to Georgia's ear. "That's very kind of you to notice, Sister, you being a nun and all, and I can certainly return the compliment," he murmured very low. "You look good enough to eat," he added for her ears only.

"Shh, both of you! Didn't I tell you to keep quiet?" Cassandra interrupted in a peevish reprimand. "If the two of you must carry on a flirtation, at least wait until we're inside the carriage."

"No one's in hearing distance. Anyway, we were just teasing," Georgia said. A few moments later, as they led Derek toward the waiting carriage, she said aside to Cassandra, "What's the matter with you, Cassie?"

"Nothing. I'm sorry. He just rubs me the wrong way. He has from the beginning."

"It seems to me there couldn't be a wrong way when it's him doing the rubbing."

"Georgia, stop it," Cassandra ground out impatiently. "Remember, you're playing the part of a woman of the cloth."

"Oh, all right, but I wish I could take your place and take him on to Nassau."

Cassandra started to say that she certainly could, but she bit back the offer and chastised herself for acting so ridiculous.

"I have a feeling that you're no nun, Miss Georgia," Derek said once they were safely inside the coach. He continued, using the same caressing voice with which he had tried to seduce Cassandra, "I can't begin to tell you how much that pleases me. Dare I hope we'll be spending some time together?"

"No, you won't be, so you can turn off the charm," Cassandra snapped, jerking down the window shade.

"I can't think of anything I'd like better," Georgia replied with a slow smile and total disregard of Cassandra's wrath. "I work at the Raven Saloon down on Camden Street. I do hope you'll visit me there the next time you're in town."

"What's wrong with right now?"

Derek Courtland would try to pick up a corpse if it were female and comely, Cassandra thought contemptuously. She especially hated the way he was drooling over her like he was a cat and Georgia was a bowl of cream!

"Did you bring disguises for us or not, Georgia?" she demanded, interrupting their irritating seduction.

Georgia turned quickly and opened the suitcase on the floor. "Cassie, you can wear what you have on. That gray dress is staid enough to belong to the wife of a missionary. I've already had a trunk carried aboard the *Rachel Ann* with extra clothes for the both of you." She withdrew a black linen shirt from the bag. "This is for you, Captain. I do hope it fits, but you're a good bit bigger than I expected." Georgia commenced to beam at Derek as if he had performed some wonderful trick by being so tall and muscular.

"Georgia, I do declare, I've never seen you act like such a ninny. Courtland, hurry up and get changed. Did you bring a clerical collar for him?"

"Yes," Georgia answered, but her eyes remained glued to Derek's bare chest as he pulled his shirt off over his head. "Oooh, my, if you really were a minister, every girl at the Raven'd get religion."

Derek laughed as he pulled on the dark shirt. "So I'm to be a man of God?"

"Yes," Cassandra muttered sourly as she tossed the stiff white collar into his lap. "As sacrilegious as that is."

Derek ignored her and winked at Georgia, who looked as if she were going to melt with delight and run liquefied under the carriage door. As their conveyance slowed among the pedestrian and carriage traffic thronging the Baltimore harbor, Cassandra gritted her teeth, wishing her two companions would quit acting like spaniels in heat.

# Chapter 7

Derek tugged at the tight clerical collar as he followed Cassandra up the gangplank of the *Rachel Ann*. The fifty-foot steam-powered sloop out of England couldn't compare to the sleek and swift *Mamu*, but all his worry and tension began to fade away when he stood with feet planted on the deck of a seafaring ship. For the first time he felt certain that Cassandra Delaney was going to succeed in her mission.

"Remember, we're supposed to be missionaries on our way back to New Guinea. We're a married couple, so don't start seducing every female aboard."

"Do I detect a tiny twinge of jealousy, luv?" Hoping it were true, Derek searched Cassandra's lovely face. She flushed slightly, rosy color rising under her creamy skin. Now that he felt safe again, he experienced a tremendous need to have her in his arms again.

"There's the captain. We'd better inform him that we've come aboard. They've probably been waiting for us. Georgia says his name is Nathan Rodgers. I'll do the talking."

The captain of the *Rachel Ann* stood at midship with several of his subordinate officers. Probably around forty, he was a stocky little man, but powerfully built with massive arms and thick legs as sturdy as tree trunks. He outstretched his hand to Derek at once. "Welcome aboard, Reverend Johnson. We were beginning to wonder if you were going to make it. I've already given orders to make ready to sail. You and your missus just made it."

"I was detained in Washington," Derek said truthfully. Captain Rodgers didn't need to know he had been detained in the Old Penitentiary at Washington Arsenal.

"You're an Aussie, I see," the man observed in a friendly way. "I've been to your country many times. The city of Sydney, a mighty fine place."

"I'm anxious to get back home. My dear wife's never been there."

When Rodgers swiveled his regard, Derek pulled her close and planted a lingering kiss on Cassandra's forehead. He winced when she pressed the heel of her leather pump painfully atop his toes.

"How do you do, Mrs. Johnson?" The captain politely inclined his head. "The ship's company is already gathered on the forecastle deck awaiting us. Shall we go there?"

Derek wondered just what they were waiting for, but he nodded agreeably and took Cassandra's elbow. The captain led them along the starboard rail, and Derek studied the passengers who were sitting on makeshift benches or leaning against the masts. He became increasingly wary as they were led to the front of the assemblage.

"I'm happy to announce that the reverend and his wife have finally arrived," he said, smiling at Cassandra. "So we'll be able to have our service after all."

"Service?" A sick feeling oozed up in the bottom of Derek's gut.

"That's right. We always have a short religious service when we weigh anchor to bless the coming voyage. I hope you don't mind giving the message. You're the only man of God among us this trip."

Derek's mind raced to think of a feasible way he could refuse the captain's request. "I really don't think that would be a good idea, Captain—" he began, but Cassandra interrupted him.

"My husband would be honored, Captain Rodgers. He is at his best at the pulpit. Go ahead, my darling, everyone's waiting."

Derek felt like choking Cassandra with his bare hands. As she moved off, smiling at the attentive captain, he enjoyed the vision of clenching his fingers around her pretty little white neck. Cassandra and the captain sat down, leaving him alone to face the sixty or so passengers and crew members assembled to hear his preaching. What the hell was he going to say?

"Let us pray," he said, folding his hands in front of him. He hadn't been to a church service since he was wearing short pants at Malmora and his mother had made sure he attended every Sunday sermon. "Our Father who art in heaven, hallowed be Thy name—"

Derek was absolutely overjoyed when everyone else joined in an oral recitation. The prayer ended too quickly, however, and once more he stared out over the pious faces awaiting his words.

"Today I shall preach on . . ." he hesitated, unable to think of one damn subject he could do justice to. "Sin," he finished rather feebly. "Aye, that's right, sin—the black, filthy, horrible sin that permeates every place on earth, even perhaps this very ship."

A few people in his audience exchanged surprised glances. "Sin clings to everyone among us like sticky, gooey . . ." he struggled for the right word, "glue."

The assemblage shifted uncomfortably. Cassandra was grinning like a crocodile; damn her. Now that the ship was moving out into the Chesapeake Bay, she felt secure enough to carry on the joke at his expense. But two could play her game, he suddenly realized. Looking down at his folded hands, he paused for a long moment, then shook his head as if overcome by emotion. He looked up.

"I'm sorry, but I just can't go on, not after the terrible thing that happened to us last night. Constance, my dear, you'll come up here and help me explain to these good people just what I'm talking about, won't you?"

A low, concerned murmur swept the group, and

Derek was pleased to see that Cassandra had lost her smug smile. Now *she* looked worried. Good. She stood, albeit reluctantly, and walked the short distance to where he awaited her. He embraced her tightly, making sure his face looked troubled.

"Good luck, luv," he murmured, then quickly sat down in her chair. As Derek sucked in a huge sigh of relief, the captain put a consoling hand on his shoulder. Derek nodded sorrowfully.

Cassandra stood silently for a moment, looking like anything in the world but a missionary. She was too beautiful for such a calling, even in her drab gray dress. Her face was very somber and sad, and Derek grinned encouragingly at her.

"I want to share with all of you the reason for my husband's distress," she began in such a low voice that everyone was forced to lean forward in order to catch her next words. "You see, together last night we witnessed the most terrible sight imaginable."

*She is definitely making this up as she goes along,* Derek thought, propping his foot on his knee and leaning back to enjoy the show.

"Just last night we stopped at the depot of Manassas Junction in northern Virginia. There was a man stranded there. His name was David Carringer." She looked down as if having trouble finding the courage to continue. She probably was, Derek thought with an inward laugh.

"Never in our lives have we seen a more pitiful, heartrending sight," she continued in a trembling, teary voice. Good God, she even had tears welling up in her eyes. *She is good,* Derek admitted, *damn good.*

"He was one of our own, a Union major, and he was a handsome man, or had been, before he sustained his terrible injuries." She paused for effect, and her audience made no sound as they awaited in somber silence for her to continue. "But he could not walk because his legs were maimed; he could not talk to us because he had been shot in the vocal cords." *Uh-oh, that wasn't so good,* Derek thought, glancing at the captain for his reaction. When Rodgers pulled out a handkerchief and then took off his glasses and wiped his misty eyes, Derek relaxed again.

"His wife was with him. A wonderful, loyal woman who had traveled behind enemy lines to save him from the horrors of a Confederate prison camp. But what did she find in the husband she loved? A mere shell of the man she had married, because, you see, artillery had exploded near his horse and injured his head. She found the love of her life, the father of her children, deaf and mute, barely able to walk."

When a sympathetic moan went up and one woman sobbed loudly, Cassandra really got into the swing of her story. "But then a miracle happened. My husband talked to her. He told her of a friend of his who was visiting this country for a short period of time. A doctor named Livingstone who operated on this very same type of head injury."

Cassandra put her hand to her mouth as if overcome by the memory. She smiled fondly at Derek. "This man before you, this wonderful, kind man of God, my husband, paid that Union hero's way to New York for that operation. He gave that couple every cent we had collected this past year to take home with us to New Guinea so we could spread the word of God among the poor primitive natives there. And now, even though we return to his country empty-handed and penniless, we go with peace of heart because we know we made a difference in this terrible, senseless war going on all around us."

Applause pattered here and there, then grew in force. People began to stand up and clap their hands toward him, and Derek watched, amazed, at the tears running down Cassandra's face as she ran and locked her arms around his waist. Feeling like an idiot, and more than a little guilty, he patted her back and tried to look humbly grateful.

"I think an offering is in order," cried a man's voice from somewhere at the back of the crowd.

"It's the least we can do," a woman concurred with tearful fervor.

Someone swept off his hat, and it was handed from one row to the next until it reached the ship's captain, heavy with coin and paper bills.

"I've always believed in the inherent goodwill of humanity," Captain Rodgers said, his voice hoarse. "Here, Reverend Johnson, take this small offering for the heathen to which you bring your blessed work."

"I really couldn't—"

"Oh, but darling, don't you see how much this will help our Cause?" Cassandra urged gently, taking the hat and crushing it close to her breast as if it were a newborn babe. "It's the answer to our prayers. I am overcome by such generosity. God does work in mysterious ways. Thank you, one and all!"

Derek waited for a thunderbolt to pierce the skies and land on Cassandra Delaney's head. Faintly surprised when no clap of thunder rolled across the water, he shook hands with nearly everyone on ship, receiving well-wishes as Cassandra pulled him slowly toward the passengers' quarters below decks.

The moment they reached their cabin, Derek shut the door while Cassandra emptied the contents of the black silk top hat onto the narrow bed.

"Good gracious, I bet there's a hundred or more dollars here," she breathed happily.

"You ought to be ashamed of yourself, but I have to admit you did that rather well," he said.

"You hardly left me any choice when you started out comparing sin to paste."

"Actually, I likened it to glue. Besides, you set me up first."

"We had to do it, or they'd be suspicious. Preachers usually ask for money, and if you think about it, little that I said wasn't true. We *were* at Manassas Junction, and you were supposedly suffering all those things."

"You're rationalizing, and you know it. You out-and-out duped those poor people."

"They're Yankees. It's better we have this money than for it to be used to buy more cannons and rifles for the northern army. These people are rich northerners who are little affected by the war, so there's no need to feel guilty." She cocked her head. "I find it a bit peculiar that you do, since you're the one with the reputation for pirating."

"Privateering, if you don't mind."

"It's the same thing, depending on whether or not a war's going on. Anyway, my story worked and we're on our way to Nassau with plenty of cash to pay for our expenses."

Derek really couldn't argue that point. He watched her sort the paper money into piles. "I'm beginning to think you *are* very good at your work. Or damn lucky. It's hard to tell which."

"Maybe I'm good and you're lucky to have me helping you."

Derek laughed. "I'm lucky to be sharing this cabin with you. I feel it's only fair to warn you that I'm the kind of man who likes my wife to share my bed."

Cassandra paused in her counting. She frowned. "I thought I made myself clear when you held me down and kissed me against my will. I meant what I said, Derek. I am not like Georgia and the other girls."

Derek lounged on the narrow cot. "I'm glad to see we're on a first-name basis at last, Cassie, luv. Come, lie down beside me, and rest awhile. There's plenty of room, and I promise I won't hold you down against your will unless you ask me to."

Cassandra looked at him where he lay on his side with his head propped in his palm. She steeled her resolve not to be taken in by his disarming smile, but she was tired. She hadn't slept on the train for as long as he had. Now they were safe and headed out to sea. All they had to do was stay below in the cabin during the short voyage to the Bahamas. That might be the most dangerous time of all—with Derek Courtland so close.

"All right, if you promise to keep to yourself. I'm too tired to argue."

Cassandra lay down next to him, relaxing back against the feather pillow. She turned slightly so she could see his face. "I've been thinking about what you said about running the blockade, and I don't believe you'd do it just for money. Perhaps you aren't a true Confederate, but I do think you took the *Mamu* through for humanitarian reasons as well as for the gold."

"So you like me better now?"

"I didn't say that."

"But you could like me a lot, perhaps even let me steal a few kisses like poor old heartbroken Stephen did in Dr. Henry's apartment—if I promise to run the blockade and not take any extra money for it?"

The way he was looking at her was distinctly unsettling, as if he knew she was willing to persuade him if necessary and he was waiting eagerly to see just how far she would go to do so.

"Something tells me you wouldn't settle for a mere kiss."

"Something tells you wrong." His voice had gotten suddenly husky as he reached over and caressed a curl where it lay over her shoulder. "I'll take a hundred dollars gold off my price if you let me kiss you right now."

Cassandra laughed. "A hundred dollars for one little kiss? You can't mean it."

"Who said anything about little?"

"Just what do you have in mind?"

"I get to hold you and kiss you as long as I want, and you respond only if you want to."

Cassandra measured him with a searching look. "And you won't try anything else?"

He shook his head, his black eyes holding her gaze. "Just think what that kind of money would buy, Cassie, darlin'. Morphine, bandages, warm uniforms. Wouldn't such a sacrifice be worth it? For the Cause?"

Cassandra remembered the kiss he had forced upon her at the White Rose and just how much it had affected her. Circumstances had been different then, though. Now they were out of danger. "Two hundred?"

"Two kisses?" he countered.

"What about five kisses and I don't pay you anything except the percentage?"

"You drive a hard bargain, but all right." He smiled in a way she absolutely could not resist.

"All right, then. Just go ahead and do it." Her

heart began to thud, hard thumps that were embarrassingly evident in the way her chest was heaving.

"Number one," he whispered, leaning over her. His mouth touched hers very gently, nibbling at her lips, softly, unthreateningly. When he quit, she opened her eyes and looked up at him in surprise. "See, that wasn't so bad. Shall we move on to number two?"

This time he slid his arm under her shoulders and brought her up against his chest, but she was thinking only of the heat of his mouth and the way he was molding her lips, but all so gentle and sweet and wonderful, she thought in dismay. He stopped again, and this time she unwittingly moistened her lips for the third kiss.

"Three. Remember, you can respond anytime you want." He held her tighter, and she could sense his growing arousal as his fingers slid up into her hair next to her scalp. This time the kiss continued for so long that she ended up putting her arms around his neck. He groaned with obvious pleasure, and she realized she liked the sound of his enjoyment. And she definitely liked kissing him.

"I think three hundred's enough for the supplies I need," she mumbled breathlessly, trying to break away.

"Medicines are very expensive, Cassie." His mouth was on hers again, insistent, demanding, his tongue coaxing her lips open, then plunging into her mouth. A strange sensation tingled in the core of her womanhood, one that caused a strong quivering through her body that she had never before experienced. Frightened of the intensity of her response, she pulled back, heaving in a deep breath as she pushed away from him.

"One more, Cassie, and this time I want you to kiss me." Derek lay back and waited.

Cassandra realized with some alarm that she wanted to continue with her disgraceful behavior. She had never been kissed in such a way, had never really had a relationship with a beau develop into this much physical intimacy. The war had taken away any kind of normal courtships for her. To her surprise, she was finding it rather pleasant, but she had the uneasy feeling Derek Courtland was the reason for that.

She propped herself on her elbow and leaned over him, but the moment she touched her mouth to his, he pulled her back into his arms and atop him, one hand clutching her hair, the other sliding under her skirt. She moaned when he found the back of her thigh, but he was kissing her deeply, draining her will to resist, making her feel weak and breathless. For a long time he continued, his mouth on her cheeks, throat, mouth and chin until she was arching against him, wanting him to continue, needing something, craving something more, wanting anything but for him to stop.

When he suddenly wrenched himself away and got off the bunk, she lay in a state of trembling arousal as he crossed the cabin and left without a word. She stared weakly at the closed door with heaving breast and hammering heart, not sure why he had left so abruptly. As galling and embarrassing as it was, she only wanted him to come back.

# Chapter 8

Hidden deep in the midnight shadows of a moonless, overcast night, Derek leaned against the starboard rail, welcoming the darkness and solitude. The decks were deserted, the passengers already retired for the night. Only a few crewmen manned the ship as she sped swiftly southward on calm seas. *It feels bloody good to be at sea again,* he thought as he puffed to flame the Havana cigar that Captain Rodgers had presented to him earlier when they talked together on the bridge. The smoke tasted good. The salty air felt good. But neither was what kept him alone in the cool night air.

The truth of the matter was that he didn't relish going below and facing Cassandra. He was feeling guilty, of all things, and with Cassandra Delaney, of all people. The situation was almost laughable, since she was the veritable queen bee of deceit and duplicity. Never in his life had he seen such a glib liar, man or woman, but that very talent had saved his neck, as she was so fond of pointing out.

Unfortunately, however, he wasn't nearly as good

as she was at lying. He had plenty of faults, but blatant dishonesty wasn't one of them. He was uncomfortable stringing her along with the assumption that he was going to take the *Mamu* back into the Confederate Cause, especially since he was beginning to enjoy having her around.

Despite her apparent lack of scruples—at least when it came to anyone wearing Union blue—he liked her. Not only was she breathtakingly lovely, she was the most intelligent woman he had ever met. Her ingenuity was impressive; God knew she had wriggled her way out of enough tight spots in the past few days. She was quick-witted when it mattered and steadfastly loyal to what she believed in. In some ways he envied Cassandra her magnificent Cause. The risks he had taken in his life had been for himself and his crew, never for any ideal or loyalty to country or king.

Any way one looked at it, Cassandra was quite a woman. Unfortunately, even more than any of the worthy attributes he had noticed in her, he liked her exquisitely molded face and silver-blue eyes. He liked the feel of her fine-textured, golden red hair sliding through the palms of his hands and the way her mouth quivered when his lips caressed hers, as if she had never been kissed before.

Derek wasn't at all convinced that she was as experienced as she let on. She might have stolen a kiss or two in the past, such as the ones she had shared with her poor physician friend, Stephen, but he would wager a pile of gold that she was a virgin.

He had been with enough women to recognize the signs—and such a realization on his part never failed to end the alliance posthaste. Cassandra was different. He burned for her, inside and out, all over. She was a flame, and he a moth, just like every other man who saw her.

Furious at his own preoccupation with the woman, he flicked his half-smoked cheroot into the roiling ocean waves. He should never have teased her into selling her kisses. God, he had acted like a half-grown, lovesick adolescent since he had met her, and he was damn sick of playing that role.

The best thing to do was to go down and tell her that he had no intention of running her blasted blockade. He was going to have to tell her the truth sooner or later, and it might as well be now. She would immediately detest him, and that would certainly cool any more intimate contact between the two of them during the next few days while they were forced to share a cabin. His mind made up, he strode resolutely toward the companionway that led to the passenger cabins.

Cassandra was waiting up for him. She was perched on the edge of the bed dressed in a scandalously revealing white nightgown. The thin, gauzy fabric clung to her slender body, and his eyes riveted on her full breasts, which swelled provocatively above two tiny pearl buttons that held the bodice together.

When Derek stood at the door and stared in fascination at her chest, Cassandra pulled up the blanket to hide her cleavage. "I know this is rather sugges-tive," she murmured apologetically. "It's Georgia's, I'm afraid. She packed it for me, and I don't have anything else to wear. She always wears this sort of gown, you understand."

As Cassandra's embarrassed explanation dwindled away, Derek absolutely had to drag his eyes off her. The gown was not even unduly immodest except for being much too tight across the bodice, certainly not nearly as revealing as some of the filmy lingerie worn by his own past lovers. But Cassandra Delaney would look like a siren wearing a gunnysack. He turned and retrieved a blanket out of a cabinet built into the wall. *Tell her now,* he told himself firmly, *right now, before you look at her again and change your mind.*

"The captain sent down trays when we didn't ap-pear at supper. I tried to keep your food warm."

Surprised by her hesitant tone, which sounded very unnatural coming from her, he glanced back at her. She smiled at him, so sweetly that he was immediately on guard. She hadn't liked him from the first moment she saw him, had certainly wasted no friendly overtures on him.

"There's wine, too, if you should want some. There, on the table. Would you like me to pour you a glass?"

She was up to something, all right, but what? Wine did sound like what he needed to get through an entire night closed up with Cassandra adorned in that skimpy nightgown. He sat down in the desk

chair and poured himself a drink. He tossed it down
in one deep draught and helped himself to another.
He didn't look at her, but he knew she had lain
back on the bed and was arranging the blanket over
her. *Good,* he thought, *turn over, go to sleep, and
leave me alone.*

"Derek? Are you angry with me?"

He hadn't expected her to say that. "Why should
I be?" he muttered, glancing back to her.

"About the way I've been treating you. I know I
was hostile and difficult when we first met." She
looked down and fiddled nervously with the pearl
buttons of her nightgown. He stared unblinkingly at
the whorls of white lace over her breasts, just sheer
enough to drive a man out of his mind. She hesitated again, obviously embarrassed.

Oh, Lord, the top button had slipped out of its
loop, he realized, angered by his continued obses-
sion with her. What in God's name was the matter
with him? Steadfastly, he turned his eyes away. One
expert flick of his fingertips and the little round
pearls would give way. One little tug, and her
breasts would swell free for his starving eyes to
feast upon.

"I can tell you're still angry," she was saying now,
sitting up and looking at him, which only put more
strain on her bulging bodice. "I won't hold you to
relinquishing your fee for the run to North Carolina
just because you wanted to kiss me, if that's what's
bothering you. You deserve the gold you'll earn as
payment for such a dangerous voyage."

Lord help him now, Derek thought, one of her straps had slipped off her shoulder. He forced a convulsive swallow down a tightly constricted gullet.

When Cassandra twisted to retrieve the lacy shoulder tie, the remaining pearl had withstood all the pressure it could take. It gave way, and Derek stared like a hungry shark at the soft white flesh of full naked breasts until Cassandra gasped and quickly crossed her arms over her open bodice.

Oh, God, he had been in jail too long for this kind of erotic torture. He needed another drink. He grimaced, but he stole another look as Cassandra pulled a soft quilt around her shoulders. Her face was flaming red. And for good reason.

Frowning, Derek doused the lamp, wrapped the blanket around him, and lay down near the door. He shut his eyes and tried to ignore her. Cassandra lapsed into silence, too, and he stared morosely into the darkness. He should tell her the truth now, he thought. There would never be a better time. If he did, though, the rest of the voyage to Nassau wouldn't exactly be a pleasant prospect. She might even be angry enough to brand him an escaped convict and turn him over to Captain Rodgers. Maybe he ought to wait until they landed in Nassau. Yes, he would tell her then, just before they were destined to go their separate ways.

Derek shut his eyes, but he lay awake with every muscle tense and straining as he listened to Cassandra move restlessly upon the bunk. He thought about the time earlier that evening when they had lain there so tightly entwined, intimately exploring each other's mouths. His throat suddenly went dry, and he wet his lips. God help him, the most delicious woman in the world lay a few feet away, and all he could think about was getting up and crossing the room, lying down beside her and taking her in his arms, and making long, leisurely love to her for hours and hours.

His loins reacted violently to that enjoyable fantasy, and he gritted his teeth so hard that Cassandra could probably hear them all the way across the cabin. If he did go to her, seduce her innocence, he wasn't sure he could refuse afterward to make the suicidal run into Wilmington that she was insisting on. One thing he knew for damn sure, the first thing he was going to do in Nassau was find a good-looking woman to put him out of his misery. Cursing, he punched his pillow, fully aware he bloody well wouldn't get any more sleep than Cassandra Delaney would. She was tossing and turning as if she lay on a bed of hot coals.

Two days later when the *Rachel Ann* sailed into the fine blue harbor of New Providence Island, Cassandra looked out over the colorful limestone houses dotting the hills behind Nassau. Throughout the voyage, she had fought against her ridiculous attraction to Derek Courtland. Time and again she had tried to analyze just what it was about him that affected her when no other man had ever sent her emotions into such turmoil.

Try as she might, she couldn't come up with any answers, and she was just pleased that he had made a point to keep distance between them after having been shaken to the bones by his draining kisses. He had spent most of his time on deck in conversation with the sailors or the other passengers, while to her chagrin, she had thought of nothing but him.

She gazed longingly at him where he stood in the bow. As they neared the wharves, he was looking intently out over the bay. Who was he watching for? A woman, perhaps, a lover? She shivered slightly and drew her black shawl closer around her shoulders.

When he turned and suddenly headed straight toward her, she found herself tensing up, and realized she was almost frightened of him now.

"G'day, luv," he greeted her, leaning against the mizzenmast and grinning down at her. All the hours spent topdeck in the past few days had given a slight reddish burn to his dark face, but that only made him look better than usual. Cassandra frowned as Derek's black eyes raked over her in an unsettling way. What was he thinking?

"Let's talk about your run into Wilmington," she said almost angrily. "Where's the *Mamu*? If you plan to sail at once, I'll need to arrange for supplies to be loaded aboard."

Derek raised a dark brow, obviously surprised by her peevish tone. "If the *Mamu* made it here without mishap, George or Big Roscoe should be watching for me. Be ready to disembark, because I intend to be the first man off this bloody ship."

"Who's Big Roscoe?" she called after him as he strode to the bow. As the crew began to bustle around the decks in readiness to maneuver the *Rachel Ann* into berth, she hurried below to get her things. Somehow she knew that if she did not make haste, Derek Courtland might very well walk off and leave her without a backward glance.

# Chapter 9

"There she is, riding at anchor. Isn't she a beauty?" Derek said as he drove the buggy down a narrow road that curved along the shining sea.

Pride infused his voice as he pointed out his ship with the carriage whip, and Cassandra felt much the same emotion when she saw the sleek sailing sloop in the distance. The famed *Mamu*, she thought, a hard lump forming in the back of her throat. The swift ship had saved many a life in the last three years. Soon she would be sailing for the Confederacy again.

"And there's the Malmora Pub, christened for my birthplace in Victoria."

Cassandra turned her attention to the two-story building just ahead. The quaint inn was constructed of pale yellow stone with fancy red tiles on the steeply sloping roof. Lily had spoken often of her family's cattle ranch in Australia, but Cassandra knew little about the real Malmora, other than that it lay somewhere near the Australian city of Melbourne.

Derek was grinning with anticipation as he slapped the reins. Cassandra held on when the horse obediently trotted at a faster gait. Shielding her eyes, she caught sight of three figures running to meet them. When she recognized Kapi and Rigi, she was pleased that her agents had accomplished their mission. Apparently they had run into no problems while smuggling the little aboriginal twins out of Virginia. With the exception of Lily's capture, her plan to get Derek Courtland back aboard the *Mamu* had worked admirably and now was close to fruition.

"Kapi, Rigi! Thank God you're safe!" Derek cried in delight, jerking the reins and bringing the conveyance to a skidding halt near the front doors of the pub. He jumped to the sand almost before the horse stopped prancing. The two eight-year-old boys jumped into his arms and clung to him. He swung them around, and as they squealed uproariously, Cassandra smiled, somehow surprised that Derek was so at ease with small children.

Her attention was diverted from the little boys when their companion lumbered up in a slow run. She stared at the giant Negro in some shock, thinking he was the most immense human being she had ever seen. As he approached Derek's six-foot-three-inch frame, he veritably towered over him. Brawny and powerful, the man's torso was as thick around the girth as a good-sized rain barrel. *Big Roscoe,* she surmised as Derek set down the two giggling children and turned to the man. To her shock, the poor man burst into tears.

"Roscoe, Roscoe, what'd I tell you about crying every time you see me?" Derek chided gently, patting the weeping man's back. Cassandra watched him soothe the Negro, surprised by yet another gentle side of Derek Courtland.

"I thought somebody hurted you and you weren't gonna come back no more," Roscoe was blubbering. He turned abruptly to the little boys. "I got some more tears now. You can have them, if you want'm."

"Tears be magic drops, Captain, 'member?" Rigi cried.

"It be good luck to catch'm," Kapi added excitedly, "and Big Roscoe always gives'm to us."

Derek laughed as the children gathered around Big Roscoe and tried to catch the tears streaming down his face. Derek was still smiling when he swung Cassandra off the seat and onto her feet. The twins immediately left Roscoe and grabbed her hands.

"We thought you was Lily, Miss Cassie, when we first saw you comin'."

"But we's glad you here with us."

"I'm glad to see you, too." She smiled down at them until Derek took hold of her arm. "Cassandra Delaney, meet my good friend, Roscoe Brown. Roscoe, this is the lady that got me out of jail and brought me back here."

Roscoe Brown could not be less than seven or eight inches over six feet, she thought, rather awe-struck by his size. Now, up close, she could see the ridges of short, jagged scar tissue that covered his face. Horrified, she realized that one eyelid drooped slightly, as if he had no control over it.

"How do you do, Mr. Brown?" Cassandra greeted him politely, smiling and reaching out her gloved hand. At the sound of her voice, however, Roscoe visibly flinched. Some awful emotion stirred upon his ravaged features. Fear, she realized, as he backed away from her. Suddenly he turned and ran toward the wall that led into the backyard of the inn.

"Roscoe, it's all right!" Derek called after him, but then a shout from the front door sent him swiveling around. A dozen men poured out of the tavern toward them, and Derek strode to meet his friends, his arms outstretched in welcome.

"It's about time you showed your landlubbing face, Captain," cried a diminutive man dressed in a striped sailor's shirt and white pants.

Derek laughed with pleasure and began to shake hands as the men crowded around him. "We'll be shipboard again before the week's out, mates, you can bet your lives on it."

A cheer went up all around, and Cassandra lifted a brow as a woman dressed in a low-cut white blouse and red skirt pushed her way to the front.

"Mabel, luv, give me the welcome I deserve," Derek cried, pulling her off the ground and giving her a hearty kiss that went on until the other men roared with laughter.

"He's been in the calaboose too long this time!" called a voice from the back.

More laughter and catcalls ensued until Derek finally seemed to remember that he hadn't arrived alone.

"Ah, forgive me, darlin'," he said, sweeping his arm toward Cassandra. "Come meet my loyal band of brigands."

Silence descended on the rowdy group as every eye turned and studied her face and figure.

"Miss Cassandra Delaney," Derek proclaimed with a sarcastic flourish and bow. "The White Rose of the Confederacy and the spy who lied and wreaked havoc on the Yankees to get me back to Mabel and the *Mamu*."

"Thank ye fer that, Miss," came Mabel's breathless voice. She pulled Derek's head down for another lengthy kiss, and Cassandra frowned as more good-natured teasing commenced. The jovial camaraderie continued as Derek moved away in the midst of his crew, still clutching the curvaceous serving wench tightly against his side.

Totally ignored, Cassandra stared after him in severe pique until Kapi and Rigi hugged her legs and looked up at her with shining brown eyes.

"We so glad to see you, Miss Cassie! When Lily be comin' here?"

Cassandra knelt down and put her arms around them. "I'm sorry, boys, but she's gone back to Washington to be with Mr. Harte."

Disappointment put an end to the happy grins

they had been sporting since the buggy had drawn into sight. They looked at each other and had a quick conversation of their own.

"Miss Lily love the green-eyed man."

"She not want to leave him."

"That's right," Cassandra agreed. "She'll be just fine there with Harte, so you don't need to fret about her."

"Come, we show you to the room Big Roscoe fixed up for us. We fix one for Lily, too, but now it can be for you."

Cassandra allowed the boys to pull her after them toward the side of the inn, then through a gate in the stucco wall where a staircase rose to a second-floor covered veranda. She saw Big Roscoe peeking around the trunk of a palm tree several yards away. Although she was more than curious about the fearsome-looking giant, she hurried along with the children, eager to wash up in the privacy of a real room in a real house on solid ground.

# Chapter 10

Much later that evening Derek clinked mugs with yet another of his crewmen toasting his safe return. He was very happy to be back in the fold. Mabel had been her usual accommodating self in his bedroom earlier in the day, and even though he had enjoyed her soft allure and the eager abandon with which she welcomed him home, she had not put out the fire burning in him for Cassandra Delaney. Derek glanced across the room where she had sat for most of the evening, frowning and giving him arch looks each time Mabel sat down on his lap or blew him a kiss from behind the counter. Was she jealous? Or just angry that he had been ignoring her?

Annoyed at his steadfast preoccupation with her, he nevertheless moved away from the bar and took a place at an empty table where he could see her better. When a new toast to the *Mamu* was shouted by a man at the bar, he raised his tankard in salute. As soon as he worked up the nerve to tell Cassandra that he wasn't going into North Carolina for her, she would be gone, out of his life and back to her own existence of secret intrigue and daredevil stunts. But did he really want that? He already knew he was going to miss her, but he was damned if he knew why. She was a troublesome wench, and that was putting it mildly.

"Captain Derek Courtland?"

A stranger was now standing beside Derek's table. The man was short and painfully thin. His hair was dark brown and combed behind his ears, and he wore a thin mustache waxed to slant down over his large lips. He wore a plain black frock coat that was too big, and a felt hat with a narrow brim. He had a bookish look about him, like a librarian or a male secretary.

"Yeah, that's right. What can I do for you?"

While Derek took a swallow of his rum, the man glanced around furtively.

"I'd like to talk to you. May I sit down?"

"Depends on what the subject is."

The man lowered his voice. "My business concerns Cassandra Delaney."

Surprised, Derek looked at Cassandra and found her interest diverted by a good-natured scuffle between two of his men at the other side of the pub. At the moment Scotty and Jeffrey were progressing from their initial shoving match into the chair-throwing stage of their brawl.

"Take a chair," he invited, more than a little interested in whatever the man had to say concerning

Cassandra. The man sat down, and he kept his conversation quiet.

"I intend to be totally honest with you, sir. My name is Edmund Colvin. I work here in Nassau as an agent for the United States government."

Derek laid his hand on his thigh near his Colt revolver. The man saw, swallowed hard, and stuttered out his reassurances. "Please, I have no quarrel with you, although I know you're highly wanted by my government. You can rest assured that I haven't come here to try to take you back to prison."

"It's a damn good thing." Derek relaxed a bit, aware that Cassandra was watching him again. She didn't give any indication that she recognized Colvin. "What do you want, Colvin?"

"Miss Delaney's brother, Harte Delaney, is my superior officer. Weekly missives from him arrive on various Union ships that dock here in Nassau. Just after your escape I received a directive from him concerning his sister."

Derek narrowed his gaze. "How could he have known we were coming here?"

"He didn't know for sure. He assumed you would make all haste to return to the *Mamu*."

"How did he know she was docked here?"

Colvin looked smug. "The *Mamu*'s whereabouts is important knowledge for the federal government, considering the times she's run through our line of defenses. I reported her arrival here the minute she sailed into port nearly four months back."

"So what's all this got to do with Cassie?"

Colvin leaned forward, his ferret face intent. "Major Delaney wants his sister out of the war, Captain. At the time of your escape, he found out that she was responsible for countless acts of sabotage while she was living in Washington. He wants her spying activities over with, once and for all."

"Then I'd say he sure as hell has his work cut out for him," Derek muttered on a sour note. He drained his mug and set it on the table. "She does whatever she damn well pleases."

"That's exactly what Major Delaney is afraid of. When she helped you escape, she committed high treason. That's a hanging offense, Captain Courtland, as you well know, since you've suffered the same charge yourself. If she goes back and returns to her previous criminal activities, chances are she'll be caught now that we in the Secret Service are on to her."

Derek leaned back in his chair. "So? What the hell's all this got to do with me?"

"Major Delaney seems to think that you will shortly set sail for Australia and cause us no more trouble. Is that true?"

"Maybe."

"If you do harbor such plans, Major Delaney wants you to take his sister along and keep her there with you where she won't be a threat to us or herself until the war's over."

Shocked into silence, Derek could only stare at him. He hadn't expected such a request, but although he liked the idea just fine, he knew well enough it wouldn't work. "I don't think the lady's going to agree to that, mate. Right or wrong, she's got a burning loyalty to the Confederacy."

A crafty look surfaced in the man's keen blue eyes. "Major Delaney thinks it best if his sister doesn't know where you're planning to take her."

Derek sat straighter. Colvin had all his attention now. "Are you telling me that Harte Delaney wants me to abduct his sister?"

"We don't like to use that word, Captain. The major considers it more of an attempt to save her from her own ill-advised actions."

Wordlessly, Derek swiveled his speculative regard to the lady in question. Cassandra gave him a dour look, then tossed her head and said something to Kapi and Rigi, who had joined her earlier. Inside, he felt a warm wave of pleasure rise and roll through his chest. He laughed to himself. If he tried for a million years, he couldn't think of anything he would rather do than spirit Miss Cassandra Delaney away on his ship where he would have her to himself for months on end. With her older brother's blessing, at that.

"What's in it for me?" he asked with a casualness that belied his curiosity.

"Five hundred dollars in gold. It's worth that much or more for our government to get rid of her. Believe me, Captain Courtland, that young woman has caused us a great deal of grief and damage."

"Oh, I believe you, all right. The lady's resourceful, that's for damn sure. She got me here, didn't she?"

"Can we count on your help?"

"When do I get my money?"

"The day you sail for Australia, with her aboard."

"You've got yourself a deal, Mr. Colvin. Please send my regards to Harte Delaney and tell him I won't let his sister out of my sight until we're in Melbourne. And tell him I'm holding him responsible for my sister Lily's welfare until I can come back for her."

"I can tell you that your sister is well and staying as a guest at Major Delaney's house, if that would relieve your mind."

"Aye, that it does. Thank Major Delaney for me."

Colvin nodded. "I'm sure he'll be quite relieved that you're taking his sister to hand, both personally and professionally. I'll arrange to be at the dock the day you depart. I'll have your payment with me. The United States government is in your debt, sir."

As Derek clasped hands on the agreement, he felt the reverse was true. Spending time with Cassandra Delaney on his terms for a change was a welcome endeavor, but he had a feeling that she wouldn't be nearly as pleased with the arrangement as he was.

For some time Cassandra had been watching Derek as inconspicuously as possible. He had been engaged in a serious discussion with a man who had entered the bar about fifteen minutes earlier. Although the man in the black coat and hat hadn't interacted with the others at the bar, she assumed he was a member of the crew. She averted her eyes when Derek suddenly rose and shook hands with the man. The next time she looked up, Derek was sauntering casually in her direction.

When he reached her, he turned around the chair across from her, straddled it, then folded his arms on its back. He smiled, slow and appraisingly, his black eyes glinting. Cassandra tried her best not to be stirred by him. As usual, it didn't work. Her heart raced.

"Hello, Cassie, luv. Miss me as much as I missed you?"

His voice was low and so huskily caressing that Cassandra felt warm pleasure seep over her skin as if she had slowly eased her body into a tub of oiled bathwater. She wet her lips with the tip of her tongue, then remembered how he always stared at her mouth when she did so. His eyes immediately fastened on her moistened lips, and she shifted uncomfortably.

"The boys have gone down to the beach," she told him, attempting a safer subject. "They like it here near the ocean. They said it reminds them of the days they spent with Harte and Lily at his house on Moon Cove."

"The aboriginals hold all of nature sacred. That's why it's so important for them to get back to their tribal lands."

"I've always wanted to visit Australia," she admitted, glad he was willing to discuss something else.

"I can't tell you how pleased I am to hear that, Cassie."

He was flirting with her again, she realized at once, but this time his smile was different, mysterious and disconcerting.

"I'd love to do a thesis on aboriginal culture," she continued, trying to ignore the way his eyes, so unbelievably black and unreadable, latched on to her face.

"Is that a fact?"

"Yes. Australia is such an interesting continent. I know a great deal about its history and the transportation of English convicts there, mainly through reading the books and travel logs of the early explorers. If I remember correctly, the first shipload of British prisoners landed in Sydney in 1679. Unfortunately, I haven't been able to uncover much information on the aboriginals, although I did search through the Smithsonian's library for such material after I met the boys. I've also interviewed Kapi and Rigi at length. They've taught me a few words of their language and how to throw a boomerang. I'm not very good at that yet, though."

She realized how nervous her chatter must sound to him, but there was still that odd gleam in his eye. She could detect it most clearly, and she felt that it had gone on long enough. "Why are you looking at me like that?" she demanded flatly.

"I'm just glad to hear you have plans to visit my country. Who knows, luv? Perhaps I'll have the pleasure of showing you around. I'll even help you write your dissertations on kangaroos and wombats."

"I daresay you'll be long gone by the time I'm able to come there. The war here could go on a very long time."

Derek's expression grew more serious. "George, my first lieutenant, says the word in Nassau is that the South can only hold out a few more months."

"That's why it's so important for us to try to get supplies in to them. Do you know when you'll be ready to set sail?"

"Don't you mean we?" he asked, arching a brow.

"Actually, I've decided to take a merchant clipper back to Boston. I saw one being loaded when we landed at the docks. I can do more good up north than behind our own lines."

"Didn't I mention my one condition? You have to go with me."

Cassandra was surprised. "Me? Why?"

He shrugged, his devilish expression back in place. "To share the excitement of running the blockade. You like danger, don't you, darlin'? We're alike in that way, I think. We both like it when our blood starts pumping through our veins and our hearts thunder until it's hard to take a breath. That's what it's like to run the blockade in the dead of night—like knocking on the devil's door."

*He* was the only thing that affected Cassandra's heart and blood in that way, but his description did sound intriguing. She could go along and make sure everything went according to plan, then slip back through the Yankee lines easy enough. She had done it more times than she could count.

"All right, I'll go with you. I'm not the least bit afraid to, if that's what you're insinuating."

"You? Afraid? I find that highly doubtful."

Cassandra glanced away from his hot eyes just in time to see Big Roscoe burst through the front doors, grab a tankard off a table, then run out again.

"Tell me about Roscoe Brown. I think he's afraid of me."

"He doesn't trust people with southern accents."

"Why?"

Derek studied her expression. "Because he used to be a slave. His owner abused him."

"Most southerners treat their people with kindness," she said defensively. "My mother never abused our slaves and neither would I."

"That's right nice of you, Cassie, but I doubt if it makes much difference to poor Roscoe, who spent all those years shackled and beaten with chains. As you can see by his face, his owner wasn't nearly as magnanimous as you and your mother." Derek's voice had hardened.

"Is that where he got all those scars?"

"That's right. Some were from beatings, but most were from the prize fights he was forced to participate in. He was quite the champion of New Orleans, I understand. He hated it, though, because, despite his size and intimidating bulk, he's a very gentle man. His master made him fight, whether he wanted to or not, and he made the consequences of losing so terrible that Roscoe dared not hold back against his opponents."

Derek paused momentarily, his voice changing, growing colder. "Big Roscoe killed three men with those big fists of his, all of them other slaves put into the ring by their greedy owners. Then one day he faced a man who was even bigger, stronger, and meaner than he was. He lost that day. He was beaten so brutally around the head that he lost an eye and most of his ability to reason. He's got the mind of a six-year-old now. His owner used him to cover a twenty-dollar bet against me in a gambling parlor in the French Quarter. That was two years ago, and he's been with me ever since. That's why he cries, Cassie, just because I'm good to him."

Cassandra couldn't hide her horror. "My God. Such things shouldn't be allowed."

Derek looked askance at her. "Isn't that a bit subversive, since you're fighting to keep the institution of slavery alive and well?"

"You don't understand the southern perspective."

"No. I don't."

"If you were brought up in the South, you'd know how important slavery is to our economy. It's an institution that's always been there. Without it our way of life would crumble—everything in our society would fall apart. It's a necessary evil."

"Human bondage is wrong under any circumstances."

Cassandra met his eyes defiantly. "I know it is. Someday it will have to end."

Derek stared at her for a moment, then pushed back his chair and stood. "I do believe there's hope for you yet, luv. The *Mamu*'s set to sail two nights from now. Make a list of what you want loaded aboard for your Confederate friends, and I'll see it's done."

Cassandra caught his sleeve as he started to leave. "Derek, I do appreciate what you're going to do for the South. I'll never forget it."

Derek gave her an enigmatic smile. "No, Cassie, I daresay you won't ever forget it."

Cassandra watched him return to the bar and rejoin his friends, but she couldn't let herself worry about his odd behavior. After all her trouble and planning, her mission would soon be complete. The *Mamu* would resume its runs into Confederate ports, and that in itself was enough to make her happy.

# Chapter 11

The night on which Derek steered the *Mamu* out of her anchorage was clear and star-spangled, with calm seas and gentle winds. Cassandra was overcome by apprehension and found herself pacing in restless agitation up the length of the port rail, then back again. To alleviate her jittery nerves, she grasped the smooth oak railing and gazed out at the dark ocean and vast night sky. Twinkling stars stretched out in endless glory like diamonds adrift in an ebony pond.

Belowdecks the holds were full of guns, munitions, and desperately needed food supplies, and all around her the crew went about their tasks with quiet sobriety, well aware of the perils they faced on such a dangerous mission through Yankee gunboats. Only Kapi and Rigi could not hide their high spirits at being with Derek again, and their happiness revealed itself as they raced down the deck and skidded to a halt at Cassandra's side. Big Roscoe had stopped a good distance up the deck when he saw Cassandra.

"Miss Cassie, come watch the captain turn the big wheel!" cried Rigi.

"He say we can hold it steady, too, someday, if we work hard and be good cabin boys!" added his brother.

Cassandra allowed them to lead her toward the stern, where Derek stood manning the watch. A lantern hung on a hook near him, and the candle flickered shadows across the chiseled lines of his face. He looked his devilish best, of course, she thought irritably.

Then Cassandra's heart softened toward him. Derek was taking a big gamble with both his ship and his crew. He was risking his own life. If any of his crewmen died from Yankee guns, she would bear the brunt of the responsibility. Shivers fled down her arms. What if Derek was killed? The thought was so awful to her that her stomach clenched, but she was too afraid to examine just what that said about her feelings for Derek Courtland.

"Can we turn it around now, Captain Derek?" one of the boys was begging.

"Not tonight. I've got to keep her steady on course. Get below, mates, and make my cabin presentable for our lovely guest."

"I'm to stay in your cabin?" Cassandra asked as the children obediently scampered away to do his bidding. Perversely, she liked and disliked the idea of sharing his quarters.

"It's the biggest and the best aboard, and you'll

have your privacy because I'll bunk in a hammock in my office."

"That's very kind, but I hardly think I'll need such accommodations on such a short voyage."

Derek shrugged. "I'd hardly be a gentleman if I didn't offer my accommodations to you, now, would I, Miss Delaney?"

"You're hardly a gentleman anyway, Captain Courtland."

"True, but please, call me Derek when you insult me."

His deep rich voice was so intimate that it felt like a kiss brushing her cheek. Cassandra fought the uncanny sensation.

"The stars seem so close out at sea," she murmured as she looked up at the vast firmament.

"Would you like to steer?" Derek's offer surprised her.

"Yes, I'm very interested in studying the maritime arts."

"Come here, Cassie."

Cassandra stepped quickly between Derek and the wheel, which stood nearly as tall as she. Unfortunately, now she was even more aware of how Derek's warmth felt pressing up close behind her.

"Just hold her steady," he whispered, his lips close to her right ear. "It's a fine night for sailing."

Cassandra did so and immediately felt the currents of the ocean against the rudder as she gripped the wheel. Derek's fingers closed over her hands.

"Lean against me, darlin', and I'll help you."

Cassandra knew better than to do that. "I'm stronger than you think, Captain. I probably know a good deal more about seafaring than you would suspect."

"I shouldn't be surprised. Have you captained your own ship in the past?"

Cassandra was amused. "Of course not, but I've studied all sorts of naval vessels, as well as the effects of trade winds and ocean currents."

"Then you can tell me about the *Mamu*, I suppose."

"I can tell you she's a steam sloop probably about two hundred feet long. I'd estimate her draft to be around twelve feet. I counted eight guns, so I'd estimate your crew at one hundred. As far as speed, she's very fast. I'd say twelve or thirteen knots with the sails hoisted."

Derek gave a low, appreciative laugh and settled his chin atop her head. "You're off on her length by twenty feet and on her draft by two. She rides at fourteen. Thirteen knots, it is, under sail and steam. I'm impressed, Miss Delaney. You probably know more about the sea than I do."

Cassandra smiled at his compliment, but she knew he was wrong. From the beginning of the war, she had heard tales of his daring feats and expert navigation, both from her Confederate compatriots and Harte's Union friends.

"When have you been aboard a ship, Cassie?" he asked, pressing his mouth against her hair. His right hand had left hers and had circled her waist to draw her body even closer against him. She didn't protest, didn't want to.

"I've been to Europe several times to study, both in England and various cities on the Continent. The longest voyage was around Cape Horn to Lima."

"You've been to Peru?" His face was pushing her head to one side so he could nuzzle the side of her neck.

"Yes," she answered breathlessly as his warm lips settled on the sensitive hollow at the side of her throat. "Dr. Henry took me there with him. He was studying Indian culture and Incan history. His wife and children traveled with him, so I was allowed to go along as his assistant."

"How old were you then?"

"That was before the war, when I was fifteen or sixteen."

"Your family didn't mind you traipsing around the world at such a young age?"

"My father died when I was little, and my mother wanted me to improve my mind."

"You've certainly succeeded in that. I suspect she's very proud of you now."

"She passed away several years ago."

"I'm sorry. That must have been difficult for you."

"Yes."

Silence surrounded them for a moment until Derek asked, "Did you enjoy your stay in Peru?"

For one terrible moment Cassandra stood again in the dirty hovel that was their hospital and saw Dr. Henry deliver a poor twisted baby from Cheopi's writhing body. Bile rose, bitter, caustic, burning the back of her throat as she remembered the mother's screams when she saw her deformed child.

"What's wrong?" Derek asked at once. "You're tense all of a sudden."

"Nothing. I'm fine," she answered, thrusting the awful memory out of her mind. "I contracted malaria when I was there. I was thinking about that."

"Did you suffer a bad case?"

"Yes," she said softly, "but I survived it."

"Thank God for that," Derek murmured, pulling her back intimately against his chest. The strong arms sheltered her from the cold sea wind, and she let down enough to lean her head comfortably against his sturdy shoulder while she lifted her gaze once again to the heavens.

"I've always found astronomy fascinating," she remarked contentedly. "I became interested when I visited the observatory in London. I think it's wondrous how the whole universe moves slowly through space from day to day with whole constellations of stars revolving in the sky like some kind of gigantic clock."

"I've always found you fascinating," he whispered in return, his lips nibbling at her earlobe.

What he was doing felt good, and Cassandra smiled dreamily, thinking she would probably regret the day Derek Courtland sailed away to Australia. He did have his good points, and suddenly she wanted to know him better, perhaps even encourage a more serious relationship between them. But it was too late for that. After this mission, they'd go their separate ways.

"I wish things were different," she said impulsively, turning in his arms. "I wish we had met before the war, when gentlemen courted the ladies and life was so much simpler."

"I can still court you."

"Do you want to?"

Derek laughed. "I haven't been the same man since you waltzed down the steps of the White Rose in that turquoise gown." His voice suddenly grew more serious. "I doubt if I'll ever be quite the same after these last few days."

Pleased, Cassandra leaned her head against his shoulder. Derek eased her back against the wheel and found her mouth in a sweet, gentle kiss. "I want you, Cassie, and you want me, don't you?"

Cassandra closed her eyes as his lips moved slowly along her smooth brow.

"Then let it happen tonight before we have to part."

His urgent whisper gripped Cassandra with the most powerful longing to surrender completely and let him take her below to his cabin and teach her all about the physical act of love shared by a man and a woman. She was shocked by the strength of her desire to do so. She could never allow such a thing. Especially not with a man like Derek Courtland, who used women and then sailed on to the next port and the next lover. She was not some trollop to be seduced and then left behind.

"I want to, Derek, but what you're suggesting isn't proper. Someday I'll marry, and I want him to be the first." What she said was the truth, but her voice trembled with her eagerness to give in. She was weakening, and she knew it. She attempted to step away, but his arms tightened and held her in place.

"Don't leave. I'll respect your wishes. I won't try to force you to do anything you don't want to."

Cassandra did relax. She believed him. Perhaps he was honorable after all, and not the hard-hearted seducer of women she had branded him. She could learn to care about him, she realized, care a great deal. Oh, Lord help her, she already did. Frightened by her own self-revelation, she looked up at the sky and forced herself to concentrate on something else.

"I can navigate by the stars," she told him when she became so aware of his closeness that she wanted to turn and pull his head down until his lips devoured hers. "The professor taught me a rhyme to help recall the order of the twelve constellations of the Zodiac."

She smiled as she quoted by memory:

"The Ram, the Bull, the Heavenly Twins,
And, next the Crab, the Lion stands,
The Virgin and the Scales,
The Scorpion, the Archer, the Sea-goat,
The Man who pours the water out,
The Fish with glittering tails."

Derek hugged her closer. She sighed and lay her head back against him, suddenly missing her studies with Dr. Henry and the other scientists of the Smithsonian Institution.

"Dr. Henry was always giving us little rhymes like that, and you can see how helpful they are." She arched her head farther back until she could gaze straight up. "Orion should be somewhere right above us. There, you can see the three stars forming his belt. The bright red star, Betelgeuse, is his left shoulder and the bright blue-white Rigel is his right foot. Sirius is the brightest star in the sky. It should be to the east of his foot, right over there. Wait a minute, I can't see it. That's strange." Frowning in confusion, she searched the twinkling clusters for the bright stars Castor and Pollux in the constellation Gemini. Instead of lying ahead of her to the west where it was supposed to be, the group of stars lay behind her, behind the stern of the ship.

"Cassie, there's something I have to tell you. Please, just hear me out before you get upset—"

The low urgency in Derek's voice alerted Cassandra that something was definitely amiss. The truth rushed over her, raw, stunning, and sent her cold with shock. They weren't sailing north toward the Carolinas at all! They were headed toward the southern horizon!

"Where are you taking me?" she cried, breaking away from his arms and whirling to face him.

"Now, Cassie, there's no need to get all riled up—"

"How dare you lie to me!"

The magnitude of his deception hit Cassandra like a plunge into icy water, and she sagged back against the rail in unmitigated dismay. A mixture of anger, horror, and disbelief laced her voice. "But I've got to get these supplies to Wilmington!"

Derek Courtland did have the grace to look guilty. "I'm sorry, but I'm doing this as a favor to your brother."

"For Harte? What are you talking about?"

"We're doing this for your own good, Cassie. Harte doesn't want you arrested and hanged for treason. I feel the same way. The idea of you putting yourself in danger the way you've been doing the last few years scares the hell out of me. I've begun to care for you, I guess." He stopped as if surprised at his own words. "Harte says it's only a matter of a few months before the war's over anyway—"

Fury such as Cassandra could never, ever remember filled her soul until she could barely draw enough breath to lash out at him.

"He's wrong," she ground out viciously, "and so are you, if you think you can do this to me and get away with it."

Trembling with rage, she drew her cloak tightly around her and stalked down the deck to the companionway that led to the captain's quarters. The crewmen she passed would not meet her eyes, and she knew that they were all in on the hoax. Her fury leaped into higher flames, and she flung open the door of Derek's cabin. It banged against the wall hard enough to make Kapi, Rigi, and Big Roscoe jump from where they were playing with a small white cat. Big Roscoe scooped up the frisky feline in his arms and backed away in fright until Derek's massive mahogany desk separated him from Cassandra's wrath.

"We're not going to the Carolinas, we're going to Australia," she snapped. "Did you two know that, too?"

Eyes round and white, the boys shook their woolly heads, then their faces simultaneously assumed expressions of pure delight.

"We go home!" Rigi clapped his hands with glee. "Now you see the dreaming time."

"Now you hunt for wallabies with boomerang!" Kapi added shrilly.

"I don't want to see any wallabies, or kangaroos, or anything else in Australia," she answered tightly. Jaw clamped hard, she crossed the floor and entered the adjoining sleeping quarters. She stopped, staring at the gigantic bouquet of white roses propped against the pillow of the built-in berth.

"They're from the captain." One of the boys giggled from the doorway behind her.

"It be his surprise for you," the other told her but his voice had grown a good bit more hesitant.

Cassandra snatched up the beribboned flowers, climbed atop the high bunk, and stuffed them through the open porthole. When she collapsed in an angry heap on the mattress, the two boys stared at her, their hands over their mouths in consternation.

"The captain gonna be mad at you," one of them said, his words muffled beneath his hands.

"He go to special place to get roses that match your name."

To Cassandra's mortification, she burst into hurt, frustrated tears. She covered her face and let herself cry but almost at once pulled herself together and cut off her despair. Weeping was stupid and unproductive, but the urge to sob threatened again when she felt the children snuggle close on either side of her. They both patted her back consolingly, their little faces filled with pity.

"We sorry you not want go to dreaming time anymore." Kapi's voice was choked with his own tears.

Rigi cupped her face in his small palms. "Don't be sad."

Cassandra leaned back against the wall, holding the boys close. She bit her lip, trying to think what to do as Big Roscoe peeked around the doorway, still holding the cat. She was astonished to see a sheen of tears in his eyes.

"You can hold my cat if you want to," he offered tentatively. "She real soft. Her name be Snowflake."

"Thank you, Big Roscoe," she managed, her heart in her throat as he brought the animal and placed it in her lap. She fought another urge to shed tears as the big man sat down on the floor and gave her a gentle smile.

How could Derek do such a thing to her after

she had gotten him out of prison and back to his ship? How could he cut a deal with her Yankee brother? She had trusted him, and he had betrayed her. That's what hurt her more than anything else. She shut her eyes, fighting her emotional distress, but she could not stop the fresh rush of tears coursing down her cheeks.

# Chapter 12

For the next few days Derek tended to his duties at the helm and gave both Cassandra and his living quarters an extremely wide berth. She had been absolutely livid the night she had discerned in the stars their change of destination, but each passing day put more nautical miles between her and her beloved Cause, and therefore, he hoped, between him and her anger. In time, she would have no choice but to accept her fate, and then Derek would make sure she enjoyed the trip so much that she would be able to forgive him.

"Well, George, we're making excellent time. The coast of Venezuela is due south of us and we'll be well out in the Atlantic within the week," he said heartily to his first officer on the morning of the fifth day. George Reynbolt had been with Derek since he had acquired the *Mamu*. The small energetic man was a good friend and, more importantly, completely trustworthy. He had taken charge when Derek had been forced to sit idle in a Yankee cell, something Derek wouldn't soon forget.

For the last hour he and George had been mapping out the different stages of the voyage and estimations to various ports of call, and he marked one last notation on the ocean chart in front of him, then rolled it up for storage. "We're in good shape, with no storms on the horizon."

"You're wrong, Captain. You've got a tempest approaching to starboard." George winked as he took the chart and turned for the bridge. "Good luck, Derek. By the look on the lady's face, I say you're going to need it."

Derek braced himself, then turned and found Cassandra bearing down on him with the two little aboriginals in tow. Big Roscoe followed at a safer distance, carrying Derek's Siamese cat in his arms.

"G'day, Cassie, luv," Derek greeted her, donning his most pleasant smile. He admired her flushed face and billowing red hair. "You do look fetching this morning."

"What you did was illegal," she clipped out in a matter-of-fact tone. "I could take you to court, you know, and I'd win my case. The cargo below is mine, every piece and parcel bought and paid for with Confederate money, and I have in my possession signed documents that prove my ownership."

"Indeed you do. Therefore, when we sell your goods at top price at our first port of call, you'll be fully entitled to the proceeds. I have no argument with your entitlement."

Cassandra's reaction to his fairness was an unimpressed glare. When Derek grinned at the boys, they smiled back until Cassandra glanced in their direction. Their little faces instantly dropped into grim solemnity.

"And just where is our first port of call, Captain Courtland?" she asked with palpable frigidity.

"Rio de Janeiro," he answered with a smile. "That's in Brazil."

"I know where it is!" she snapped furiously.

"Rio's one of the most beautiful cities in the world," he told her, blithely disregarding her flashing blue eyes. She was spoiling for a fight, but he knew better than to give her one. "They'll be celebrating Carnival while we're there. I do hope you'll allow me to take you ashore and show you the sights. Quite an interesting culture to study." He couldn't resist mocking her love of all things scientific.

"I'd rather be escorted by Attila the Hun."

Cassandra's remark struck him as funny. He shook his head, trying not to laugh. "Now, Cassie, you might as well stop your fretting and fussing and learn to accept your lot graciously, like a good girl."

"Accept my lot? Like a good girl?" she repeated with such derision that he almost flinched. Her lips tightened and her eyes narrowed dangerously. "You really are a wretched human being, aren't you? Is there anything you wouldn't do for a high enough price?"

Derek pondered the question. "Not much," he answered regretfully, then chuckled when he realized her unflattering assessment was fairly true to the mark. "Maybe I just wanted some time to court you properly, the way you suggested a few nights ago. Did you ever think of that?"

Cassandra's eyes moved out over the sea, and she took a deep breath, obviously trying to control herself. Derek enjoyed the way her breathing moved her bodice until she returned her wintry gaze to his face. "If you'll turn this ship around and head back to America, I'll pay you double whatever Harte promised you. Surely that triggers that colossal greed of yours."

Derek quirked a dark brow. "We're a long way from the Bahamas, Cassie, and your brother paid me in advance."

"You are despicable."

"And you are beautiful beyond compare."

"Me think you be, too," Big Roscoe broke in, then averted his eyes and shuffled his feet in self-conscious embarrassment.

"Us, too," the twins cried together, their heads nodding vigorous agreement.

"You see, Cassie, it's unanimous."

"Do you actually think a few flowery compliments will make me forget that you kidnapped me?"

"Now, Cassie, you know that's not true. I didn't abduct you. Harte paid for your passage." He smiled. "When you're angry, your eyes sparkle aquamarine like the lagoons in Tahiti."

"You're insane."

Derek looked down at her tightly clenched fists. For a moment he thought she was going to slap him across the face. Her features held in rigid control, she inspected his face. "All right, Captain. Just tell me what I have to do to get you to take me back home, and I'll do it."

"I find you highly attractive," he answered softly, leaning close to her. "Why don't you try to seduce me?"

"What's 'seduce' mean?" Kapi whispered to Rigi where they stood a few feet away.

His brother shrugged.

"It be a card you play in poker," Big Roscoe volunteered in a low voice.

"Seducing you wouldn't be much of a challenge, now, would it, Captain Courtland?" Cassandra was answering through set teeth.

Derek wanted to laugh because she was right.

"Is that what you want? To bed me?" she asked, very low so the children wouldn't hear. She surveyed his face thoughtfully as she awaited his answer.

Derek wondered if she might think his suggestion a viable exchange. "Surely that's not an offer I hear, Miss Delaney?"

"Of course it isn't. I just wondered how low you really were."

"Sorry to disappoint you, but I'm not that much of a cad." He lowered his voice even more. "If we ever decide to become lovers, darlin', it'll be by mutual agreement. Tell me, my pet, have you ever been to Brazil?"

"Stop calling me stupid names. I'm no lapdog to be coddled and stroked or rubbed behind my ears.

My name is Cassandra. Is that so hard to remember?"

Nothing about Cassandra Delaney was hard to remember, that was for damn sure, Derek thought as she turned on her heel, her unlikely entourage following her around like the obsequious courtiers of a royal princess. True, she hated him with a vengeance at the moment, but the trip to Melbourne was a good three months in duration. Surely he could win her over in that length of time. In any event, the idea was a challenge, and one that most definitely appealed to him.

A fortnight later, Derek wasn't so sure he would be successful in smoothing down Cassandra's ruffled feathers. She was not coming around in the least. They had rounded Cape São Roque, the westernmost tip of Brazil, and she had yet to utter a word to him, other than a cool nod if they should pass each other on deck.

Fortunately, however, she was keeping to herself or spending her time with Kapi, Rigi, and Big Roscoe, and Derek was glad for that small favor. His crew were a decent lot, and loyal to him, but they were red-blooded men. If Cassandra had taken on a flirtatious manner, the likes of which Derek had witnessed firsthand in the White Rose Tavern, there might have been violence aboard, even bloodshed. It would be better if she stayed below and out of sight. He had to admit, though, he missed her company—even her sharp tongue and irritating propensity for citing detailed knowledge of every subject he mentioned.

"Captain, come quick!"

One of the twins was running up the planked decking toward his position in the stern. The child looked frightened.

"What's wrong, boy?"

"Miss Cassie be sick, real sick. She need you."

At once Derek was suspicious. Cassandra was up to something and using the child to lure him into it. He would bet gold on it. "What's the matter with her?"

"Don't know. She say she gonna hafta go to bed and she need you to take care of her."

"Yeah, I'll bet," Derek muttered under his breath, but his curiosity was piqued. He would go see her, all right, but he would be ready for whatever game she had in mind.

Following the boy belowdecks, he opened the door to the captain's quarters and found the other twin and Big Roscoe standing near the bunk. Cassandra sat on the edge of the bed. Her face was ashen and beads of perspiration shone from her forehead and chin. She was sick, all right, enough so to cause Derek immediate alarm.

"Cassie, what is it? What's wrong with you?"

"I have medicine I can take. Please, come over here and let me show you how to administer it."

Derek hastened to her side and watched her dig with palsied hands into a large velvet satchel. She pulled out a flat silver flask with an attached medicine vial. She opened the top and quickly poured a small amount of fine white powder into the flask.

"What is that?"

"Water. The powder's quinine."

Derek instantly knew her malady. "Your malaria's recurring?"

"Yes," she murmured weakly as she shook the bottle to dissolve the powder. "Please don't be concerned, no one's in danger. It's not catching, I promise." She stopped speaking as she drank some of the medicine.

"I've seen malaria before."

"Then you know I'll be incapacitated for a few days."

"How bad will it be? Do you know?"

"Very bad." She wiped her hands across her brow and gazed beseechingly at him. "Will you help me while I'm sick? I don't have anyone else to turn to. I'll pay you."

"Don't be insulting, Cassie. I'll do what I can for you, but I'm no doctor."

"I don't need a doctor. I can tell you what to do. The quinine will reduce the fever, but I'm usually too sick to dose myself after the delirium starts. I'm sorry. I can't tell you how humiliating this is for me. The fever comes on so quickly sometimes that I can't make the necessary preparations. So I carry my medicine with me all the time. I'd let the boys help me, but they're scared and so is Big Roscoe. You might want to keep them out of my cabin until I'm myself again."

"You heard the lady, boys. Run along and let me help her get well."

"We don't want to go," Kapi said, tears threatening. "We can shake up white powder, too."

"Please, darlings," Cassandra said. "This happens to me every now and then, but I'll be fine, I promise. You go on with Big Roscoe and play on topdecks."

Derek watched Roscoe take the boys by the hands. After they were gone, he looked at Cassandra.

"Can you get undressed by yourself?"

Cassandra gave him a slit-eyed look that was definitely more like herself. "Yes, and I do hope you're gentlemanly enough not to molest me while I'm unconscious." She glared at him. "Are you?"

Derek grinned at her less than complimentary opinion of his scruples. "I've never ravished a woman on her sickbed before, so as attractive as I find you, Cassie, I suspect I'll be able to restrain myself."

"Please turn your back while I put on my nightgown. The chills will start soon. I just pray the fever lasts only a day or two."

Derek moved to the porthole and gazed out at the ocean swells. Behind him, he could hear the flutter of her clothes as she disrobed and climbed into the bunk. How unfortunate that a young woman like Cassandra was saddled with such a violent recurring illness. He had to admit, though, that she certainly approached it with the same practicality she adopted toward everything else in her life. Cassandra Delaney was no shrinking, sampler-stitching female—that was abundantly clear.

"You can turn around now."

Derek did so and approached the bed. He sat down on the end and observed the high-necked nightgown of plain white cotton that she had donned. She caught his gaze.

"I do appreciate this, Derek. I know it's improper, to say the least, but since you stole me away and deposited me on a ship full of strange men, I really had no choice."

"Believe it or not, you can trust me." Derek watched her pull her silky hair over her shoulder and braid it into a long queue. When she was finished, she lay back against the pillows. "Does your malaria recur often?"

Cassandra closed her eyes. "Once or twice a year. Sometimes I'm lucky and it's less than that. Dr. Henry taught me how to administer the quinine. The drug derives from the bark of the cinchona tree that grows on the eastern slopes of the Andes, you know. The Peruvian Indians have been using the medicine since before the Spaniards came in the 1500s."

*Even when she was sick Cassandra attempts a dissertation on the history of her disease,* Derek thought in amusement, but now her breathing was becoming labored. When she began to toss and turn fitfully, he moved to the washbowl and pitcher set in a built-in shelf near the bed. Watching her, he poured fresh water into the large porcelain bowl and retrieved one of the linen towels stacked beside it. He returned to the bed, moistened the soft cloth, and pressed it against her sweat-drenched cheek.

"I hate this," she whispered, her eyes brilliant with fever. "I hate it when someone else has to take care of me—"

"Shhh, I know. I wouldn't like it, either, but you might as well lie back and get through it. You can rely on me, Cassie. I'm not the monster you seem to think."

"Lily always said you were kind," she muttered hoarsely, her body suddenly wracked with chills. Derek tucked a blanket around her, gently cooling her hot skin with the wet cloth until she closed her eyes, eventually lapsing into the fitful delirium of malarial fever.

Cassandra was burning up. Her body felt as if flames smoldered just beneath her skin. Her mouth was dry, her throat parched and swollen. Why was she so hot? She was painfully thirsty, but she didn't think she could swallow. She would give anything for a drink of water, cold and clear—

"Hot—so hot—"

Something was touching her brow and face, so soft and cool and then wetting her lips. A voice came to her, low and thick with a strange accent, and she tried to force open her heavy eyelids, tried to remember who was with her, who was helping her. Was it her mother? No, she was gone now.

"Dr. Henry? Where are you? Am I going to die—"

Then her mind swirled with vivid colors and sounds and blurred images, and she knew she was rushing through the jungles of Mexico, the vines catching her hair and scratching her face, and she saw the ancient Aztec temples where the sacrifices were held—

"No, no, not my baby, don't take my baby—"

But the chief in his feathered headdress was holding the baby aloft, high in the air. Someone was screaming, it was her, she realized, screaming shrilly and full of terror—

"Cassie, Cassie, you're all right. It's just a nightmare."

The strange but familiar voice again; who was he? Then the images began to spin again, changing from one picture to the next like inside the kaleidoscope her brother, Stuart, had given to her when she was eight years old. Pieces of memories were whirling in a confusing maelstrom that made her dizzy until they formed a clear image, and she was walking through the ancient Incan capital of Cusco, over unpaved streets choked with weeds. She entered the hut of Cheopi.

"Cheopi? Where are you? Has the baby come?"

She ducked through the heavy blanket hanging over the door, saw Dr. Henry holding the infant. Full of dread, she lifted back the red blanket woven with yellow geometric patterns. The child lay stillborn, twisted, misshapen, grotesque in its deformity. Cassandra screamed.

"No! No, Cheopi! Poor baby, poor little thing—"

Heartbroken, she wept for the baby and for Cheopi and for herself until the primitive hut faded into a rushing river of blackness. The man's gentle voice came back and the cool water soothed the coals lodged beneath her flesh, and she stopped weeping and dropped down, down, down into a vast sea of cool black nothingness where there was no deformed babies, no fiery pain, no screaming—only calm, quiet peace.

When Cassandra finally quit her thrashing and slept calmly under the effect of the quinine he had administered nearly an hour earlier, Derek leaned back in the desk chair he had drawn up to the bunk and contemplated her delirious ramblings.

For three days and nights he had stayed beside her, bathing her burning body and feeding her spoonfuls of water and medicine. She had been wracked with horrible dreams that clearly terrified her, and he was still trying to make sense out of some of the words she had cried out with such anguish.

Most of her dreams concerned a baby, one who was born dead, but who's child was it? Cassandra's? He didn't think she had made love, much less delivered a child, but maybe he was wrong. She had led a strange, unconventional life and visited many different foreign lands on scientific excursions. What terrible events had she witnessed that tortured her subconscious mind in such a way? She had shown much more vulnerability than he ever would have expected. Inner devils haunted her mind, and he knew how that felt. He carried his own images of horror deep in his soul. His, too, concerned an innocent baby. He shut off his thoughts of that long-ago day before they could get started.

He moistened the towel with cool water, squeezed out the excess, then pressed it to Cassandra's forehead. Despite this last violent delirium, she was getting better. The quinine was finally bringing her out of her nightmares.

Groggily, Cassandra became aware of splashing water. She swam toward the surface of awareness until she could open her eyes and see the light. Everything seemed to sway in a relaxing rhythm, and when her gaze focused on the porthole across the cabin, she remembered she was aboard a ship.

Water tinkled again, and she turned her aching head and found Derek Courtland a few feet away. Naked from the waist up, he was bathing his chest and arms from a washbasin recessed into the wall. She watched him until he saw her in the mirror.

"So you've come back to us, have you, luv?" He toweled off as he came toward the bed. He smiled broadly.

"Yes, I think so." Her gaze settled on his chest only inches from her face. As weak as she was, her face burned with embarrassment. "You really should be wearing a shirt."

"Indeed I should, darlin', and I would, if you weren't wearing it."

Cassandra was shocked to find she did have on his white shirt. "But I wasn't wearing this . . ." Her voice trailed off and her eyes widened.

Derek looped his towel around his neck. He grinned. "Your nightgown was wringing wet. See, I'm not so greedy. I gave you the shirt off my back."

"You don't mean that you— I mean, surely you didn't actually take my clothes off me!"

Derek shrugged, and Cassandra was horrified. "I can't believe you would actually do anything quite so— so scandalous," she managed weakly.

"Would it make you feel better if I said that I didn't look?"

"Not unless it was true," she answered, but she was suddenly too tired to argue with him. If he saw her, he saw her. Besides, it wouldn't have been the first time. And she still owed him a debt of grati tude. Wearily, she lay her head back against the pillow.

"How do you feel?" Derek reached out and laid a cool palm across her forehead.

"Tired and hungry and embarrassed."

"You were a very sick lady. I was beginning to get worried."

For the first time, Cassandra realized that he, too, looked exhausted.

"How long has it been?" she asked as he poured a glass of water for her. He supported her head and helped her to drink.

"Three days."

"Usually it's just a day or two."

"Who takes care of you when I'm not around?"

"My mother used to." Deep inside, she mourned again her mother's passing. "After she died, I'd usually go to Harte's house, where Hannah would take care of me."

"Hannah?"

Cassandra smiled. "She was our mammy when my brothers and I were babies, but Harte was always her favorite, too."

"Too?"

"My northern grandmother doted on Harte so much that she finally ended up taking him to Rhode Island to raise. When Mother let him go, she devoted herself to my other brother, Stuart. Papa was the only one who paid any attention to me. He told me I was smarter than everyone else in the family." The moment the words left her mouth, she wondered why on earth she had shared such a personal memory with Derek Courtland.

"And he was probably right."

Something in the way Derek was looking at her made Cassandra's heart come up into her throat. She felt the burn of tears and immediately blinked them back. *How absurd*, she thought, but then she did always become weak and overemotional after her relapses.

"Who's Cheopi?"

Cassandra looked quickly at him. "Did I dream about her?"

"Yes, quite a lot, I think."

"She was an Indian girl I met when I accompanied Dr. Henry to Peru."

"Was?"

"She died while we were there." Cassandra put her hand to her aching temples. She didn't like to think about her Indian friend. "I should be up and around tomorrow, so I won't have to trouble you anymore."

"No trouble."

He smiled, but she remained serious. "Thank you, Derek. I won't forget how kind you've been."

"Do you mean that?"

"Of course."

"Then you wouldn't think of refusing me the pleasure of showing you around Rio, would you?"

"That's blackmail."

"First you accuse me of kidnapping, now blackmail. I'm beginning to wonder if you have a low opinion of me."

Cassandra smiled. "All right, I'll go with you."

Derek rubbed his bearded cheek. "Then I'm going to leave you to your rest. There are three people outside who have been dying to see you."

To Cassandra's shock, he leaned down and pressed a tender kiss to her forehead. He left with long, masculine strides, closing the door quietly and leaving Cassandra to ponder over his gentleness.

# Chapter 13

Cassandra Delaney sat in the maroon leather desk chair in the office area of Derek's quarters. Swiveling slightly, she gazed out the wide mullioned stern windows over the deep blue waters of Guanabara Bay to where a long curve of dazzling white beaches edged the Brazilian port of Rio de Janeiro. Low mountains rose behind the sprawling city, gray and indistinct in the deepening twilight, but the famous Sugar Loaf Mountain loomed massive and impressive against a sky swirled softly with the pinks and violets of late sunset.

As Derek had promised her weeks earlier, yesterday, when they had dropped anchor, the cargo she had purchased with Confederate money in Nassau had been winched into boats and transported to the wharves for sale. The thought of her supplies, so desperately needed by the South, being sold to foreigners rankled her, but there was little she could do about it now.

The fact that he was returning the profits into her hands helped assuage her resentment to some degree. As soon as she could get back home she would simply repurchase the goods and run them through the blockade herself, if necessary. On the other hand, Derek's treachery was hard to forget even though their relationship had changed for the better since she had been ill. He had tricked her vilely, and instead of doing her part to ensure the Confederate victory, she now sat idle and helpless aboard his ship. The well-oiled cogs of her spy network would grind to a halt without her leadership and coordination, so it was imperative that she return to Virginia.

During the last few weeks when she had been recovering from her bout with malaria, she'd had plenty of time to think. Despite Derek's kindness and solicitous concern, she knew she had to find a way to leave the *Mamu* before they set sail across the vast oceans to Australia. She didn't know exactly how she could accomplish such an escape, but she knew her best bet was right here in Rio, especially since he had made a point to coerce her into accompanying him into the city.

Such an excursion would get her off the ship and enable her to find someone with pro-southern sympathies. The Confederate Navy had ships continually sailing from port to port, and she knew for a fact that President Jefferson Davis had sent diplomatic delegations to all the major capital cities of the world. Rio de Janeiro was surely one of them.

Her primary concern now was that Derek might change his mind. He had gone ashore the day before on business and had taken Kapi, Rigi and Big Roscoe with him. He had told her he was coming back today, but she had yet to see the launch return. What if he changed his mind? What if he had decided to leave her aboard the ship?

A knock at the door caused her to turn her chair around, and she breathed a quick sigh of relief when she saw Derek standing in the doorway. He was dressed in a long black leather vest over a white shirt and tight black breeches. Tall black boots reached to his knees, and he carried a long white dress box in his hands.

"How are you feeling, luv?" he asked, smiling at her as he came forward.

Of all things, Cassandra felt suddenly guilty about contemplating flight. She could *not* let the fact that she was becoming fond of Derek Courtland get in the way of what she had to do.

"I'm much better, thank you. In fact, I feel wonderful."

"That's just what I wanted to hear." He placed the box on the desk in front of her, then dropped a small leather pouch beside it. When it hit, the coins inside jingled. "Your money, madam. As you see, I always keep my promises. You'll be pleased to learn that I got top dollar for your merchandise. Two hundred sixty-five American dollars and thirty-seven cents, to be exact."

As Cassandra lifted the purse and gauged its weight in her hand, he lounged with easy grace into the chair opposite her. He propped his booted feet upon the desk and observed her over his steepled fingers.

"There's a present for you in the box."

"Are you trying to bribe me into forgetting how I came to be a prisoner on your ship?"

"Aye." The way he grinned made her want to smile. She had fought his charm during their entire association, but she could not deny her attraction to him. In any case, she had better encourage him at every turn until he took her ashore.

"It will have to be an impressive gift to vindicate your dishonorable actions," she said playfully.

He shrugged a shoulder. "Have you ever been to Carnival?" he asked. "You seem to have done everything and been everywhere."

"I was in New Orleans during Mardi Gras before the war started. Stuart and I accompanied my mother there on holiday."

"Rio's celebration is similar except there's more dancing and feasting, and the women wear provocative costumes that drive men wild."

"Then I'm quite sure you make a point never to miss it."

Derek placed a hand over his heart in mock despair. "You wound me with your sharp tongue, Cassie."

His dark eyes were laughing, and Cassandra's lips twitched with the desire to laugh with him. Derek was so hard to resist, and he had shown a different side to his nature when he had nursed her back to health. At the moment, however, she needed to concentrate on her escape plans. Should she bring up the idea of going ashore or let him?

"Even without Carnival, Rio's a fascinating place to visit. The city was founded by the Spanish in the 1600s, I believe—"

"Actually," she corrected him, "it was the Portuguese and it was on January 1, 1502. Rio de Janeiro means 'River of January.' I studied all the countries in South America before I went to Peru."

"Then you must know there are all kinds of fascinating ancient buildings just waiting for you to explore. One church is said to house the breastplate of a Spanish conquistador. You are still planning to go with me, aren't you?"

Pleased that he was making it so easy, she smiled. "I thought you'd changed your mind, since you left yesterday without inviting me."

"Not a chance. I just wanted to get rid of your three bodyguards so I could have you to myself. The two boys have clung to your skirts constantly since we left Nassau. Big Roscoe's nearly as bad. Now he's as protective of you as he is of me."

"They're all very sweet. I missed them today. Did you leave them alone in the city?"

"No. George has agreed to take them under his wing for the night. Don't you want to open your present?"

Cassandra plucked the red satin ribbon and when it fell away, she lifted the lid. Crinkly white tissue paper lay inside, and she carefully unfolded it.

"Oh, Derek, it's beautiful." She gasped with genuine delight as she stood and took the garment from the box. Fashioned out of soft black velvet, the dress was constructed in an unusual fashion with a tight-fitting tunic long enough to reach to midthigh and tied together on each shoulder with velvet straps. She placed the strange gown across the desk and smoothed her palm reverently over geometric designs made of shiny silver jewels and gold beads that must have taken countless hours of tedious needlework. But the skirt was quite outrageous—consisting of nothing but long strands of black and silver beads. As she picked it up to examine it closer, the beads clicked together like Oriental curtains.

"I've never seen any garment like this," she murmured with genuine fascination. "The designs look almost like the fish and birds the Incans wove into their fabrics and painted on their pottery."

"You're close. The design of this costume was taken from one depicted on a king's tomb. The Brazilian Indians wore it in their Jaguar dance. Originally, the mask and robe were both made out of bark cloth instead of velvet and beads. There's a mask that goes with it."

Cassandra was intrigued. She retrieved the mask from the bottom of the box and found it to be an elaborate re-creation of a jaguar's face made from black velvet and glossy black feathers with golden beads outlining the eyes. "This is beautiful, Derek, but where is it worn?"

"To the costume ball we're attending tonight."

Cassandra turned to him in surprise. "You're taking me to a ball?"

"That's right. I ran into an old friend of mine today, and she invited us to come. It's quite the social event of Carnival, and the gardens of the house overlook one of the best parade routes. It's quite exciting. Everyone comes in costume."

For a moment Cassandra couldn't believe her luck. Derek was not only offering her a chance to escape, he was providing a costume in which to do so. "That sounds wonderful, Derek."

"There is a condition."

Cassandra waited fearfully, expecting the worst, and she got it. "You have to promise me you won't do anything stupid like trying to slip away and board a ship bound for America."

Cassandra tried valiantly to keep an innocent look on her face. "I think that would be a bit difficult in a getup like this."

Derek eyed her appraisingly. "Do you give me your word, then?" he asked bluntly.

Cassandra looked him in the eye. She nodded. To her relief, he smiled and stood up.

"Good. Then put on the costume and I'll see you topdecks as soon as you're ready."

When he was almost to the door, Cassandra called a question. "But Derek, what am I supposed to wear under the beads?"

"Nothing," he told her, then laughed at her expression before leaving her to contemplate the indecency of that idea.

\*     \*     \*

A little more than an hour later Derek looked out over the city where lamps were just beginning to twinkle along the broad avenues radiating from the shore. He was so eager to spend time alone with Cassandra, he was ashamed to acknowledge it even to himself. He had grown to care about her a great deal—too much, in fact. He craved her company more than he should and against his better judgment. She fascinated him and had from the beginning, not just her irresistible beauty but also her intellect. Hell, except for her blind passion for the southern Cause, he liked everything about her. That's why he was going to show her a good time and hope she would forget their past squabbles.

When Cassandra stepped into sight a moment later, he straightened slowly and stared at her. She looked so exquisitely lovely in the feathered, bejeweled costume that for a moment he couldn't find his voice. The wind stirred the beads and he got a glimpse of her shapely white legs.

"The beads are sewn together down past my thighs, in case you're wondering," she said when she saw where he was looking.

"I was wondering."

She frowned as she looked down over his black vest and breeches. "Why aren't you wearing a costume?"

"I am. I'm Blackbeard, the bloodthirsty pirate of old."

"How appropriate."

"You look so beautiful it takes my breath away."

His compliment seemed to fluster her, and she turned slightly and looked around the deserted deck. He hoped she was completely well. She had been sick enough to cause him some fright.

"Are you sure you're feeling better now?" he asked, taking her arm and leading her to the ladder.

"Oh, yes, I'm very eager to walk on solid ground again."

Derek assisted her into the bobbing longboat where several of his crewmen awaited to row them to the dock before they set out to enjoy their own shore leave. The sweet scent of gardenias enveloped him as he took his seat in the boat beside her, and in that moment he decided that they were going to become lovers that very night, or he was going to die trying.

By the time the longboat had deposited them ashore and Derek had assisted her into a hired carriage, Cassandra was a bundle of nerves. At her first opportunity she was going to give him the slip, but at all costs, she could not let him know her intentions. As she settled the lovely, glittering costume around her, Derek swung into the seat across from her and intently admired her bare knee showing through the beaded skirt.

"I guess you know that I intend to show you such a good time tonight that you can't possibly resist me."

Cassandra's tensed muscles relaxed. She pondered her best tactic and decided she should remain a challenge. She had a feeling that Derek Courtland had been irresistible to a great many beautiful women in the past. No doubt he enjoyed the pursuit but was bored with the capture.

"Good luck, Captain. You'll need it."

Before she could object, Derek leaned forward and caught hold of her fingers. He brought her hand up tightly against his mouth, and Cassandra gasped at the feel of hot masculine lips against her sensitive palm. A sensual chill swept up her arm, then faded when she jerked her fingers out of his grasp.

"Please don't do that. I don't like it."

"I think you do."

"How dare you think that every woman is dying for your affections," she replied with some breathlessness, folding her hands together in an effort to remain calm.

Derek relaxed back against the seat. "I know you like me more than you'll admit. Why don't you just let it happen? You might enjoy it as much as I know I will."

"Can you blame me for being resentful of what you did?"

"But will your resentment fade away if I agree to take you back to America?"

Cassandra eyed him with renewed interest. "Are you considering that idea?"

"And cheat myself of your charming company? Not a chance, I'm afraid. Anyway, Harte might have me arrested again."

Cassandra set her gaze out the window, not wanting to show her annoyance with his glib reply. Derek was staring at her the way he always did. She fought the desire to squirm like an amoeba under her laboratory microscope. She decided to involve him in a neutral subject that would take his mind off seducing her, before she decided to give in and let him.

"Did the design of this outfit really come from etchings on a burial tomb?" she asked, smoothing her fingers over the crisscrossed lines of beadwork down the front of her bodice.

"Yes. Would you like to hear the Indian legend concerning that particular costume?"

Cassandra nodded, always interested in ancient legends and Indian folklore. She had written an essay once on the subject of Irish ghost stories.

"A gown like the one you're wearing was given to the most beautiful young virgin in the village. She would carry a flute in one hand and a spear in the other as she danced before the strongest and bravest of the warriors." He paused for effect. "When the drums died away, she would untie her shoulder straps and the gown would drop around her ankles as she stood naked before the man she wished to marry."

"You're lying, Derek."

Derek's black eyes gleamed with mischief. "It's said that wearing such a costume throws a woman into a state of uncontrollable arousal. Apparently, no man is safe from her voracious appetites. Should I be concerned?"

At that point she knew he was making the whole thing up. She laughed at his audaciousness. "Sorry to disappoint you, Captain Courtland, but I've had on this outfit for some time now, and I have no urge to dance nude or choose a husband."

"Too bad for me."

"I'd offer you the opportunity to don this costume yourself," she said then, "but it hardly seems necessary, since you always seem to be in a state of uncontrollable arousal anyway."

Derek grinned and rubbed his whiskered jaw, as was his habit. "Only since I met you, Cassie, darlin', only since I met you."

The way he was looking at her filled her with undeniable pleasure, and when her loins quivered in response to the highly provocative conversation, she quickly glanced away, glad the coach was slowing to a stop.

A white liveried servant rushed to open the door and Derek stepped down, then reached up to assist her. "Welcome to Carnival."

Cassandra was hesitant to touch him, for obvious reasons. His long fingers closed warmly around hers and he tucked her hand in the crook of his elbow. She looked up a set of white marble steps to where four gigantic Corinthian columns crossed the front of a large mansion. Every room was lit, and figures could be seen moving past the windows. Soft violin music drifted out to them on the mild evening breeze.

"It seems the party has already begun," he told

her, looking up at the magnificent facade. "Shall we don our masks and join the festivities?"

Cassandra set the feathered mask in place and looked eagerly around her as they climbed the steps. "Who lives here?" she asked as another servant appeared to open the tall front doors.

"Senora Magdalena de Queiros, the White Rose of Rio."

Cassandra looked at him quickly. "Is she a spy, too?"

"Not exactly. Come, I'll introduce you to her."

Inside the spacious marble-tiled foyer Cassandra realized the house was of palatial proportions, the entrance hall alone adorned with six glittering crystal chandeliers. Guests milled about the hall and adjoining rooms at will, all dressed in bright, befeathered costumes similar to her own, though most of them far more revealing. She silently thanked Derek for his discretion. The hostess of the party stood near the base of a curving marble staircase. She smiled and walked forward when she caught sight of Derek.

"*Querido*, you did come," she cooed to Derek. He kissed her on both cheeks, and Cassandra stared in some shock at the woman's attire. Though she went unmasked, her costume was made of white lace so sheer that every inch of her body could be glimpsed beneath the fragile fabric. Although she wore some sort of black corset and pantalets underneath, her lush figure was on display for anyone who cared to look. Cassandra noted sourly that Derek certainly didn't miss the opportunity.

"You do look fetching, Countess," he murmured with a shake of his head and a crooked smile. "I am glad I decided to come."

The countess laughed softly and touched his face in an openly intimate caress. "You are welcome anytime, as you well know, my love." She turned her full attention to Cassandra. "You look very pretty, my dear. I was pleased to provide a costume for you and I must say you do it justice with those long legs of yours. The fertility symbols you're wearing are said to arouse the wearer. Did Derek share the legend with you?"

Shocked by the woman's comment about her legs, Cassandra nodded and murmured some bland reply, glad when Derek led her away as a newly arrived party entered and claimed the countess' attention.

"She might as well go about naked," Cassandra remarked, glancing back and finding the countess' costume even more scandalous from the back.

"Maggie's never been shy," Derek answered with offhanded interest. "Pedro doesn't seem to mind."

"Who is Pedro?"

"Pedro II is the emperor of Brazil."

"Emperor? Is she of royalty, then?"

Derek chuckled. "In a way. She's his favorite mistress and the most famous *cortesana* in Rio. He'll be arriving here later at a more discreet hour."

"A courtesan? You seem to know her quite well."

Derek looked faintly surprised, and Cassandra realized her words had been pointedly accusatory. "I told you we were old friends."

"Are you sure you don't mean old lovers?"

His lips curved slightly as they stopped beside a pillar supporting the entrance to a large salon where couples were dancing to a small orchestra. "Sometimes, Cassie, the two can be one and the same."

"I'm sure that's nearly always the case with you," she replied, shocked to hear such words leave her mouth. *Why, I'm jealous,* she thought, instantly appalled at the transparency of her remark.

"Why, Cassie, darlin', what's come over you? I do believe that Jaguar costume is beginning to take effect."

"You're right. I'm sorry. It's none of my business."

"Not at all. I'm flattered. Dare I hope you might not hate me anymore?"

"I don't hate you," she answered truthfully.

"Then may I have this dance?"

Cassandra let him take her in his arms, and as they waltzed away among the whirling couples, she marveled at Derek's great height. He looked so much like a swarthy bearded pirate in his black mask and cape that she felt a glimmer of excitement as if she indeed danced in the arms of Blackbeard the buccaneer. She was not unaware of how many women turned to watch him guide her around the floor, and she felt a certain pride at being his partner.

At once she chastised herself for becoming so

attached to him. Her first priority was to get away, and she had better not forget it. With a stern rebuke fixed firmly in her mind, she began to observe the other costumed guests for any signs of a potential ally.

# Chapter 14

As the evening progressed, Cassandra realized with some dismay that she was having a wonderful time mingling among the glittering elite of Rio de Janeiro. When she remembered how the war was still being waged back home with endless heartbreak and bloodshed, she burned with shame because she was so enjoying her frivolous night out with Derek Courtland. She couldn't remember the last time she had attended a ball when her sole intention had not been to elicit information from the Yankee officers in attendance.

After an exhilarating whirl across the mirrored ballroom in Derek's arms, she was breathless and happy to allow him to lead her out onto a long outdoor porch supported by elegant columns. She preceded her escort to the balustraded wall and breathed in the cool night air as she gazed over the series of manicured terraces and flagstone walkways that swept down to a busy plaza. Parades were going on continually on the streets below, and she could hear shouts of laughter over the distant strumming of steel guitars and beating of drums.

When Derek placed his palms on her shoulders, she reminded herself again to forget his charming manner and to recall her duty to home and country.

"Are you having a good time tonight, Cassie?"

His words were low, and his fingers had begun to knead her tight shoulders.

"Yes, of course. Will we be able to go down to the plaza and watch the parades before we return to the ship? It looks as if everyone is having a wonderful time."

"If you like. I warn you, though, the people in the streets have a tendency to become wilder and more drunken than Maggie's sophisticated guests. The plaza there is called the Praca Maua, and nearly all the parades proceed along the Avenida Rio Branco to the Avenida Beira Mar, which curves along some of the most beautiful beaches of Rio."

"You seem to know the city very well," she commented as he drew her down beside him on a marble bench overlooking the lights of the city.

"It's been three years since I was last here, but I always try to stop on my way to and from Melbourne. I have friends here in the import business. One of them is always ready to purchase whatever cargo I have at the time. I usually buy their goods to sell when I reach Africa."

"Are we to anchor there?" she asked quickly, excited by the prospect of visiting the dark, mysterious continent. She belatedly remembered that if she had her way, she wouldn't be with him after tonight.

"What? I've found a place you haven't visited?"

He was trying very hard to be pleasant and agreeable. Unfortunately, he was succeeding admirably. She bit back her rash desire to ask him all sorts of questions about his life aboard the *Mamu*. Suddenly where he had been and what he had done before they had met seemed important for her to know.

In the back of her mind, she knew what her curiosity meant—that she was beginning to admire him as a person and consider him her friend. Even worse, she burned for him to touch her and kiss her, over and over again, the way he had when they had lain together on the bunk in the cabin of the *Rachel Ann*. Deep, sensuous longings flooded her, and she desperately tried to shake such traitorous needs away.

"I was in Algiers once on my way home from Rome," she answered in a rush, uncomfortable about her growing feelings for him. "I didn't really get to explore the Casbah the way I would have liked, though. Northern Africa has a strong Arab influence, but I'd like to see the south, where the elephants and lions are. I particularly would like to study the Zulus. I've heard they're warlike and hostile."

Derek laughed. "I wouldn't advise an expedition into Zulu country. You might end up in one of their stewpots."

Cassandra looked quickly at him. "Are they cannibals?"

The amused glint in his eye betrayed him. "No, but they don't mind killing white men who invade their territory. In any event, I'm afraid you won't get a chance to meet any Zulus this trip because I intend to round the Cape of Good Hope and weigh anchor on the island of Madagascar."

"I've certainly never been there."

"Good. I'll take you ashore and let you meet an old friend of mine."

Cassandra decided to pave the way for a future escape attempt in case her plans did not meet fruition in Rio. The vigilance with which Derek had watched her since they had disembarked the ship was making the prospect of slipping away from him appear increasingly bleak. "Do you promise?"

Derek caught her hand and pressed his lips to her fingers. "It will be my pleasure."

Cassandra swallowed hard and gently disentangled her hand. "I'm glad I decided to come along with you tonight. It's beautiful here, and I'd almost forgotten what it's like to dance and laugh without any ulterior motives. The war took that away from me."

"What about before the war? I suspect you were quite the belle of Virginia."

At first she thought he was being sarcastic, but he appeared only interested. "We used to entertain a great deal. There's a beautiful ballroom on the third floor at Twin Pines, and Mother prided herself on being the best hostess in the county. When we were little children, Stuart and I used to hide in the balconies overlooking the dance floor to watch Mama whirl about in her beautiful gowns."

Bittersweet nostalgia twisted her heart. Those days had been safe and peaceful. Now her mother was dead and gone, and she hadn't seen Stuart since he had left to fight with his Virginian unit nearly five years ago. For all she knew, her brother could be dead on some faraway battleground. And if Grant had advanced far enough along the James River, Twin Pines Plantation could be burned to the ground.

"That war will end someday." Derek placed his hand over hers. "Then you can go home and enjoy life again." His voice was so gentle and understanding that she felt the prickle of hot tears, and she averted her face so he wouldn't see how much he had touched her heart. He put a finger beneath her chin and turned her face back to him.

"I want to apologize to you, Cassie, right now, tonight. I shouldn't have agreed to bring you with me without telling you. It was wrong, I know, but believe me when I say that I didn't do it to hurt you. I saw the dangerous life you were leading, and I didn't want you harmed." He paused, but she couldn't look away from his intense eyes, so deep and black and warm. "And I admit I wanted to be with you, Cassie. I wanted to get to know you better. I just wanted you, period." His mouth was a breath away, and Cassandra's heart hammered wildly as his lips touched her cheek, then slowly tasted their way to her trembling lower lip. Memories of her devastating response the other times he had kissed her set off all sorts of warning signals inside her mind. She should pull away! She should tell him to let her go! She should say that she hadn't forgiven him!

"Take me back home, Derek, please," was all she could utter as her breath caught and her eyelids drifted closed. "Help me return to fight for what I believe in."

"I can't let you go," he murmured. Then his lips took possession of hers—gentle, warm, firm, unthreatening, but wonderful, and oh so pleasurable. She forgot her escape plans, forgot her will to resist. All conscious thought swayed and swirled away in some awful, delicious kind of incoherent confusion until she was overcome with pure tingling sensation.

Against her will, her arms twined around his neck and she clung to him. He groaned and continued the deep, draining kisses, and when he released her, it took her a moment to return to rational thought. She opened dreamy eyes and found that he was on his feet staring down at her.

"I'm going to go get us some champagne to cool us off a bit," he said, his breath coming as fast as her own. "I learned the hard way in a certain saloon back in Virginia that you're not to be treated as a loose woman, so we'll continue this later in a more private place if you've a mind to."

He kissed her hand, then disappeared through the open French doors of the ballroom. Oh, Lord, did she ever have a mind to! How could she have allowed her feelings for him to get to this point? Every hour she spent in his company she became more entrapped by his masculine appeal. If she didn't escape him soon, she was afraid she would quit trying. She put her hand over her mouth and tried to think.

This was her opportunity, of course, while he was busy inside. All she had to do was make her way down the back lawn and disappear into the crowded plaza. Once there, she could find her way to the nearest foreign embassy and get the help she needed. She spoke Spanish and had enough gold in the leather pouch tied beneath her dress to buy passage anywhere in the world. She could take care of herself. Hadn't she taken more dangerous risks in the past? Why didn't she want to go through with her plan now that the time was at hand?

She stood and looked around. One couple was having an intimate tête-à-tête in the shadows on the other end of the balcony, but most of the guests were still inside, dancing or visiting the refreshment tables. Derek's dark cape was nowhere in sight among the colorful costumes. In the distance she could hear the insistent throb of drums that matched the rapid thudding of her own troubled heart. This was her only chance before they crossed the Atlantic. Rio was the last port of call where she might find a Confederate delegation.

Rising, she made up her mind to flee and ran quickly to the end of the house where a long stone staircase led to the first of the grass terraces that sloped down to the Praca Maua. She ran on, keeping to the flagstone paths, but she only passed a few other people. Continually looking back for any sign of Derek, she finally found the gate in the high brick wall separating the de Queiros estate from the plaza. An armed servant bowed and opened the wrought-iron gate for her, and she stepped out among the people following the parade. A babble of Portuguese surrounded her, and she held her mask in place as she threaded her way deeper into the throng of merrymakers.

According to Derek, the Avenida Rio Branco was a central thoroughfare of the capital. Perhaps one of the foreign dignitaries would keep a residence in the houses lining the wide street. If so, a foreign flag would be flying on the stoop, such as was the practice in both Washington and Richmond. As soon as she was a safe distance away from Derek, she would begin to inquire for directions.

As she neared the actual parade in the center of the avenue, she was jostled and knocked about by the excited participants, many of whom were intoxicated and carried either wine bottles or tankards of beer. She was glad she had tucked her derringer in her purse.

Swept along like a chunk of driftwood in a swollen river, she felt more secure as she continued to put distance between herself and Derek. She searched every storefront and apartment facade for the Confederate Stars and Bars, hoping she would eventually end up at the waterfront where the foreign ships were anchored.

After some time, she drew up in surprise when she heard someone nearby shouting in English. Turning quickly, she picked out a group of men wearing the striped shirts and bell-legged trousers of the British navy. They stood watching the parade and quaffing beer under the muted light of a corner lamppost.

Immediately she veered toward their position, but she knew that, derringer or not, one woman was no match for so many men, not if they were inebriated. As a precaution, she hovered nearby and tried to judge by their conversation if she would be foolish to approach them.

"I'd jump the bloody ship and live here gladly," said one man heartily, swigging whiskey from a gourd-shaped, green bottle. "Ain't no Englishwoman I know who'd dance half-naked in the streets like these Brazilian tarts."

"There won't be none paradin' through the streets of London, neither, that be for sure."

Cassandra edged closer and examined the men for signs of criminality. All four sailors were burly and well-muscled, as seaman usually were, but none of these men was drunk or dirty. Her instincts told her they wouldn't molest her. When a short wiry man with blond mustache and beard noticed her loitering nearby, he politely tipped his peaked cap. Encouraged by his manners, she took off her mask and asked for their help.

"Please pardon my intrusion, gentlemen," she began courteously, knowing from experience that behaving in a genteel manner with ruffians often caused them to react in kind. She prayed that would be the case in this instance. The men appeared shocked that she spoke to them in English; they quickly snatched off their hats.

"We'd be honored, ma'am," said the young blond. He had the ruddy, sunburned face sported by many of Derek's crew. "Ye're American, ain't ye?"

"Yes, I'm from Virginia," she admitted, searching the faces of the other three. They were all dark-haired and rugged, but none seemed in any way threatening to her person. "I'm afraid I must ask for your help. You see, I've become separated from my party in the course of the evening and turned around a bit with my directions. We were to join some American friends tonight shipboard, but I can't remember the name of their vessel. Could you tell me how to get down to the waterfront?"

"Why, yes, ma'am, we'd be glad to, but there be only one Yankee frigate docked here in Rio that I'm aware of, by the name of *St. Louis*. The truth is we passed by her berth comin' down here this very night. We're headin' back there; we could show ye the way if you like."

Cassandra debated whether or not she should take them up on the offer, then decided such a course would be the quickest, easiest way to find a ship headed home, and as long as they kept to crowded streets, she would probably be safe enough.

"That's very kind, sir. Thank you, I believe I will."

Things were working out quite well for such an impromptu escape plan, she decided, glancing back one last time for any sign of Derek. His tall black-caped form was nowhere to be seen, and she knew he could never find her among such a large, boisterous crowd. Regret plagued her heart until she forcibly shook away thoughts of the handsome Australian and his breathless kisses. She had to stop thinking about him. She was needed at home, and she couldn't let her growing affection for Derek stop her.

"What makes you think this woman will come here?"

Derek leaned back in his chair, a glowing Cuban cheroot held idly between his fingers. He gazed across the desk at Theodore Mosler, the captain of the federal frigate *St. Louis*.

"Because your ship is the only American vessel in port and the only way for her to get back to Virginia so she can continue her espionage activities. She'll be here, all right. Actually, I'm surprised she hasn't made it yet, as resourceful as she is." He took a moment to knock ashes into the copper ashtray beside him before he continued. "I've seen her in action, Captain, and I assure you that before dawn lights the sky, Cassandra Delaney will walk through that door and beg your help. Furthermore, I predict that she'll offer to pay the price of passage out of a brown leather pouch containing over two hundred dollars, the pouch which she stole from me earlier today."

Captain Mosler shook his head, then absently scratched his graying sideburns. "I do appreciate you coming here to warn me, Courtland. I'd hate to think we would make the same mistake you did and set sail with a southern spy aboard, especially a conniving female."

"I couldn't agree more. There's nothing more unlucky than having a woman shipboard," Derek answered calmly, though in truth he was more than anxious to get Cassandra back on the *Mamu*. He had been a complete fool earlier that night when he had been distracted by Cassandra's curvaceous body and honeyed words, and even more stupid to leave her alone in the garden. She had duped him with her soft kisses just the way she had her poor doctor friend, Stephen, and God only knew how many other unsuspecting saps. He gritted his teeth so hard that his jaw almost locked, but he hid his rage from the Union sea captain.

"And this woman heartlessly betrayed her own brother, you say? Good God, there's no end to the evil spawned by this damnable war."

Derek nodded agreement, but when Mosler went on with his tirade about the innate treachery of womankind, he only listened with half an ear. He hoped to God he had guessed right about Cassandra's plans, but the truth was he'd had little choice other than to try to waylay her at her eventual destination. The moment Magdalena's guard had shown him the spot where Cassandra had melted into the crowd thronging the plaza, he knew he hadn't a chance in hell of finding her in the streets.

His instincts told him she would waste no time seeking out a ship headed for America, and in that pursuit he had one advantage she didn't have. He had a carriage to transport him quickly to the wharf, and he was damn glad now that he had inquired about which American ships were in port the day before when he had come ashore to dispose of Cassandra's cargo. The *St. Louis* was the only one, and therefore her logical choice. Cassandra would come, and Derek would be waiting. For once, her clever little schemes would backfire, and he could not wait to see the expression on her lovely little face when she realized he had outsmarted her.

After twenty more minutes of waiting for her to turn up, he wasn't so sure that she hadn't second-guessed him and gone elsewhere for help. When there was a tap on the door a few minutes later, he sat up eagerly.

"The lady you have been waiting for has come, Captain Mosler. She's asking to see you," said a young officer the captain had introduced earlier as Lieutenant Harry Shelton. "Shall I bring her down?"

"Yes, but don't mention the fact that Courtland's here with me." Captain Mosler smiled grimly at Derek as he rose and buttoned the jacket of his dark blue uniform. "Well, sir, it seems your hunch has been verified."

Breathing a sigh of relief, Derek stood and

crushed out his cigar. "I better stay out of sight until she brings out my money. I daresay it won't take her long to incriminate herself."

A single oil lamp burned on the desk, and its dim flickering shrouded the walls of the cabin in darkness. Derek stepped into the shadows and leaned back against the wall. He crossed his arms over his chest and waited patiently for the show to begin.

Moments later Cassandra opened the door and swept into the room with the beads of her costume clicking and the sweet essence of her perfume bringing back all too clearly the delicious memory of her trembling mouth. Anger came swiftly, but now, probably for the first time in her life, she was trapped like a rat, and he was enjoying it immensely.

"Please, sir, forgive me for asking you to receive me at this late hour, but you must believe me when I tell you I had no other choice."

*Yeah, that's for damn sure,* Derek thought sourly, wondering what outrageous tale she would spin for Mosler.

"Do not concern yourself, madam. The truth is that I was already awake. Please sit down and tell me how I can be of service to you."

Cassandra sank down into the chair that Derek had just vacated. She placed the back of her hand to her brow in a theatrical flourish as if perhaps she might swoon at any moment.

*Cassandra? Fainthearted? Not a chance,* Derek

thought, impressed nonetheless by her flair for the dramatic.

"I've been through the most horrible ordeal imaginable, Captain. It's very hard for me to relate, but I know I must in order to gain your trust. You see, I've just escaped from the most dreadful man who has been holding me captive aboard his ship. He abducted me from the streets of Washington and forced me away from my friends and loved ones." Her trembling words stopped, and a sob caught pitiably in her throat. "I can't tell you how awful the past few months have been."

*That's the understatement of the century,* Derek thought, but he continued to listen to her most interesting plea.

"Madam, please don't distress yourself so," the captain was saying sympathetically, clearly beguiled by this damsel in distress despite what Derek had told him.

"I must return to America as soon as possible. You must take me with you before he can find me again. I can pay you. I have over two hundred dollars, and I'll give every cent of it to you if you'll take me home to Mama and Papa."

*Mama and Papa?* Derek thought, then smiled triumphantly when she brought out the brown leather pouch and dumped out the contents on Mosler's desk.

The American stood up, the sight of the money snapping him back to reality. When he spoke, he didn't mince words. "Madam, I'm afraid I'm going to have to place you under arrest."

Cassandra literally froze in the act of gathering up the money. "What did you say?"

"Hello, White Rose," Derek said, stepping into the light.

At the sound of his voice, Cassandra jerked around. He watched in satisfaction as stark horror drained all the color from her face. Unfortunately, she got over her initial shock in a hurry.

"What lies has he told you about me?" she cried indignantly, whirling back to Mosler. "You mustn't believe him! He's the one who abducted me! Don't you see what he's trying to do?"

"He says you're a southern agent," Captain Mosler said uncertainly, glancing at Derek.

"No, no, I work for the Union! That's why he kept me locked up on his ship! He's the enemy! You don't even know who he is, do you?"

"Shut up, Cassie. Your tricks won't work this time. I'm taking you back to the ship."

"He's Derek Courtland, the captain of the famed *Mamu*," she went on, obviously pressing her advantage while Mosler appeared to be wavering. "Surely you've heard how many times he's run the blockade! He's sunk more Yankee ships than anyone can count! You should be arresting him, not me!"

"I've heard of the *Mamu*," the captain admitted, a perplexed frown riding his brow. "I've even given her chase a few times."

"For your information, the *Mamu*'s right here in

Rio. This traitor dropped anchor out in the bay where no one would be likely to board her."

If Cassandra didn't shut up, she was going to get both of them hanged, Derek decided as Mosler's hand settled over the butt of his pistol. Dammit, he hadn't expected Cassandra to be able to turn the man against him so easily, but he should have known better than to expect her to go along meekly.

"Don't believe her, Mosler," he said slowly, not sure what the man intended to do. "She's the spy, just like I said. I told you how clever she is. She's trying to turn things around and place the suspicion on me."

Derek didn't like the look on the captain's face. He liked it even less when Mosler drew his gun and pointed the barrel dead center on Derek's chest.

"All right, get back against the wall, both of you."

"Goddammit, Cassie," Derek muttered furiously under his breath. "Now look what you've done."

"Me? You're the one who ruined my plans."

"Get your hands up, I say," Mosler ordered harshly. He barked a command loud enough to bring his young lieutenant running into the cabin. "Disarm him," he said, "then take them down to the brig until I can find out just who the hell's telling the truth. If the *Mamu* is anchored in the harbor, it shouldn't take me long to find out."

"Yes, sir."

Lieutenant Shelton cautiously slid Derek's six-shooter from his holster, then herded them outside at gunpoint. He pushed them ahead of him down the dark gangway, and Derek was relieved to find the ship silent except for the creaking of timbers as the hull rocked at anchor. It was the middle of the night, so the majority of the crew were probably sleeping. Chances were that only a skeleton crew manned the topdeck, which boded well for an escape, but he had no time to waste.

As Mosler had pointed out, it wouldn't take him long to find out the truth, and Derek would be damned if he'd rot again in an American prison. After descending a narrow companionway and moving down a dark passage, Shelton stopped in front of a wooden door with a barred grate. He held his gun on them as he took down a ring of keys from a hook on the wall.

"Okay, get inside."

"Ladies first," Derek said mockingly, deciding that if he didn't make a move now he wouldn't get another chance.

Cassandra glared at him, but Shelton kept both his gaze and his gun centered on Derek.

"No. I won't share a cell with him."

Her refusal obviously startled Shelton, and when his eyes darted to her, Derek hit him with a short, hard jab square on the nose. The young officer went over hard and lay still.

"My, lord, he's out cold," Cassandra said, kneeling beside the unconscious man. "Did you have to hit him so hard?"

"I thought it the thing to do under the circumstances," he answered sarcastically, going down on his knee and taking Shelton's gun.

"I can't believe you were reckless enough to come here when the Yankees want you for treason!" she exclaimed in a subdued whisper.

"They didn't know I was wanted until you opened your big mouth," Derek returned angrily.

"What did you expect me to do, just sit there and let you spoil everything?"

"Just shut up and come on, unless you want to stay behind and swing from the yardarm. I know a way to get us topdeck without being seen."

"How do you know so much about this ship?"

"Because I spent months aboard a prison brig in New York Harbor until your brother got me transferred to a jail in Washington."

When he stepped over Shelton and swiftly headed to stern, Cassandra followed without a word. Thank God she was using her head for a change. They were both in a hell of a lot of trouble, and she no doubt knew it as well as he did. He ran down the gangway to the companionway at the stern, then climbed the steps slowly. He lifted the companion hatch and peered outside.

"Wait here until I see if it's clear," he warned Cassandra, then climbed out and crouched motionlessly behind the hatch. The night was damp with fog and still except for the sound of low voices somewhere at midships. He reached down and yanked Cassandra bodily up beside him.

"They'll be guarding the gangplank, thanks to you,

so we'll have to go into the water. Try to hold those bloody beads still, will you?"

"You're the one who asked me to wear this stupid dress," she whispered back.

Grimacing and cursing her rattling skirt, she kept close behind him as he moved stealthily along the railing until he came to the opening where metal bars had been bolted to the side of the ship as access to boarding craft.

"Go on down and slip into the water as quietly as you can," he said urgently. "Head for the pilings under the wharf, then to the beachfront on the other side. Go on, dammit, hurry it up!"

Cassandra obeyed, but her foot hadn't touched the first rung when a loud voice split the quiet night.

"Hey! You there! What are you doing?"

"Jump, Cassie!" Derek gave her a shove that sent her flying out into the air. She waved her arms for balance and cried out as she fell, and Derek turned quickly to follow her into the water. A shot rang out and hot lead ripped through his shirt into the flesh of his side. He leaped out into the darkness and plummeted deep into the sea, his pain intensifying tenfold as salt water invaded the open wound. He fought his way back to the surface and gulped in a lungful of air.

Bullets were still being fired; he could hear the spattering sounds on the surface of the water. He could hear Cassandra splashing somewhere in the water behind him. He set his jaw against the excruciating burning and tried to put distance between himself and the ship.

The night was pitch-black, and he followed the sounds Cassandra was making as she swam, hoping to God he had the strength to make it to the wharf. When his fingers finally touched the slimy surface of the pilings, he clung to it with his good arm. He felt rather than saw Cassandra come up beside him. The shots from the ship had stopped, but he could hear voices yelling and see the lanterns being lit along the railing where they had jumped.

"What are you waiting on? We've got to get out of here. They're shooting at us!" Cassandra was pulling on the back of his shirt now, and he pushed off and labored to follow her through the pilings toward the beach. Grunting under the effort, he groaned when his feet finally touched bottom. Holding his side, he waded into the shallows and collapsed to his knees on the sand.

"What's the matter with you? Why do you keep stopping?" Cassandra demanded as she came up beside him. "Oh, my God, Derek, you've been shot! You're bleeding—"

"Never mind that. The carriage is in an alleyway not far from here. We've got to get there before they can get to shore and send out a search party."

He struggled to his feet, and they moved up the beach and across the dirt road that edged the ocean. He soon led them to the entrance to the alley and staggered into the darkness where he had ordered the driver to wait. The man was stretched out asleep on his perch, and Derek slapped the side of the coach to awaken him as Cassandra opened the door and scrambled inside.

"Take us back to the ship," he muttered hoarsely, "and make it quick."

Biting off a groan of agony, he pulled himself inside and slumped down on the seat opposite Cassandra. Breathing hard, he gritted his teeth and tried to stanch the flow of blood with the palm of his hand.

"Derek, I'm so sorry," Cassandra said in a low, concerned voice. "I never dreamed you'd get hurt."

"Shut up, Cassie."

"Please let me help you. You're losing so much blood!"

When she reached out to touch him, Derek's anger exploded with a viciousness he couldn't control. "Stay away from me, Cassie, do you hear? You're poison. Wherever you go, whoever you touch, you're nothing but pretty poison. I'm going to take you on to Melbourne like I promised Harte, and then you're on your own. And I'll be bloody glad to say good riddance to you."

His words had been uttered with such cold, absolute fury that Cassandra retreated and huddled into the corner. Derek leaned back his head and shut his eyes. He had meant what he said. At that moment he was sorry he had ever laid eyes on Cassandra Delaney.

# Chapter 15

Cassandra sighed deeply where she sat on the bench beneath the windows at the stern overlooking the churning wake. She laid the astronomy book she had been perusing facedown on her lap and gazed out over the water. Although the incident in Rio had happened weeks ago, Derek still had not spoken one word to her. The crew had been collectively unfriendly as well, and even her friends the faithful twins had deserted her to spend their time in Derek's company. Big Roscoe had been sweet, had even played his flute for her, but she was lonely and bored. Most distressing of all, however, was the guilt plaguing her conscience.

She wanted to make Derek understand how sorry she was, but he treated her like a pariah and ignored her presence until she wanted to scream with frustration. He acted as if everything were all her fault when he had been the one who had tricked and kidnapped *her*! Where was the fairness in that?

Moreover, she was continually torn with ridiculous, contradictory desires and stupid romantic yearnings that had no place whatsoever in her life. She was sorry he had been shot and felt grateful the wound was healing well. Big Roscoe had told her that the ship's doctor had put thirty stitches in Derek's side the night of the altercation. At times when she took air topside, she would watch him longingly from afar and wince each time he grimaced with pain.

Often she had thought of the sweet things he had said to her on the terrace that night in Rio, but always those memories were eclipsed by the cruel taunts he had thrown at her later aboard the carriage. *Pretty poison,* she thought, biting her lip. What a terrible thing for Derek to call her. Maybe she was. She had lied to and manipulated people a bit too much and too often since the war had begun. Never before now had she felt ashamed of what she had done. She had considered her espionage work as her duty and an honorable way for a woman to fight for her country. But was it?

Confused and unhappy, she leaned her forehead against the thick glass of the windowpane. Far away over the rolling gray waves, she caught sight of a dark blue hump rising against the misty horizon. Immediately alert, she sat up and sharpened her gaze. Land? The tip of Africa, perhaps? She had been charting their progress the best she could and had predicted that landfall would be sighted sometime in the next few days.

As she gazed at the shadowy mountain, a knot of disappointment formed inside her breast as she thought of the Zulus, and zebra and giraffes, and all the other exotic sights she would miss if Derek did not choose a port of call somewhere along the shoreline of South Africa. Perhaps, though, he would drop anchor briefly to replenish their coal or water stocks, as he had done often on the voyage. If he did, she was determined to be among those granted leave to go ashore. Her jaw set with resolve, she rose and went in search of Derek.

The moment she stepped out into the sunshine, the fresh sea wind billowed her unbound hair and her full rose-sprigged white skirt, and she held the soft fabric with one hand as she scanned the decks for Derek. She found him on the bridge with Kapi, Rigi, and Big Roscoe. When he saw her, he glanced away as if he hadn't seen her—the way he had done since their disastrous night in Brazil. She drew in a deep breath and clenched her fists. Their quarrel had gone on long enough. He was going to listen to reason and begin to acknowledge her presence, whether he liked it or not.

With bold step and lifted chin, she strode straight up to him. She faced him squarely, doubled fists planted firmly on her hips. "You're being unreasonable to harbor this grudge for so long. I offered an apology about what happened, didn't I? More than once. Why aren't you gracious enough to accept it?"

Derek looked her up and down, the amused grin he had sported so often at the beginning of their relationship replaced by a humorless scowl. "Like a lot of other people, your own brother included, I find being around you detrimental to my health. Therefore, I plan to keep my distance from now on."

"You're never going to forgive me for getting you shot, are you?"

Without answering her, Derek swiveled his brass-plated telescope toward the shadowy red-hued mountains looming to the north.

"Are you sighting in on the coast of South Africa?"

"We navigated the Cape of Good Hope at second watch two days ago."

"Then that must be Madagascar on the horizon," she said when he didn't elaborate further.

"That's right."

"Thank goodness. I was beginning to think we'd never see land again."

Studiously ignoring her presence, Derek made several notations on his chart of the Indian Ocean.

"I read the book you have on your shelves about the Malagasy," she continued as if he were listening. "I was surprised the inhabitants derive from Indonesian rather than from African tribes. I can't wait to see them for myself."

"You aren't going ashore," he said flatly without deigning to glance at her.

Cassandra couldn't hide her disappointment.

"You mean you're not going stop and visit your friend?"

"I mean that *you* are not going ashore. I intend to visit Kahlel alone, just like I always do."

"Kahlel? Isn't that an Arabic name?"

Derek turned around and shouted a slight change of course. George called back in the affirmative.

"Please, Derek, let me come with you. I've been counting the days until we got here."

"Look, Cassie," Derek said with the sharpest tone he had ever used with her. "I'm not sure I could survive taking you anywhere with me again. I've got an ugly, half-healed bullet hole in my side to prove how trustworthy you are."

Cassandra flinched at the graphic reminder of the pain she had caused him. "I don't blame you for being angry with me. If the man's aim had been true, you could have been killed—" her voice caught, further revealing her remorse over her responsibility. "I couldn't have lived with myself if that had happened. I swear I won't do anything stupid and irresponsible like I did in Rio. I regret it now, truly I do."

For the first time in days, Derek leveled his full attention on Cassandra's face. "You're admitting that running off like that in a strange city was stupid and irresponsible?"

Cassandra nodded. "I was desperate to go home. And I was still angry with you for lying to me, and for tricking me. But I never dreamed you'd come to harm. Surely you know that I care what happens to you."

"I guess the fact that you convinced Captain Mosler to arrest me made me wonder."

Cassandra withered under his stone-cold sarcasm. "I promise I'll do whatever you say without a bit of argument. I've now resigned myself to making the best out of going to Melbourne. Perhaps I can even solicit funds for the Confederacy while I'm there. At least that would make the voyage worthwhile."

Derek wore a dark frown, but she somehow sensed he was wavering about not taking her ashore. "Your presence might complicate things."

"How?"

"Then again, having you along might smooth things over from my last visit."

"Smooth things over? Are you at odds with this man named Kahlel?"

"We parted on a bit of a sour note the last time I visited. No one is ever sure exactly what Kahlel will do next."

"Perhaps I could help ease the tension between you."

For one brief instant Derek's dark eyes shone with the old glint of humor. "Kahlel's going to like you, I have no doubt about that much."

"Then take me along. I am well versed in the tenets of Islam, so it's unlikely I would do anything to insult him. Please, Derek, I'm going crazy cooped up without anything to do or anyone to talk to. I've already read all your books and deciphered all your ocean charts, so there's little else to occupy my mind."

"I have nearly three dozen books in my cabin, Cassie. You're not telling me you've read them all?"

"Yes, and I was impressed with the wide variety of subjects in your personal library. I had no idea you were so well read. I was particularly fascinated with the meticulous accounts you detailed in your past ship's logs."

Derek shook his head and looked away, but when she detected a half smile hovering on his lips, Cassandra knew she had won. "I won't cause you one moment's trouble, I swear it, Derek."

"All right," he said after such a long hesitation that she had begun to fear she had claimed victory too soon, "but you're to do exactly what I say when I say, without one word. Is that clear? We'll go ashore tonight, so be ready."

Cassandra nodded eagerly as he rolled up his chart and strode off to stern. She pivoted her delighted gaze to the landform now gathering height and width. *Madagascar,* she thought, wondering if it was as wonderfully romantic as the name promised. Perhaps time alone together would turn Derek back into his old, teasing self. More and more, that's what she wanted. She wanted him to kiss her again, pursue her as he used to, but this time she wanted him to catch her. She blushed at herself, then smiled as she made her way below to bathe and dress for what she hoped would turn out to be an intimate night with Derek on a mysterious tropical isle.

As was Derek's wont, the *Mamu* did not sail into port but anchored offshore in a calm, sheltered cove. Though night had fallen, inky black and impenetrable, lights twinkled on the far point of the bay, indicating a town of some size. She had donned her favorite evening gown for the excursion, the icy blue silk that matched her eyes, and she held the full skirts in one hand, not missing in the least the unmanageable hoopskirts she had discarded as too cumbersome since they left the States on the *Rachel Ann*. Derek climbed down into the bobbing launch ahead of her, then handed her aboard before he pushed off the hull with an oar.

"Isn't anyone else coming with us?" she asked in surprise.

"Nope."

"You're going to row us in to the beach yourself?"

"That's right."

"Isn't that a bit unusual?"

"This is an unusual situation."

"Why?"

Derek set the oars in the locks and leaned his weight into the first stroke. The lightweight craft skimmed over the smooth water away from the sloop's mooring. "You ask a hell of a lot of questions, don't you, Cassie?"

"My Grandmother Delaney said that's the way one learns things. She also told me that there's no such thing as a stupid question. So do tell me, why are we slinking in to shore like thieves in the night?"

"That just about hits the nail on the head."

A thrill coursed through Cassandra. "Do you mean Kahlel's a pirate or something like that?"

"Wanted in just about every country this side of the equator."

"How many countries are you wanted in?"

"Are you contemplating turning me in for the reward?"

He had remembered his anger with her. She could tell by the hard edge that had crept into his voice. She lapsed into silence so as not to annoy him further. Nevertheless, she was wonderfully happy to be alone with him and on her way to terra firma again. She was not as seaworthy as Derek; she liked her feet planted on something solid and sturdy. The surf was wild and pounding, and she was relieved when the bottom finally scraped sand. Derek jumped lithely into the waves and beached the boat, then scooped Cassandra into his arms and carried her to shore.

"Doesn't picking me up like this hurt your side?"

"I'll live."

When he put her on her feet, she looked up and down the dark beach, confused.

"But there's no one here," she said, her voice nearly obliterated by the roar of the breakers.

"Kahlel's sentries are. They watch the coast day and night, so they'll have seen the *Mamu* in plenty of time to send out an escort. They're probably somewhere up there." He pointed to dark palms lining one end of the beach.

"This is certainly a clandestine tryst."

"You should feel right at home, then, since you're used to lurking around at night and spying on people." Derek turned as if he had heard a strange noise over the crashing waves. "There they are."

Cassandra peered futilely into the dark until a figure finally loomed before them. The rider led a second horse by its bridle, and his black attire made him nearly indistinguishable even when he came close enough to hail them. To her surprise, Derek answered and spoke fluently with him in a foreign tongue.

"You never told me you spoke Arabic," she accused when he took her arm again.

"There's a lot I haven't told you, Cassie. Kahlel only sent one horse because I've never brought anyone here with me. Do you know how to ride?"

"Of course. I won blue ribbons nearly every summer at the county fair on an Arabian thoroughbred named Tantrum—"

Derek cut her off. "Fine. Spare me the details. Here, I'll help you mount."

Cassandra reached out and took hold of the magnificent silver bridle. Long silky tassels flowed down either side of the low-slung Persian saddle. "Look at these macrame knots, Derek. Someone must have worked on this saddle weaving for months to make anything so intricate."

Derek interrupted her admiration of the trappings by unceremoniously boosting her backside into the soft leather saddle. He swung up behind her, pulled her back tightly against his chest, and kicked the horse into motion. Their escort had galloped away at once, and they followed his example, riding hard in the opposite direction. Cassandra smiled with pleasure and held on tightly to the low saddle horn as they rode like the wind down the white sand beach. She was on Madagascar, in the arms of the most handsome man she had ever seen. And he was transporting her off to a hidden pirate's lair. Never in her life had she been so exhilarated, not even when she had helped Professor Henry translate the *Iliad* from a two-hundred-year-old tome written in Greek.

After ten minutes or so, Derek turned away from the pounding surf and urged the spirited stallion up an incline that edged the beach. As they crested the hill, Derek reined in the steed, and Cassandra gazed in amazement at the myriad of white tents spread out across the wide plain below. She could see robed figures moving among the fires that burned throughout the camp.

"It's like a small city," she murmured.

"More like an army encampment. Kahlel likes to protect his interests."

Cassandra twisted around in the saddle. "How did you get involved with such a dangerous man?"

Derek only laughed as he guided the horse carefully down the steep embankment. He skirted the edge of the desert dwellings until they approached the largest of the tents. Derek slid off as an Arab, in flowing black robes, strode forth to meet him.

While they spoke their greetings, embraced, and kissed each other on both cheeks, Cassandra looked at the other guards surrounding the domed structure. Each wore the same flowing black garment, called an *aba,* if Cassandra remembered correctly. Leather bandoliers containing bullets crossed over their chests, and they wore long curved scimitars at their waists.

Derek took his time greeting each man courteously, seemingly very good friends with the entire band of brigands. Cassandra began to feel some worry about the nature of Derek's own past deeds. In truth, she knew next to nothing about him, other than his habit of running the blockade and a few tidbits his sister, Lily, had told her about his home in Australia.

At last he turned and lifted her to the ground. She hesitated slightly when he held back a flap of rich scarlet silk and motioned her inside the tent. Something akin to fear squirmed inside her breast. All her life she had heard tales about the lustful sheiks of Arabia and how they kept harems and dealt in white slavery in order to fill them. Poor Lily had nearly suffered such a terrible fate when she had run into slavers on her way to America. If it hadn't been for Harte, Lily might have become the plaything of some pasha.

Surely Derek wouldn't bring her into that kind of danger, would he? Unless he was still enraged over what had happened in Rio. She remembered him saying that morning that Kahlel would like a woman like her. Oh, lord, what if he were planning to sell her to his Arab friend?

# Chapter 16

"You're not afraid, are you?" Derek whispered softly close to her ear.

"No," she denied quickly, but she was. At the same time she was excited to be entering a dangerous den of thieves.

Once inside a tiny vestibule constructed with walls of silk fabric, Derek took her arm and spoke in a low tone. "Arabs have different customs than we do, Cassie. The men do the talking here, so don't start asking Kahlel a lot of nosy questions about his lifestyle and especially not about Islam. And *please* don't let him find out how smart you are or he might be offended."

*Men are the same the world over*, Cassandra fumed inwardly, *always intimidated by a woman who knows how to use her brain*. Before she could respond, however, a deep, heavily accented voice called out from the other side of the purple silk.

"Derek? Is that you, my friend? Come, let me see you."

Derek ducked through the flowing panels ahead

of him, and Cassandra followed more slowly. She hung back as he strode forward, without waiting for her, toward a man sitting on a zebra-skin rug at the far end of the tent. While the two men embraced warmly, she examined the astonishingly lavish adornments of the interior.

Shimmering sheets of silk and lustrous satins of the richest hues of topaz, ruby, and emerald draped from carved ivory poles, and plush dark blue and crimson Persian rugs carpeted the floor. Brass braziers burned in the corners and large silken pillows were scattered about as the only means of seating. The lush mix of textures and soft waving of the scarves overwhelmed the senses, and Cassandra admired every detail until she caught sight of a group of women sitting cross-legged at one side of the chamber.

They, too, were dressed in a lovely array of rainbow silks, and each wore a semi-sheer veil over the lower half of her face. Only their eyes were visible, lined with black kohl to appear huge, and to Cassandra's surprise, all their gazes were focused on her instead of on Derek, the opposite of the Brazilian women at the ball in Rio. "Kahlel, my sheik, you do me great honor by offering such a magnificent feast," Derek was saying in English, gesturing at a low table set with bowls and dishes. "I am undeserving."

"Humility becomes you, my friend, but do you not best me at all our contests of skill? Few other men can boast of such victories against Kahlel. I have looked forward to your return with great anticipation."

"You'll never win the *Mamu* back from me. I've grown much too fond of her."

*Win the Mamu back? Surely Derek hadn't won such a ship on a wager?* Cassandra thought as Kahlel laughed and clapped Derek on the back. When the other man finally moved into her line of vision, Cassandra got her first good look at the feared Arab pirate.

Unlike his guards or his women, Kahlel was dressed in pure white, both his aba and the voluminous headdress secured by a rope of white beads that encircled his forehead. Shocked, Cassandra estimated that he couldn't be much over fifteen or sixteen. Though so young, he was strikingly handsome, with swarthy dark skin and a strong, slightly hooked nose. When he caught sight of her near the entrance and let his gaze linger on her face, she was shocked to find that his eyes were emerald green.

"Derek, what lovely creature is this that you have brought to me?" he murmured slowly, his regard still riveted on Cassandra.

"I have brought gifts from America, but she is not one of them. She's mine, so keep your hands off her, my friend."

Kahlel chuckled, but his eyes burned with a more intense emotion as Cassandra bristled at Derek's proprietary remarks. He made it sound as if she were his slave! She remembered Derek's warning, however, and her promise to obey him if he brought her ashore, so she held her tongue as the young sheik swept toward her with a rustle of robes. Up close, he looked younger and even more handsome. He moved and spoke with supreme self-confidence, rare in an adolescent boy.

"I have never beheld an angel who trod the earth until this moment. *Ahlan wa sahlan,* welcome to my humble abode," he murmured with oily ooze, his emerald green eyes scorching her face as he lifted her hand to his lips. He then adopted such an openly lascivious expression that Cassandra felt the urge to laugh.

"Does this sweetest of desert blossoms have a name?" he inquired with the same unctuous charm as he reached out and caught a loosened tendril of her hair. Cassandra opened her mouth to reply, but Derek stepped between them before she could speak. He took Cassandra's hand out of Kahlel's grasp and held it between his palms.

"Her name is Cassandra Delaney. She's American."

"No," Cassandra corrected, more out of habit than annoyance. "I'm Confederate."

Surprise flickered across Kahlel's dark face. He threw back his head and barked an appreciative laugh. "So you have not tamed your woman yet, Derek, my friend. I envy you that task."

"I think that task will be too long and tedious for you or him to enjoy overly much," Cassandra snapped, forgetting herself when they talked around her like she was a dessert on display.

Derek gave her such a black, quelling look that Cassandra quickly bit back a whole string of vituperative comments on his superior attitude.

"Come, Cassandra Delaney, meet my wives." The youth puffed his chest with pride. "Each has borne me a fine, healthy son."

Cassandra stared disbelievingly at him, wondering how long he had been fathering children. Derek gave her another warning frown and gripped her arm tightly to reinforce the sentiment as Kahlel presented the girls one at a time, touching the top of their veiled heads with a forefinger when he spoke their name. *Like a father would introduce his children,* Cassandra thought. His wives stared at Cassandra as if she were some exotic creature Derek had delivered from the planet Neptune. She wondered if they were allowed to speak.

"Sit down, my sweet," Derek said with deadly emphasis on the endearment, "and hold your tongue while Kahlel and I converse."

Cassandra sat down cross-legged on a gold silk cushion, then arranged her full skirt modestly around her. She hadn't folded her legs in such a scandalous position since she was a little girl playing checkers with her brother Stuart. It felt rather good to be unladylike for a change. Kahlel carelessly waved one hand, and his six wives rose gracefully and subserviently fetched bowls of food and placed them on the priceless Persian rug in front of his guests. Kahlel lounged down directly across from them, lying on his side, his head propped in his open palm. He stared unblinkingly at Cassandra.

"Tell me, Kahlel, has Allah watched over you since last we met?" Derek said, selecting an orange from a gold-rimmed black bowl.

"My coffers are full of riches and my house is full of beautiful women and male children. What need have I to plunder for more?"

"Plunder?" Cassandra repeated in surprise, then bit her tongue when both men swiveled their eyes to her. She couldn't help it; she wasn't used to sitting silent during interesting conversations.

"Kahlel's the scourge of the seas," Derek informed her with an air of indulgence, "as was his esteemed father before him."

"My father is one with Allah now, but he was the first to bring your master to Cairo to enjoy the hospitality of our home." *Master?* Cassandra thought, lowering her lashes so Kahlel wouldn't see her amusement.

"That's how we became brothers of the blood," Kahlel went on. "Even though he stole my favorite ship from me, I hold great admiration for him."

"You stole Kahlel's ship?" Cassandra asked Derek. If Kahlel continued to draw her into the conversation, why should she sit around like she was deaf and mute?

"I won the *Mamu* fair and square in a game of dice," Derek replied, smiling warmly at one of Kahlel's wives as she filled his silver goblet with red wine. "Kahlel is somewhat addicted to games of chance."

"But I have yet to best you, my friend, when I find no other man kissed with your good fortune while sitting opposite me." Even as he spoke, he stared at Cassandra.

Derek shrugged and braced his elbow on his bent knee. "Is your mother well? And have you found suitable husbands for Riyada and Tarina yet? You were beginning to inquire after dowries the last time I was here."

"My uncles are protective of my little sisters and think them too young to wed so they still reside in the old house in Egypt," Kahlel answered, his eyes examining Cassandra's face and curling golden red hair, then boldly exploring her modest décolletage. "I am surprised Derek brought you here. He does not usually allow his concubines to travel with him but leaves them in port so the bad luck innate in womankind will not befall the *Mamu*. I have heard him say as much many, many times."

Derek merely grinned, and Cassandra flushed with anger. "I am not a concubine," she informed him acidly. "I'm only with him because he saw fit to kidnap me."

Kahlel did not appear shocked in the least. "Ah, it is good when a man takes what he desires by force. It adds much to the excitement, eh?"

Cassandra had to garner every ounce of her will-power to contain her resentment. To think she had thought her brother, Harte, was condescending toward women! Kahlel certainly won that prize hands down, and now Derek, too, seemed to have adopted the youthful Arab's preening air of male superiority. She knew from her studies, of course, that women were considered little more than chattel in the Arab culture, and she glanced sympathetically at the silk-veiled women. Their identities were hidden from the world, each a mere facet of their husband's existence but otherwise worthless in their society. She pitied them.

"I must have you in my bed," Kahlel suddenly decreed, pushing himself into a sitting position. "Now. This very night."

Cassandra's hand froze in the act of choosing a ripe fig from the platter in front of her. Derek, on the other hand, didn't look particularly concerned. He casually fingered one of Cassandra's long curls. "Sorry, my friend, I told you she belongs to me. You know that I never share my women, not with you or anyone else."

Cassandra wondered what women he spoke of, but Kahlel's face twisted into an infantile pout. "But you owe me a contest this night, one of my own choosing. It is the law of the camp. Honor requires you to accommodate my wishes, does it not? If you are partial to her among your other concubines, perhaps the prize should consist of but a single night in which I might enjoy her beauty and womanly charms. Would that satisfy your possessiveness?"

Reduced now to a state of full alarm, Cassandra

waited with bated breath for Derek's indignant refusal.

"All right," he agreed thoughtfully, "but it'll have to be tonight, providing you win, because I intend to ride out of here at dawn. What contest do you have in mind this time?"

"I will not allow this!" Cassandra tried to rise, but Derek planted a firm hand on her shoulder and held her in place. He leaned closer and nuzzled her earlobe. "Hush, luv, and trust me. Kahlel will not be denied his games."

The calm reassurance in his eyes relieved Cassandra's anxiety. Derek knew Kahlel well and was obviously handling the situation the only way he could . . . unless this was Derek's way of extracting revenge on her for what she had done. A chill passed down her spine before she hastily chided herself for harboring such a ridiculous fear. Derek was a civilized man. He would never hand her over to a mere boy whose prime intent was to ravish her! "All right, Kahlel, how will we cross swords this night? Dice? Cards? I have bested you at both many times before."

That was certainly encouraging news, Cassandra thought, relaxing a bit. Derek sounded more than confident that he could win any of their little competitions, and why not? He no doubt had spent many hours gambling and carousing at dockside taverns. He was so sure he would win, in fact, that Cassandra wondered if perhaps he was particularly adept at cheating.

"This time I have chosen to challenge you in a different arena. This time we will compete in a test of strength."

Derek was twice his size, and Cassandra's whole outlook grew rosier until she remembered Derek had a recent gunshot blast in his right side which was not fully healed. He couldn't fight at his full capacity with such an injury. She waited for him to reveal his weakened condition and demand a different contest.

"All right," he replied, smiling. "What do you have in mind?"

"We will use our arms to fight for the proud Confederate flower." Kahlel's handsome face lit up with the fire of competition. "Come, let us begin. My night with the lovely Cassandra grows shorter with each passing moment."

It took a great deal of self-control for Cassandra to sit idly by while two stupid, strutting males took turns insulting her. She had to trust Derek, however. He would never enter into such a wager unless he knew he could win. She bit her lip. Or would he?

Nerves aflutter, she watched Kahlel wave his hand in another imperious command. The woman who was dressed in jade-green hurried to draw back a black silk panel which revealed an alcove set with a marble table inlaid with onyx tiles. Two black leather gold-studded arm chairs were placed on each side. Derek and Kahlel sat down facing each other.

Cassandra glanced uneasily at the two black-garbed, rifle-toting guards. *How could Derek involve me in such an untenable situation?* she thought furiously. Why had he even brought her along in the first place if this sort of thing could happen? She frowned, recalling with regret the way she had begged him to let her accompany him.

Smiling grimly, the two men gripped their hands together. It was then she saw that two wicked-edged knives had been strapped to the table, blade up to impale the hand of the loser.

"The dirks are just to make our duel more interesting," Kahlel was saying, his eyes glowing with excitement.

To Cassandra's shock, Derek was grinning, too, as if he were having a wonderful time. "Ever bloodthirsty, aren't you, my Egyptian friend?"

*Men must have some sort of genetic defect that makes them play stupid, violent games,* she thought, shaking her head and glancing helplessly at the other women. They all stared calmly at her, as if a bloodletting were not about to commence.

Cassandra returned her attention to the contest. Derek's wound was on his right side. Even though he was much bigger and more powerful than Kahlel, his strength was bound to be impaired. Though young, Kahlel had a lean, wiry physique.

Kahlel smiled into Derek's eyes. "*Inshalla,* my captain?"

"That's right," Derek answered. "If God wills."

The challenge of strength began, both men holding steady at first. Several minutes passed with their connected arms not moving so much as a fraction of an inch. As time went on, the effort taxing them became more visible. Sweat began to bead on their faces as they held their jaws locked with concentration, their minds focused solely on forcing their will upon the other. To Cassandra's horror, a spot of crimson blood suddenly appeared on Derek's white shirt near his waist as his grueling efforts reopened his recent wound.

She came to her feet. "Stop! This has gone far enough!"

Neither man paid heed to her admonishment, both staring defiantly into each other's eyes until blood vessels began to bulge in their temples, blue and throbbing.

"Stop it, I say!" she cried in a more forceful voice.

A low titter of Arabic erupted among the veiled wives. To Cassandra's dismay, Derek's grip slackened a degree, and Kahlel was quick to exploit his advantage, pressing down with renewed pressure until the sharp blade touched the back of Derek's hand. When the sharp point pierced far enough for blood to trickle down Derek's wrist into his shirtsleeve, Kahlel suddenly let go and jumped to his feet. His face was filled with glee.

"I am the victor at last, my friend. Tonight I am your equal as a man, and I am honored. And I have won the most wondrous prize of all." He turned and beamed at Cassandra.

"But you only get her until the sun rises over the sea," Derek told him equably, calmly holding out his punctured hand and allowing one of Kahlel's wives to wrap a coral-colored silk scarf around the slight wound. "You have won honorably. I bow to your strength."

To Cassandra's absolute stupefaction, he turned and strode from the tent, leaving her behind without a backward glance.

# Chapter 17

Kaleel clapped his hands. Cassandra was instantly surrounded by the flock of veiled wives. Before she could prevent Derek's departure, the tittering girls swept her away in the opposite direction. Her first impulse was to wrest herself from their clinging hands, but then she realized they were whisking her away from Kahlel and whatever lecherous designs he had on her person. So she went willingly into the night with them, still hoping that Derek would have a change of heart and rescue her from such a ridiculous predicament.

Once she had been drawn unresistingly into a nearby tent, the women gathered around her, laughing and chattering in rapid-fire, indecipherable Arabic. Almost at once they rid themselves of their facial veils, and Cassandra realized that most of them were younger than her own twenty years. Several appeared to have scarcely left their early teens, but all were quite beautiful, with jet hair, almond eyes, and smooth olive skin of the desert Bedouin, with the exception of one woman who was a tall, striking-featured black African.

Cursing herself for not learning the Arabic language when she had taken the time to master so many others, she first greeted them in French, thinking perhaps one might have had contact with Europeans. A trill of amused giggles met her attempts to communicate, and she pushed away several pairs of hands examining her gown and petticoats. When they continued tugging and pulling, she realized with some consternation that they intended to undress her.

"Stop!" she cried in Spanish when the buttons holding the back of her bodice gave way. A German plea to desist did not faze them as they pulled her sleeves off her arms, nor did the few syllables of Russian she gasped out halt their endeavors, and her dress was stripped over her head. The entire disrobing had been accomplished among a great deal of chattering and smiling as if they were very pleased and happy with their task.

Her corselet caused some stir and was examined with cries of curiosity as it was unlaced. Her petticoats and pantalets followed until she was left wearing only a short chemise of thin pink satin. One diminutive girl with huge brown eyes and hooped gold earrings swept back a hanging silk curtain and revealed a copper hip bath. The sweet scent of jasmine wafted up from the steamy water and permeated the draped chamber.

The ramifications of being bathed in oils did not

escape Cassandra's notice. On the other hand, she had been on a ship at sea for weeks, her daily ablutions administered out of a bowl and pitcher. A hot, fragrant bath sounded like a dream come true. Why shouldn't she indulge herself? Derek had told her to trust him. He would surely concoct a plan to get her away from Kahlel before the unthinkable happened. Until he did so, she would take advantage of the hospitality and amenities of Kahlel's fancy harem tent.

"Thank you, ladies," she told the wives with a smile, stepping eagerly into the bath and slipping out of her chemise. She emitted a low moan of ecstasy as she sank to her neck in the deep, silky bathwater. When she leaned her head back against the cushioned headrest, one of the girls unpinned her chignon and began to brush long strokes through her thick hair with a jade brush carved meticulously into the shape of a cobra. Some of the other Arab women knelt around the tub and fingered her red-gold curls as if fascinated by the bright color.

Sighing, she watched them argue among themselves about, she deduced, who should have the honor of shampooing her hair or adding more oil to her bath. There was no doubt in her mind about what Kahlel expected from her that night. His eyes had burned with lust. She had better come up with an alternative plan to get out of Kahlel's clutches with her virginity intact, in case Derek had truly taken leave of his senses.

Perhaps she should tell the Arab pirate she had a dreaded communicable disease which left a man impotent, she ruminated with a vindictive smile. That should make Kahlel's desire wither and droop a bit. Her amusement didn't last long. As Derek had warned her, the Arabs were a different lot. If she told that particular tale, Kahlel just might have her beheaded or sold off to slavers for being unclean or some such thing. Damn Derek! How could he just walk out and leave her to fend off the sheik by herself?

While she soaked, several of the girls gathered up her gown and undergarments and carried them out of the tent. Two others entered from behind a silver-and-crimson-striped curtain, one holding a beautiful flowing garment, the other a veil to wear over her hair. When they laid them out for her to see, she saw that the costume consisted of a tight turquoise silk bodice with long sleeves, but low-cut enough in front to almost completely bare her breasts and short enough to expose her entire midriff. The matching silk trousers were designed with full loose legs of semitransparent fabric cinched around the ankle with silver braid. All in all, not likely to cool the sheik's ardor.

The girls gestured for her to stand. She obeyed and was quickly patted dry with soft linen towels. Then she was led to a velvet-seated backless teak chair with ornate scrolled arms, where every inch of her skin was massaged with yet more scented perfumes as if she were the Empress of China. Her hair was dried and brushed gently until it shone, and her eyes were lined with thick black kohl. Reverently, the women placed a short turquoise silk scarf over her hair and secured it around her forehead with a silver chain wrought with diamonds and rubies. As a last touch, wide gold bands were clasped around her upper arms, and dozens of thinner gold bracelets were clipped over her wrists and ankles.

When the wives were finished with her transformation from American scientist to female prize of the evening, Cassandra gazed sourly at her reflection in a hand mirror they presented to her while the bevy of wives exclaimed over her appearance with a great deal of clapping hands and nodding heads. Without delay, she was herded outside like a lamb to sacrifice and into yet a third tented chamber. While she stared at the absolutely huge round bed draped with enough soft white furs to warm an entire Eskimo village, the excited girls fluttered out of the tent en masse.

Absolute silence settled around her like gossamer threads floating to earth. For the first time, panic nibbled at the edges of her calm. She sank down on a low silk divan. Derek wasn't coming back. What on earth would she do now? Her chin jutted up a notch. One thing she would certainly *not* do was climb in that big furry bed with lusty little Kahlel. She would *not* be a blue ribbon in a man's trophy case.

"Ah, my flower, now you are so beautiful that my breath is snatched from my beating heart."

Cassandra whirled around and found Kahlel right behind her, clutching his chest for dramatic effect. She tensed, prepared to fight off his advances tooth and nail. To her relief, however, he merely smiled and sat down at the other end of the couch. His black hair was damp and slicked straight back, indicating he had bathed and groomed himself for her deflowering ritual. He had changed attire as well, though he still wore pristine white, but this flowing aba was sewn with golden thread and edged with woven gold and black braid. She had a terrible feeling that underneath his robe he was as naked as a satyr and ready to proceed at a moment's notice.

"Please don't look so distressed, Miss Delaney," he murmured in his heavy accent as he lifted a bottle of champagne from a brass urn held by a wooden tripod. "Derek saw fit to leave us this gift to enjoy during our brief night together. Ah, from France, I see, and the very best quality. Derek always brings me the best. You are the ultimate proof of that, my jewel."

Cassandra's teeth came down hard. She had not wanted to believe it, but Derek really had gone off and left her at the boy sheik's bedpost. Anger smoldered, sparked hotly, then raged violently inside her breast. "I do hope you don't think you can force me to share your bed," she informed him in as conversational a tone as she could muster through her fury, "because I will not."

Kahlel stopped in the process of uncorking the sparkling wine. He assumed a facial expression that looked as if she had just thrust a sword through his heart. "Force you? Kahlel? Oh, my Confederate beauty, I have no need to coerce any woman. I will seduce you with the heat of my masculinity and you will melt like warm butter into my embrace."

Cassandra stared incredulously at him. *Good luck, buster,* she thought, but she was more than relieved to hear he had no violence in mind. Derek must have known that Kahlel wouldn't force his attentions on her, but she was still going to kill him for putting her through such an ordeal. She smiled grimly as she relished the pleasurable fantasy of squeezing her fingers tightly around his thick Australian neck.

"Here, my flower, my sweet jasmine love, champagne to sweeten those ruby-red lips that tempt me to madness."

Wondering where he had learned his melodramatic dialogue for seduction, Cassandra accepted the silver chalice he offered, though she had no intention of drinking a drop. She pretended to take a sip as she asked casually, "Is Derek still here in the camp?"

"You are in love with him, no?" Kahlel observed, cocking a regally arched eyebrow. He shrugged expansively. "Derek is to women like the sweetest lotus blossom is to the honeybee. I cannot blame you for finding him attractive and desiring his attentions. He is a magnificent man. I have never bested him in any contest until tonight."

*Lucky me*, Cassandra thought sardonically, giving Kahlel a vinegary look. She was in no mood to hear praises sung about Derek Courtland's virility. A change of subject was in order, and from what she had observed, Kahlel was not exactly the humble sort. Somehow she knew that he wouldn't object in the least to allowing himself to be their sole topic of conversation.

"Tell me about yourself, Kahlel. Are you really a pirate, as Derek said?"

As she had predicted, Kahlel looked thrilled with her choice of topics. "The father of my father's father sailed the seas for plunder and bounty. For generations we have been the masters of men and rulers of great harems filled with beautiful women of our choosing."

Although Cassandra was no stranger to the belief most men held concerning the inferiority of the female gender, she thought Kahlel certainly won the prize for touting the theory. "Your two sisters were also born from the loins of the father of your father's father, were they not? Are they allowed to keep harems of beautiful men?"

Kahlel threw back his head and laughed with jolly abandon. When he sobered from what he obviously considered a joke of uproarious proportions, he looked askance at her. "You are most different from our desert flowers. You are outspoken and perhaps even able to read, I fear. In my culture, such attributes are not admired in females, but I want to sleep with you very much, so I will overlook your shortcomings."

The urge to smile tugged at Cassandra's lips. "And I take it I am to be pleased that you are willing to forgive any trace of intelligence I might display?"

Kahlel looked shocked by her question. "But of course. You are to be complimented by everything that I say and do."

Cassandra had to laugh, but she no longer feared the arrogant young sheik. "You are a straightforward man, Kahlel, so I will be as well. Please don't be offended, but I will never lie with you. If it will make you feel better, I haven't lain with Derek Courtland, either, as magnificent a man as you think him to be. After his despicable behavior here tonight, you can bet I never will."

"He has not bedded you yet? How very unlike him. Especially since you are such an extraordinary beauty. Perhaps your surrender should be the greatest contest of our manhood."

Cassandra shook her head in disbelief. Kahlel was as addicted to gambling as he was to desert flowers, but this was one bet he would never win. But neither would Derek Courtland, the lousy traitor. She watched Kahlel rise like a fluid wraith in his voluminous white robe and move to a legged brass brazier and take his time lighting a stick of incense from coals smoldering inside it. He walked back, smiling like a hungry crocodile swimming toward a wildebeest with a broken leg. He stuck the incense into a small vase made of hammered gold that was filled with sand and engraved in Arabic script.

"I have a special treat for you," he murmured, lifting with care a lute from a small chest covered with scarlet leather. He held the instrument out for her to examine.

"It's very beautiful," she murmured truthfully, running her fingertips lightly over the smoothly polished wood shaped like a gourd sliced in half and affixed with seven pairs of strings.

"Yes, this *oud* is very ancient. For generations it has been passed down from father to eldest son as one of our family's greatest treasures. My father's father and his father before him have used its sweet melody to seduce the women they desired. I will play for you until you melt with love for me."

*Not only are you an egotistical peacock,* Cassandra thought, *but your father's father and his father before him were, too.* Then she wondered how Kahlel's forebears ever had time to do any pirating with all the seducing going on behind their silk curtains. She relaxed back in her chair, more confident now that her dilemma wasn't nearly as precarious as she had first thought.

Kahlel was charming in his own self-centered, male-dominating way, and he could attempt to seduce her until he sprouted horns as long as he kept his distance. She had withstood an overwhelming attraction to a man like Derek Courtland for all these months, had she not? Not many women could boast that kind of self control; not many women would want to, she realized unhappily.

"This ballad is old and sweet," Kahlel was telling her in a honey-coated murmur chock-full of sensual promise. His green eyes held hers, warm and persuasive, as he strummed the strings and sent a rippling wave of urgent nasal tingling sounds through the tent.

When he began to sing Cassandra did not cringe into the cushions, but only because of extreme force of will. The notes coming out of his mouth were the most discordant, off-key, unmelodious noises she had ever heard vibrate off human vocal chords. She had heard mating bullfrogs who sounded better.

Stifling the laughter trying to bubble up her throat and out her mouth, she listened to the garbled English words of lyrics obviously written for Arabic interpretation. No wonder his wives were so pleased that Cassandra had shown up. Now they wouldn't have to suffer through a night of Kahlel's cacophonous serenades in the cramped confines of the harem tent.

Filled with silent mirth, she endured his first song without an outburst of giggles but was inordinately pleased when he paused to drain his goblet. As he refilled his glass with Derek's gift of wine, resentment streaked through her. Kahlel gave her a long leer of lovelorn lasciviousness then began his painful moaning again.

Behind her the smoldering incense was pouring out a heavy cloud of exotic perfume, the fragrance of which she did not recognize. For the first few minutes the scent was pleasant to the senses, but then as the tent gradually became saturated with the cloying smoke, she began to feel giddy and light-headed.

"Kahlel, I don't mean to be rude, but this incense is making me dizzy."

Kahlel's long, slender fingers paused on the lute strings. He eyed her blearily, grinning as he slurred out his answer. "But of course it does, my desert angel."

"It's supposed to make me sick?"

This time Kahlel looked mightily offended. "This incense is specifically made for nights of intimacy. Soon it will touch your heart and body, and even your soul. You will swoon in my arms, and we will join our bodies in the dance of love."

For a moment Cassandra could only stare blankly at him; then the truth came rushing up to crystallize inside her brain. The incense was an aphrodisiac! He was fumigating her like a pig in a smokehouse!

"Love potions are useful with proud virgins such as yourself," Kahlel was murmuring as if his tongue were thick and unruly and had a mind of its own. "I have used this incense many times with wonderful results."

Cassandra was shocked that he had dared to do such a thing to her, then groggily wondered why she was surprised. The entire evening had been as bizarre as a chapter out of Scheherazade's tales of the *Arabian Nights*. Aphrodisiacs had been used for centuries in various forms, of course, but she had certainly never been subject to one herself.

Holding the blue veil tightly against her nose, she inched as far away as she could from the golden bowl billowing forth its love fumes. Kahlel didn't seem to care or even notice, concentrating on his wailing, which was even worse now that he had indulged in several goblets of champagne. So woozy now that her arms felt weighted with iron chains, she was thankful she felt no all-powerful urge to press herself up against the randy young sheik.

"Come, my desert rose," Kahlel was mumbling incoherently. "Enough time has been wasted. I need you, I want you, I must have you. I will die if I do not possess you."

Kahlel had come up on his knees, and Cassandra found herself so heavy-limbed and weak that she feared she could only lie back and watch objectively as he ravished her. *So that's how incense works,* she mused dully. *The woman lies half-conscious like a slab of ham while the man feasts on her.* As if she were floating above her body, she watched Kahlel loom over her like a great white albatross. She blinked in surprise when he suddenly disappeared from view.

*Why, look at that, he's lying facedown on the rug,* she thought thickly, her reasoning slowed to a snail's pace inside the dense fog of incense. She pondered various reasons why he would adopt such a posture while smack-dab in the middle of his seduction, but her thoughts swam slowly through her mind like a sea bass trapped in an underwater cavern.

Only when she heard his loud, reverberating snores did she realize that he had passed out. If only she could move her body, she would get up, find Derek Courtland, and strangle him with her bare hands. When she got tired of holding her eyes open, she let her lids drop down until she was enclosed in some warm, dark place.

"C'mon, Cassie, darlin', time to go home."

The words were low, close to Cassandra's ear. Someone was shaking her. Somehow she forced open her eyes as she was pulled upright. With difficulty she focused her vision on Derek's smiling face. She ought to slap him, but his white teeth were gleaming against his bronzed face, and she wanted him to kiss her, more than anything she had ever wanted in her life.

"Cassie, wake up. It's me."

"You left me here to get smoked," she accused foggily as he got her on her feet. He was dressed in black desert robes now, like the ones Kahlel's guards wore, with a gun strapped around his hips. He looked dangerous and handsome.

"You look nice in that aba," she slurred out of lips that were burning to be kissed.

Derek gave a low laugh. "Thanks. Now let's get out of here before someone realizes I drugged Kahlel's wine."

"I'm going to kill you, Derek, but first I want you to make love to me, all night, until dawn comes." Her mouth gaped open as soon as she heard what she had said.

"No, I don't," she countered her own remarks in confusion, but when she looked at his sensual mouth and the way his lips were slowly forming his words and his black beard that scratched against her cheek when he kissed her, she wanted to press her mouth on his, to force open his lips and taste his tongue. "Kiss me, quick," she demanded huskily, then shook her head in denial.

"I see Kahlel's been using his favorite incense again," Derek said, swinging her easily into his arms and making her bracelets jingle. Cassandra couldn't fight him, and her body lay limp and relaxed against his chest. "It's as potent as hell, luv. You probably won't remember any of this in the morning. I sure as hell hope not."

Cassandra wanted only to press herself up against the great, sculptured muscles of his chest. She wanted his arms around her, wanted to touch his skin. Weak and warm and woozy, she barely felt the coolness of the night air as he ducked out the tent with her and strode with silent tread through the darkness to his waiting steed.

"I love you," she astounded herself by saying. "But I don't like you one bit," she added quickly.

Derek only laughed as he settled her in his arms and spurred the stallion into a gallop. They seemed to fly away, up off the earth into some unknown plane, swallowed by a strange, whirling world of dark, desperate desires that made her body ache and burn and writhe with fires that only Derek could quench.

# Chapter 18

Derek rode due south toward the village of Fara-fangana. Cassandra was arching against him and pressing warm kisses along the side of his neck, and he wasn't exactly unresponsive. Kahlel's incense was potent; Derek had found that out firsthand the night Kahlel had fired up a stick of it during one of his wedding feasts in order to seduce his reluctant African bride. Cassandra was ready and more than eager to give herself to a man, and he sure as hell wasn't going to take her back to a ship full of able-bodied seamen who hadn't had shore leave since the far side of the Atlantic.

"Where are you taking me?" she purred, her lips nibbling just beneath the angle of his jaw.

"Somewhere you can get the incense out of your system."

"I want you," she murmured, her hand seeking entrance among the folds of his aba until he laughed softly, struck by the irony of the situation.

"Cassie, stop that, or we're going to end up in the bushes along the side of the road. Go to sleep and leave me alone."

Mumbling vaguely, she laid her cheek against his chest, but her hands continued to roam. His own desire was hard to ignore—literally, he thought with grim humor. By the time they approached his house in Farafangana, he knew he had to get her off his lap quick before he forgot his good intentions.

After the mess she had gotten him into in Rio, he had sworn to stay away from her. Having her aboard the *Mamu* and in plain sight day after day had robbed him of sleep and his inclination to stay angry with her, especially when she was so openly penitent. Not that he didn't know her to be perfectly capable of using her charms to get her own way— God only knew how many men she had wrapped around those long, slender fingers of hers— but he had never been so obsessed with a woman. Now that she was throwing herself at him in a way he had previously only dreamed of, any response on his part would be inappropriate, if not dishonorable as hell.

"I think I love you," she whispered against his throat. "I really think so."

Derek knew he was not going to last much longer. Thank goodness he had a place to go where he could put her to bed and let her sleep it off. The room he kept in a small adobe boardinghouse on the edge of the village was dark and shuttered, and he swung off and flipped the reins over the hitching rail. When he lifted Cassandra down and set her on the ground, she quickly reached up and locked her arms around his neck. She was unsteady on her feet so he swung her back into his arms with enough clanking of gold bracelets to wake up the neighbors.

"Hush, now, darlin', or my landlord'll hear and come running."

"I love your body. It's so hard all over."

*That's for damn sure,* he thought wryly. *Do the right thing, do the right thing,* he kept repeating, but by the time he got inside and locked the door, she was all over him and breathing hard. Even so, she was not as affected as he was.

The room was pitch-black, and he made his way to the bed and dumped her unceremoniously into its soft feather mattress. He strode away to light the candle he always left on the table by the window. Fumbling with the tin box, he finally was able to strike a match. When the flame flickered, sending his shadow snaking up the wall, he looked back at Cassandra.

She had lost her veil on the ride, and her golden red hair hung wild and tangled around her shoulders. She might as well have been naked because the outfit Kahlel had provided clung provocatively to every lush curve of her body. Her smooth white skin shone through the sheer fabric, and she looked like a beautiful Egyptian queen, a reincarnated Cleopatra, with her silver-blue eyes lined so heavily with black kohl.

For a moment he could not move. God help him, he absolutely ached for her. Cassandra suddenly smiled, slowly and seductively, as if she knew of the battle raging inside him. Every fiber of his body leaned toward her as if she were reeling him in with some invisible cord. He wanted to go to her, strip off her clothes and bury himself in her silken flesh.

"Dammit," he muttered, turning away by sheer force of will. He flung open the casement window and breathed deeply in the cool night breeze. Damn Kahlel. Derek should have known better than to take Cassandra there with him tonight. But he had wanted to be with her, alone and away from the confines of the ship. The truth was he had missed her during their weeks of estrangement, missed her smile, her voice, the way her eyes changed color with the gowns she wore. Now he had her to himself, and his blood was boiling like water in a hot cauldron.

"Derek?"

Before he even knew she was close, she was pressing against his back, her arms clamped possessively around his waist. He stiffened, then turned quickly and locked his fingers around her wrists. He swung her around where she would be forced to breathe in the crisp air.

"I'm not made of steel," he whispered in a thick voice. "I've wanted you too damn long for you to do this to me."

She leaned her head back against him, her chest heaving above the arm he had clamped around her naked midriff.

"I didn't burn for Kahlel like this, but I do for you. I always have, from the beginning, when you held me down and kissed me at the White Rose, but I didn't want to. I hate you sometimes, but then I can't resist you. I can't fight this awful yearning inside me anymore, please—"

A tide of emotion began to swell inside Derek's chest, a feeling he had never encountered before, a wonderful, frightening tide of tenderness. He cared about her more than he should. His feelings were deeper than he wanted them to be. Oh, God help him, he was in love with her.

He let go of her wrists, amazed and appalled, and Cassandra turned in his arms and strained up to brush his mouth with her soft lips. He put his hands on her shoulders, still trying to do the chivalrous thing. He had thought of little other than possessing her since the first day he had seen her. Deep inside his soul he knew he had been waiting for this moment—hungering for the point when she was his for the taking.

Derek crushed her body against him, squeezing his eyes shut and trying to sort out his own emotions. He could feel the beating of her heart, could feel his own. He grasped a fistful of her flowing hair and gently pulled her head back where he could look down into her face. She smiled so angelically, her love for him warming her eyes. An absurd tremble flashed across his heart. *Oh, God help me, I'm lost to her,* he thought, then his mouth was on hers, hungry, starving, desperate.

Cassandra was eager, clutching him with unbridled passion. He picked her up and she wrapped her legs around his waist. Derek took her mouth again, his palms molding her hips. He collapsed on the bed with her, his loins burning with need, his heart thundering. "I shouldn't be doing this, dammit, not now," he breathed out hoarsely, half disgusted with himself. "You're going to hate me in the morning."

"No, I could never hate you, not when you make me feel like this."

Their mouths met, clung, caught fire until they broke apart with ragged breathing and heaving chests. Derek came to his knees, unbuckling his gun belt and jerking open the front of his aba. Cassandra tried to help but only fumbled with his pants in her haste and inexperience. Derek tore off the rest of his clothes, never taking his eyes off her moist, parted lips. There was no doubt that she was ready for him to make love to her. If he had her now, if he took her virginity from her, there was no going back, he knew that.

For a long, agonizing moment of soul-searching he held her clinging hands at bay, then he crushed her body tight against him and lowered her back down into the soft bedclothes. He pressed his lips against her throat as he slowly pulled down the brief scrap of silk bodice, baring her breasts for his pleasure. Cassandra moaned audibly and clutched his hair between her fingers. He wanted to give her pleasure such as she had never known before. He tasted the soft flesh of her breast, took the hardened tip between his lips.

Cassandra cried out weakly, and Derek slid his

hand lower, caressing skin that felt like a length of fine Persian silk. He pressed a kiss against her flat belly and her body jerked. She was reacting to each gentle touch of his fingertips with heightened, virginal sensitivity. She was untouched, pure, he knew that for sure now, and he was glad she was. He wanted to be the first; he wanted to be the only man to have her.

"You're too beautiful, Cassie, too perfect." Derek rolled with her, bringing her atop his loins as he had fantasized endlessly since they had shared a similar embrace briefly at the White Rose Tavern. But this time she was naked, her long, silky hair flowing down over his chest, and she was warm and soft and eager. When she leaned down and pressed her bare breasts against his chest, he caught his fists in her silken tresses and brought her head down to his mouth. Their lips crushed together, and he wanted to devour her, to slide his hands over every inch of her body, to possess her until her soul cried out with joy.

"Derek, Derek," she murmured over and over again, and he slid his hand up her inner thigh. When he touched her lightly with his fingertips, she gasped with pleasure. He caressed her until her arousal brought her up against his hand. When the pleasure came, she clutched the sheet in her fists and cried out in wonder.

He came back atop her, pressing her down on the bed, his mouth on hers. "I do love you, Cassie," he muttered, entering her gently and finding the resistance of her maidenhood. She went stiff when he pressed harder, then he groaned as he finally was able to make her his own. She cried out in his arms, and he murmured soothing words until she undulated slowly with him, her fingernails digging into his shoulders, and he was overcome with such fierce, uncontrollable pleasure that a hoarse cry tore from his throat. Ecstasy such as he had never known before rocked through him, tossing his body like hurricane winds and leaving him trembling and shaken. He lay against her softness, sated emotionally and physically, but more than anything else, shocked by the power of his own response.

"I love you, I do," she whispered, and he held her tightly, tenderly until she lay still, her fingers still tangled loosely in his hair.

Cassandra snuggled closer against the warmth surrounding her. She felt wonderfully content and happy, and she stretched luxuriously as she slowly began to awaken. Someone was massaging her bare back, and her muscles were relaxed, gloriously and completely.

"G'day, darlin'."

Derek's husky drawl against her earlobe brought her eyes wide open. She sat up in alarm. Derek lay beside her, naked except for the sheet around his waist. Blushing with embarrassment, she stared down at him in something akin to astonishment. When his regard fastened to her torso, she realized with dismay that she was nude, too. She snatched up the sheet to cover herself. Even the room was unfamiliar, and she couldn't remember how she had gotten there.

"Where are we? What happened? How could you do this to me?" Faint recollections of their intimacies welled up in strange wisps of dreamlike memories. She felt her face burn as the color rose in her cheeks.

"You seduced me." Derek smiled and tugged at the end of the blanket. "Come back and let me show you how you did it."

"No!" She moved away, shivering as more vivid pictures formed in her mind. "You went off and left me at Kahlel's mercy."

"But I came back for you, didn't I?"

"What if it had been too late?"

"I've known Kahlel for years. He prides himself on his powers of seduction. I knew he wouldn't force you to do anything you didn't want to do. And I knew you wouldn't let him touch you. Just to be safe, though, I put some sleeping powder in his wine." He grinned. "If I had refused to compete for you, Kahlel would have been insulted. Arabs don't overlook insults from their friends. Whoever loses the last competition chooses the new one and the prize. I had to agree, and I would have won if you hadn't gotten me shot in Rio."

"So now all this is my fault?" she said sarcastically.

For the first time he had the grace to look slightly

contrite. "I tried my damnedest to resist you last night, but you just kept after me until I gave in."

Cassandra started to deny his outrageous accusations, but then a hazy remembrance floated into her mind—she saw herself walk to a window and embrace him. Turning her head, she saw the open window and recognized it only too well.

"It was the incense, I assure you," she said defensively.

Derek moved so fast that she could only gasp before she was lying flat on her back with him holding her down. He caught her hands beside her head. "You were affected by the incense, darlin', and well I know it, but you love me. You told me so last night. More than once."

"No, I didn't."

"Oh, but you did. You enjoyed every minute of our lovemaking. You moaned the most when I did this"—Cassandra's lips fell apart when he slowly slid his hand up the inside of her naked thigh—"but what I found the most amazing is that I love you, too. Despite all the trouble you've brought my way."

Cassandra's heart stopped. She stared up at him, and he smiled at her expression. "Do you really love me?"

"That's the godawful truth, Cassie. God help me."

Pleasure, pure and simple, rolled over Cassandra. He had admitted it. She hadn't thought him capable of that, even if he did have such feelings for her. But did he say the same thing to every woman who woke up naked in his bed? "Just when did you start loving me?" she demanded as suspiciously as a police interrogator.

"When did you start loving me?" he countered with a challenging grin.

Cassandra was given pause. When had she started loving him? Derek didn't wait for her answer.

"I stole you away on my ship so I could take you home with me, didn't I?" he whispered, winding a long lock of her hair through his fingers.

"You were paid well enough."

"That's right, but the money only made it a legitimate kidnapping. I wanted you from the first time I saw you without your fake beard. Last night you were willing, and I was too weak to stop myself."

He had been whispering his words, his black eyes holding hers, his forefinger caressing her lips. Weakly, Cassandra closed her eyes. "But I missed the whole thing," she said, her voice heavy with a disappointment she couldn't hide.

Derek laughed softly then his lips touched her again. "This time you won't. This time you'll remember everything I do, everything you feel—"

Cassandra couldn't move. She wanted that, too. She wanted him to kiss her mouth and touch her body. She felt captured in an enchanted spell. Despite the fact that he had stolen her away from her home, had left her with Kahlel, she wanted to be held in his arms. He was touching her so gently, with tender reverence, and he had told her he loved her. Despite the fact that they weren't husband and wife, and their union was a dreadful sin, she was glad last night had happened. She was surely becoming the most wicked, terrible woman, but for the first time in her life, she was in love.

# Chapter 19

"That's a very interesting painting, Kapi," Cassandra remarked to the little boy several days later aboard the *Mamu*.

Kapi looked up from where he sat behind Derek's desk. His lips parted wide and revealed his funny, gap-toothed grin. "Thank you, Miss Cassie. It show the footprints of a great ancestor."

Cassandra walked around the desk and peered intently over his shoulder. She had found an old box of paints in one of Derek's sea chests, and the boys had used the backs of discarded ocean charts for their canvases. Kapi especially liked to create art. He would still be sitting and drawing long after Rigi got bored and ran topdeck to play with Big Roscoe and Snowflake.

His current masterpiece was about two feet square, and he had used his finger to spread the different colors of paint. In the background he had dabbed on dots of unmixed ocher that seemed to blend together in the eye of the beholder and produce an unusual luminous effect. At the center of the yellow points he had smeared a big blue circle with several smaller circles of the same color scattered around it. Each circle had a scarlet rim and a maze of squiggly, bright pink lines connected them like beds of baby snakes.

"What exactly do you mean by the footprints of your ancestors, Kapi? Can you explain your picture to me?"

"It be a honey-ant dreaming."

"Honey-ants? Are those like the little black ants we have in America?"

Kapi shook his head. "It big and red and feed on sap of mulga tree that grow in desert where Kapi and Rigi got life from mother."

"I see," Cassandra said, eagerly pulling up a chair. She had long been interested in aboriginal art and had seen other drawings Kapi and Rigi had done of birds and animals, but none were in abstract form as was this one. "Exactly what is going on in your picture?"

"It show the journey of the Honey-ant Ancestor."

"How do you know about his journey?"

"The elders who live in the hills on Malmora teach us the paths of our ancestors."

"Do you and Rigi have a special ancestor?" She knew that many tribes of Indians, both in South America and North America, had animals which they identified as their personal totem, but she didn't realize that the aboriginals of Australia had similar beliefs.

239

Kapi nodded as he carefully added another squiggly line with his crooked little finger.

"We call them totems where I work," she said. "Is your totem the honey-ant? Is that why you're drawing it?"

Kapi looked horrified at such a suggestion. He shook his head in vigorous denial. "No man can paint his own dreaming. It too powerful. It kill him. Not eat his ancestor, either. I can draw honey-ant dreaming because it be totem of Tjilkamata."

"Who is Tjilkamata?"

"He old man who teach us about the Creation."

Cassandra was fascinated. "The aboriginals have a legend concerning the creation of the world?"

The child nodded. "The ancient ones wandered over the land in the dreamtime, singing out name of everything they came upon. They sang names of birds and animals, the plants and rocks and streams of water."

"And in so doing they sang the world into existence?"

Kapi nodded soberly.

"What is your totem, Kapi? Are you allowed to tell me?"

"Kapi and Rigi have wallaby dreaming. We cannot kill wallaby or eat it meat. It be part of us."

Cassandra knew wallabies to be like small kangaroos, some of which were no larger than rabbits. "I see. Show me what the honey-ant is doing in your picture."

Kapi placed a small forefinger on the large blue

circle. "It be eternal home of Honey-ant Ancestor at Tatata. He start journey there."

"What are the circles?"

"They be places for ceremonies of his ancestors."

"And the wiggly lines?"

"They be dreaming-tracks that show path of ancient one when he name things."

"Will you show me these dreaming-tracks when we reach Malmora?"

When Kapi shook his head, Cassandra was disappointed. "Cannot see them," he told her. "They be inside here." He pointed to his forehead. "Elder with same ancestor sing them to us and then we know where they go."

"So the legends and visible paths of each great ancestor are passed down from one generation to the next by memory?"

Kapi was already busy making more curvy lines, and Cassandra felt excitement growing inside her at the prospect of landing in Australia and being introduced to more undocumented aboriginal customs and legends.

"Where did Rigi run off to?" she asked, picking up the other child's art, which had barely been started. His picture also had many dots and circles scattered over the paper.

"He like being with Captain Derek best."

Cassandra certainly knew that feeling well enough, especially since the night they had spent in Farafangana. They had returned to the ship after a whole day of lovemaking, and Derek had set sail at once. He had been busy with his duties throughout the days since then, but each night he had come to her. A shiver coursed through her at the thought of the hours she had spent enfolded in his strong arms.

Almost as if he had sensed she was thinking of him, he appeared in the doorway. He was dressed in a clean white shirt, fawn-colored pants, and black leather knee boots. When he gave her a rakish grin, his face burned by the sun and his black eyes filled with erotic promises, her heart leaped and began to thud with anticipation.

"Kapi, George's going to show Rigi how to rig the jib. Why don't you go up and watch, too?"

Kapi shook his head. "I telling Miss Cassie about Way of the Law and footprints of the honey-ant."

Derek walked forward. "You can tell her about the songlines later. I have some business with Miss Cassie that can't wait. In other words, Kapi, scram."

Kapi grinned when Derek winked at him; then he jumped to obey. As soon as the child had scooted out the door, Derek slid the door bolt behind him. His eyes, as hot and black as a summer midnight, locked on Cassandra's.

"Get your clothes off, darlin'."

A thrill started at the base of Cassandra's spine and rippled its way to the roots of her hair. She felt a deep, agonizingly acute stir of raw desire erupt in the core of her womanhood. Her throat went dry. She shouldn't allow this, she thought, she couldn't let this scandalous love affair continue. She was a decent woman, not some trollop to be had by a man without the blessings of wedlock. She shivered again as he walked toward her, pulling his shirt over his head as he came.

"Derek, we really ought to talk about what we've been doing," she began nervously as he took her hands and pulled her up from the chair. He sat down and drew her atop his lap.

"I didn't come down here to talk." His mouth found her quivering lips. "I want you. I always want you."

"Derek, please," Cassandra said, then gasped as he pulled her astraddle his loins. "We can't do this every time you walk into this cabin."

"Why not?" He was unbuttoning her white shirtwaist now, his lips seeking flesh, and when he found the curve of her breasts, she moaned and quickly lost all will to discuss the impropriety of his advances. His hands were intruding beneath her skirt, finding her and preparing her for him, and she moaned and tangled her fingers in his long hair.

"I—just think—oh—that we should—ah—consider—"

"Stop thinking about anything but this," he murmured breathlessly as he continued to caress his fingertips over her sensitive flesh with the utmost gentleness.

"Oh, my, please, Derek, don't—"

"Hush, and kiss me, Cassie," he ordered, his voice gruff and low. Cassandra lowered her mouth to his, so overcome by the exquisite sensations he was causing inside her that she labored for breath. His mouth seemed to fuse with hers, and she was hardly aware that he was undressing her until he had tossed her clothes aside and brought her down atop him.

She cried out as he made her body undulate with his own slow rhythm. Then he leaned her back across the desk, molding her lips so forcefully that she was lost in the magic of what his hands and mouth could do to her. The pleasure built with each slow thrust, higher and higher, until she felt she couldn't bear the joy of it another minute; then the fiery starbursts shot through her, over and over, so intense that she cried out his name as he rose above her, head thrown back as he groaned with his own ecstasy.

Afterward he pulled her back atop his lap on the chair and held her tightly. Cassandra leaned her cheek on his wide shoulder, her body and mind limp with contentment as he stroked her hair and pressed kisses against her forehead.

"Now give me one good reason why we shouldn't do this every time I come down here."

Cassandra thought of the stillborn child she had seen, so twisted and pitiful, but she couldn't bring herself to explain her inadequacy to him, not yet. Derek would want sons, every man did, and she couldn't give him healthy ones, couldn't give him children at all. She didn't like to think about it. "Do you plan to set me free once we're in Melbourne, as you promised?"

Derek stiffened. He pushed her back and searched her face. "Do you still want to go back?"

"I have to."

"Stay with me, Cassie. I've got some problems to work out at home, then I'll take you back to America, I swear."

"What problems?" she asked, realizing she knew very little about his reasons for making the long voyage into the southern hemisphere. All she knew was that she loved him to distraction.

"My father was murdered. I promised Lily I'd find out who did it and bring him to justice."

"Do you have any idea who did it?"

"I think it's a man named Strassman. He owns the cattle station adjacent to ours in Victoria. He drove Lily off Malmora. That's why she came to America to find me. Didn't she tell you anything about this?"

Cassandra remembered once when Lily had tried to talk to her about her father's death, but Cassandra had hardly listened because she had been so preoccupied with gathering information about Harte's whereabouts. In retrospect she felt ashamed of her insensitivity to her friend's grief. She couldn't bring herself to admit that to Derek, either. "I knew your father was killed and that's why she came to America looking for you. Do you know this man Strassman?"

"Yeah." Derek's voice tightened and his face took on an angry expression that she hadn't seen since they had left Rio. "He's capable of murder, all right, but I don't know why he wanted my father dead. The two of them always got along well. But you can believe I'll find out and see him thrown in prison if he did it."

"This is very important to you, isn't it, Derek?"

"Yes, as important as your war is to you."

"Will you take me back after you've dealt with this man?"

Derek nodded.

"And run the blockade?"

Derek smiled and shook his head. "Always the enterprising spy, aren't you, darlin'?"

"I love the South."

"More than me?"

Cassandra hesitated. "I'm beginning to fear not."

"Then you'd marry me if I asked you?"

His question startled her. She couldn't marry him without telling him she was barren. Would he still want her? She was afraid to find out. "Are you asking me?"

Derek smiled. "I can't believe it, but I am considering that very thing."

Cassandra decided to respond in the same light manner. "If I should marry you, what's in it for me?"

"This," he whispered, his mouth caressing her lips softly until he ignited her passion as he always did and everything was forgotten except the fires burning in their hearts.

On the fourth day of June, the *Mamu* sailed into the narrow mouth of Port Phillip Bay. As they steamed onward toward the smaller inlet of Hobson's Bay which embraced the city of Melbourne like a lover, Cassandra stood at the rail flanked by Big Roscoe and Kapi and Rigi, who were so excited they could barely contain themselves.

The port was bustling with a forest of masts where ships from throughout the world lay at anchor. They were guided to berth at Railway Pier, a long wooden docking area set with railway tracks to transport arriving cargo to the warehouses lining the harborfront. Ships crowded either side of the pier, but Cassandra's gaze was drawn to the Australian city of several hundred thousand; she was amazed at its size and cosmopolitan air.

Reminiscent of Richmond and other southern ports, church steeples rose in the distance, one of particular size and beauty, while many smokestacks on nearby factories poured their vile black smoke into the sky. Farther away, along streets radiating uphill from the edges of the bay, she could see buggies moving among the brick houses of a residential neighborhood.

Hardly had the gangplank fell with a thud against the pier before the boys took Big Roscoe's hands and pulled him ashore. They had insisted on their friend coming with them to Malmora, and he seemed as eager as they to step upon the soil of their beloved homeland.

Cassandra's meager luggage was packed and beside her—demonstrating her own eagerness to explore the wild unknowns of Australia. The ocean might be Derek's first love, but Cassandra did not share his passion. She had grown up loving the land, almost as much as Kapi and Rigi did. She loved green grass and pine trees and black Virginia soil. *And now Derek, too,* she admitted with a secret smile. She glanced at him where he gave last-minute orders to George and some of the other men. She knew he was going over instructions to unload and sell the goods taken aboard in Brazil, and to negotiate for contracts with the Melbourne wool merchants to transport their product back to England. By the time he returned from Malmora to resume command, the *Mamu* would be loaded and ready to sail.

When he did join Cassandra, he, too, seemed gripped with a barely contained urgency. His first words to her, however, were not what Cassandra wanted to hear.

"I think you should stay here on the ship where George and the crew can protect you. I don't know what's waiting for me at Malmora. But it's damned certain Strassman won't welcome me home with open arms."

"I'm going with you," she insisted, raising her chin to a defiant angle. "I've been on this ship for nearly three months, and that's long enough."

"Cassie, listen. Strassman hires convict labor to do his bidding. They terrorized Lily until she was scared enough to take off for America on her own. You'll be safe here with my men, and I won't have to worry about you."

"I promised the boys that I'd go with them and see their totem. I intend to write a thesis on aboriginal songlines and their legends of creation while you're tending to your affairs, so I won't be in your way. Besides, I don't think you can last that long without me."

Derek reached out and caressed her cheek. "You do have a point there, luv. My bed would seem cold and lonely indeed without you in my arms."

"So enough about my not going," she said in brusque dismissal of the idea. "How do we travel to Malmora from here? If I remember correctly, the interior is quite wild and unsettled. Didn't a man named John Stuart cross the continent from Adelaide to Darwin just two or three years ago?"

Derek nodded. "We call the interior the outback down here. It's going to be a long, hard journey to Malmora, the last leg has to be on horseback. Are you sure you're up to it?"

"If I am able to study the aboriginals and be with you, the hardship will be worth it. Lily told me how vast and beautiful the land is."

Derek took her elbow and led her toward shore. "I just hope the house is still standing. Strassman might have torched it."

Cassandra heard the change in his voice. "You hate this man, don't you?"

"I hate what he has become. He was a good mate once. We used to be friends."

Cassandra was intrigued. "Friends? What happened?"

"We parted ways." Derek's face adopted an expression which she had come to recognize as one that effectively closed whatever topic was being discussed. As Derek assisted her off the gangplank and onto Railway Pier, she looked at the brick shops and wool warehouses lining the wharves.

"How long will it take us to get there?"

"Several weeks of hard traveling through every kind of terrain."

"I've got the heart of an explorer," she answered, and it was true. She couldn't wait to see the strange and wondrous land where herds of kangaroos leaped and crocodiles lay hidden in the rivers, waiting for unsuspecting travelers. It sounded romantic and fascinating, and besides, she would be with Derek.

# Chapter 20

The first leg of the journey into the outback was by rail but only as far as the town of Echuca. There, Derek bought passage for the five of them on a paddle-wheel packet that chugged slowly up the wide, impossibly brown Murray River. Along the banks passed thick forests and tiny settlements which grew farther apart as the steamer churned in a steady course northwest on the muddy winding stream.

From the topdeck of the packet, Kapi and Rigi had pointed out a platypus on one occasion as it swam away from the boat, but mostly Cassandra had observed great flocks of birds such as the beautiful galahs—pink-crested cockatoos which at times flew hundreds strong out of roosts along the river to wheel over the paddleboat and paint the sky with the rosy color hidden on the underside of their wings.

To Cassandra's surprise, she did not glimpse even one aboriginal, and she was happy to step off the boat at a place called Cohuna because from there they would proceed by horse and wagon. Now farther inland she would have an opportunity to study the Pitjantjatjara tribe in their natural habitat.

She and Derek had their own mounts, and it felt good to don a white shirtwaist, tan suede riding skirt, and boots, and climb into a saddle. Often she had need of her soft suede jacket as well. The weather was cool but not cold, and it seemed very strange to experience the winter of the southern hemisphere in the month of June, which was so warm back in Virginia.

Big Roscoe drove a small supply wagon, with Kapi and Rigi perched on the seat beside him. They were happier than she had ever seen them and often jumped down from the slow-moving rig and pointed out the name of the dreamtime ancestors of the various boulders or giant ghost gum trees that marked their journey inland. Cassandra found the entire trip delightful, and her own warring country seemed very far away as she asked the boys endless questions about the especially unusual flora and fauna sighted among the dense vegetation.

Derek rode ahead by himself, his eyes continually scanning the trees and trail ahead. He had become serious and introspective since they had disembarked the paddlewheeler, entirely caught up with his own thoughts. She knew he must be thinking of his father, who had died so violently while Derek was halfway around the world. She hoped he would be able to find peace of mind about his father's death once they reached Malmora.

Cassandra knew how it felt to return to the home where one had grown to adulthood. An old ache filled her heart when she remembered the last time she had been to Twin Pines. Her mother had been laboring for breath on her deathbed, succumbing at last to the consumption which had made her a thin, gaunt shell of the beautiful, graceful woman she had once been.

As Cassandra knelt beside her great rosewood four-poster bed, Charlotte Harte Delaney did not weep for her youngest son, Stuart, who valiantly fought the Confederate cause for her, nor with the regret of giving over her firstborn son, Harte, to her mother-in-law to raise. Her tears had not been shed for her grieving daughter weeping at her side, but only for the survival of her beloved Twin Pines Plantation.

That night she had signed a document with palsied hand, assigning the ownership to Cassandra in case Stuart did not survive the war. She had made Cassandra swear not to let the Yankees step foot in its hallowed chambers, no matter what she had to do to prevent such desecration. She had closed her eyes and died peacefully afterward, leaving Cassandra alone and desolate and determined to help win the war. And she had single-mindedly pursued that end until Derek had stolen her away. Now she was thousands of miles away from Virginia with no idea of the status of the war. Now for the first time in her life, she loved a man, so deeply and completely that Twin Pines seemed only a beautiful, empty house.

"Cassie? Are you all right?"

So deep had been her thoughts that she had not heard Derek rein in at her side. She smiled at his concerned face. "I was thinking about home."

Derek leaned closer and put a consoling hand on her thigh. "I'll take you back to Virginia, I promise you, Cassie. Just give me time to do what I have to do here."

"I'm afraid Harte might have been right about the war ending before we can return. I can't bear to think about the South falling."

Derek nodded, but he had no comforting words of reassurance, and she knew he believed the North would win the war. She had seen it in his eyes. A chill of foreboding passed over her.

"We've been on Malmora land most of the morning," he was saying now.

Cassandra darted a quick look at him. "But it's nearly noon!"

Derek smiled. "This is a land of vast, open spaces."

"Twin Pines is over four hundred acres. Is Malmora larger than that?"

"It's a thousand or more, but not in acres." His grin widened. "Down here, we tend to measure properties in square miles."

Cassandra's jaw nearly dropped. "Square miles! Are you telling me you own over a thousand square miles of land?"

"That's right, if Strassman hasn't overrun it. Australia's big enough to go around, especially out here in the bush," Derek answered. "I'm going to ride ahead again. We're getting closer now."

As he spurred his horse forward, Cassandra held her mount in check and contemplated the immensity of Malmora. The dimensions he had quoted were absolutely mind-boggling. In a way Australia was similar to the Great Plains stretching out west of the Mississippi River. She wondered if the aboriginals here would resist the whites' expansion with bloody raids and massacres the way the red warriors were doing in the Colorado Territory.

"Do the Pitjantjatjaras fight the whites?" she asked, guiding her horse closer to the wagon where the boys had climbed up next to Big Roscoe.

"Only when they destroy mother earth and the dreaming sites of our ancestors," answered Rigi.

Kapi smiled happily. "Soon we will be at our dreaming of the wallaby where we belong, Miss Cassie, and you will see where our ancestor sang his songs."

For most of the afternoon they made slow progress through thick glades of the strange gum trees from which small, odd-looking bears that Derek called koalas hid and peered through thick branches at them. In time the forests became interspersed with great open pastures and grazing lands, and by the time Derek finally galloped back and reined in beside her, Cassandra was ready to climb down and rest. She hadn't ridden such a long distance since she was in pigtails.

"The house is just through the trees. There." He pointed a finger to where the road dropped away into a deep, tree-spiked valley. On the floor of the basin she could see a large house surrounded by several outbuildings and a series of empty stock pens.

"Do you think anyone's living there?" she asked, shielding her eyes and trying to ascertain any life about the place.

"I don't know. I'm just glad it hasn't been burned. I better ride ahead first and make sure we don't meet up with some of Strassman's men."

Derek galloped off alone, and Cassandra picked her way over the rocky, overgrown road as the wagon rumbled slowly behind her. As they neared, she surveyed the house where Derek and Lily Courtland had grown up, but the boys jumped down and disappeared into the bush without a word. Cassandra smiled at Big Roscoe.

"It seems we're alone again, Big Roscoe."

"Don't you be afeared. I won't let nothin' happen to the captain or you, neither."

"That's very good of you, Big Roscoe," Cassandra answered, well aware the huge black man considered himself their self-appointed protector. He often followed one or the other of them around in his zealous vigilance. Suddenly she wondered what the former slave would think of the aboriginal tribesmen. He was black of skin as they were, but he would certainly find their ways as primitive and mysterious as she did.

By the time they neared the white picket fence that surrounded the weed-choked yard, Derek had dismounted in front of the house and was staring silently at its dilapidated facade. Kapi and Rigi reappeared in the edge of woods at one side of the house and called loudly for Big Roscoe to come see their cave. The huge black man climbed down and obediently lumbered away to join his little friends, and Cassandra dismounted and tied her horse on the fence.

Derek turned when she pushed open the gate and its rusty hinges squealed her arrival. "Welcome to Malmora, Cassie. I guess Strassman didn't kill Father for the house. It doesn't appear that anyone's been here since Lily left."

Cassandra gazed up at Derek's ancestral home, which was constructed in a long, single-storied design. Wide wooden verandas were built around all four sides, with many doors opening onto each one. Someone had added white latticed panels along the roof and crossbucked the porch rails. A few dusty couches and a wicker table and chairs were placed at various spots along the porches, and many potted plants, now brown and dead, adorned the wide railings.

"It's lovely, Derek."

"Lily would cry to see what's become of her plants." Derek tore a dead leaf off the nearest one and crumbled it in his fingers. He stepped up a low step onto the front veranda. "She always loved to grow things. Even when she was little, she used to lug a bucket of water from the creek to keep her plants green and healthy."

"Do you have a key?"

Derek turned to look at her, and she realized he found her question amusing. "Nobody locks up their places out here. It's so isolated that any swagman is welcomed with open arms, stranger or not."

"Swagman?"

"Itinerants or stockmen in search of jobs. Usually they'll work for food and a place to sleep. I suspect all our men moved on when Lily took off."

Derek's boots clomped hollowly on the boards as they walked to a pair of double doors. The knob turned easily, and Derek preceded her inside. Cassandra followed, watching him closely as he glanced around the room. He placed one hand on an ancient upright piano positioned beside the front door. A small white vase atop a crocheted lace doily rested on its lid. Three dead roses still drooped over its side. For the first time, Cassandra realized in just how great a hurry Lily must have fled her home for the safety of Melbourne. She must have been terribly frightened.

"My mother used to play for my father every night after supper. He'd sit right there and smoke his pipe and listen for hours."

He patted the back of an easy chair covered in blue-flowered chintz, causing dust to cloud up into the air. "After she died, he would sit here anyway and just stare at her piano. He never really got over her death."

"They must have been very much in love."

Cassandra's voice seemed to bring Derek back to the present. "Everything needs a spot of dusting, but I suspect we can make it livable enough. Chances are we won't be here long."

"It's a fine home, Derek. I know it must be sad for you to see it in such disrepair."

"It seems dead to me—like someone sucked all the life out of it."

"Once we clean it up and get a fire going in the stove, it won't seem so lonely," she said consolingly. He was feeling the loss of his family; she knew that and wanted very much to comfort him.

Derek seemed to shake off his despondence. He smiled. "I better be about getting us some firewood. I wonder where Kapi and Rigi took Big Roscoe."

"They said something about showing him a cave. Is it close by?"

"It's down by the creek. They used to spend a lot of time there. Sit down and relax while I bring in the supplies and stable the horses."

After he had gone outside, Cassandra looked around the dusty parlor. Through an open door she saw a kitchen. Another door opened into a bedroom. Rolling up her sleeves, she looked around for work to be done and found plenty. On the other hand, she hadn't slept on a full-sized bed with a feather mattress since that one memorable night in Derek's rented room in Farafangana. The idea of cuddling up with him again in such a cozy, comfortable bed was definitely a strong incentive to get things tidied up before nightfall.

Later that afternoon as shadows began to lengthen across the valley, Cassandra felt much better. She had discovered a draped bathing alcove complete with white porcelain hip bath, and had pumped and heated water herself, which was a new experience for her. She was used to the help of servants, but her efforts were worthwhile. Now that she had enjoyed a long soak and washed her hair, she felt rejuvenated and ready to face whatever came her way.

Stepping from the tub, she dried quickly and wrapped a towel around her, then peered out the lace-draped window of the largest bedroom. Derek was nowhere in sight, though earlier she had heard him filling the woodbox and bringing the supplies into the kitchen. Big Roscoe and Kapi and Rigi had yet to reappear.

She had found a clean gown made of soft red wool in the armoire of Lily's bedroom, and grateful they were near the same size, she donned it and stepped out on the veranda in search of Derek. Malmora was different than she had expected. Australia seemed a land muted in browns, grays, and dark greens instead of the lush emerald grass and trees of Virginia and Maryland. The outback seemed huge and untamed, a vast, uninhabited wilderness that was hard to comprehend. She leaned her palms against the board railing, then gasped with delight when she saw a small kangaroo grazing at the edge of the woods. Several even smaller ones hovered nearby, but as she watched they bounded gracefully back into the cover of the bush.

She strolled down the porch and turned the corner of the south veranda. She saw Derek then, his tall, lean form silhouetted against the sky. He stood about a hundred yards away, and she stepped down off the porch and walked toward him. Halfway there, she realized that he stood inside the fence of a small family cemetery. He had removed his hat, and his dark head was bowed. He didn't see her even when she stood just outside the wrought-iron gate.

"Derek?"

He turned, smiled, and held out his hand to draw her inside the fence with him. He held her close and nuzzled her damp hair. "I'm sorry. I meant to come back sooner."

"I've been soaking in a deliciously warm bath."

"You smell like Lily."

"That's because I used her rose-scented bath oil."

When he spoke next, his voice had lowered somewhat, become gruff. "I didn't get to say good-bye to either of my parents. I was at sea when they both died. The last time I saw my father was nearly three years ago on my last visit before I started running the blockade. We argued bitterly about my leaving again. We parted in anger, and I regret that more than anything."

Needing to know more about his life before they had met, she asked gently. "He wanted you to stay here on Malmora?"

Derek nodded. "He thought I should be content to run Malmora, but I had just won the *Mamu* off Kahlel, and I was anxious to sail on her. I never had much interest in raising cattle, anyway. Lily was the one who loved this place." He gave a small laugh. "She talked about the green-eyed man of her visions coming here for her someday. But she ended up going to him, didn't she?"

"She told me about seeing Harte in her dreams when she was a little girl."

Derek nodded. "Her visions were always very clear and exact. The first time she described him to me we were standing right down there where we used to swim in the creek." He gestured vaguely at a rippling stream curving through the trees and around a wooded rise.

"How old was she?"

"Around six, I think. She saw him many times after that."

"What about you? Did you know I was in your future?"

Derek's arms tightened around her. "Not until Harte paid me to get you out of his hair."

"How romantic," she said with mock disdain. "You could have at least sensed I was going to be your true love."

"Oh, I sensed I was going to love you, all right, the moment I saw you in that low-cut blue dress you had on in the White Rose. I haven't stopped wanting you since you sat down in my lap and told me to kiss you so no one would suspect us."

Cassandra pressed closer into his embrace, thinking that that night seemed an eternity ago. "I wanted you, too, and I didn't like it."

"Do you like it now?"

"More than I should admit," she whispered.

Derek kissed the top of her head with the kind of affection that warmed her heart, but for the next few minutes they stood without speaking, listening to the wind rustle the branches of the huge red gum tree shading the gravestones.

When she felt his arms go tense where he held her against his chest, she looked back at him. He was staring down toward the creek, a peculiar expression on his face, one that seemed almost painful.

"What is it?" She turned to look and was surprised to find a woman leading her horse up the grassy hill toward them. She was young and slim and wore a tight-fitting black velvet riding habit. A flat-brimmed white hat decorated with a black plume was hanging by its strings down her back. She proceeded until she was only a few yards from them before she finally saw them half hidden by the gigantic tree trunk. She stopped in her tracks, and her face drained of color.

"Derek?" Her shock was evident in the way her voice faltered. Her lips were trembling. "I can't believe it's really you."

Derek didn't answer, standing so stiff and unyielding beside her that Cassandra was immediately aware that something was not right between the girl and him.

"Hello, Becky," Derek said at length, his voice so quiet it sounded unnatural. The tension was now so thick it was almost tangible. This woman, Becky, had once been very important to him, Cassandra realized, and perhaps still was. A terrible kind of fear filled her, even though Derek kept his arm around her. "How did you find out I was back?"

The girl looked straight at Cassandra, and Cassandra was startled to see a flash of something unsettling in her dark blue eyes, some fleeting emotion that was gone so quickly that Cassandra couldn't be sure she had seen it at all.

When Becky turned her regard back to Derek, Cassandra decided she was pretty in a tomboyish sort of way, with her russet-red hair pulled back with a black ribbon. She had freckles across her small nose, and her face was slightly sunburned as if she always went about with her hat down her back instead of shielding her face against the harsh sun. Cassandra noted with some relief that she wore a wide gold wedding band on the third finger of her left hand.

"I didn't know you were here," Becky was saying in the same breathless way. "I come here once a week to put flowers on your parents' graves. I promised Lily when she left that I would do that. Did she find you?"

Derek ignored her question. "Isn't that a bit hypocritical, since your husband was the one who had my father killed?"

Cassandra gasped. Derek's accusation was bitter; his eyes darkened with some intense emotion. Her heart trembled. What had gone on between Derek and Becky? She had the most terrible feeling that he still cared very much for the girl wearing black.

"Is she your wife?" Becky asked bluntly, without looking at Cassandra.

"Not yet. Cassie, this is Becky—" he hesitated slightly, "Strassman." He took Cassandra's hand. "Allow me to introduce my fiancée, Cassandra Delaney."

"How do you do, Miss Delaney?" Becky looked as uncomfortable as Cassandra felt. "Will the two of you be staying here long?"

"Long enough to find Father's murderer."

"Don't be cruel to me, Derek, please. I can't bear it after all that's happened." Becky's words were conciliatory and cautious, as if she knew his moods well. "I can help you. I want to."

"How?"

"I think you're right about Karl killing your father. Maybe I can help you prove it."

Derek released Cassandra's hand and took a step closer to the other woman. "How?"

"He keeps his important papers in his office safe. I think he might have wanted access to Malmora because he believes he might find gold on your land."

"There's no gold on Malmora."

"I overheard a couple of the convicts talking about some caves near the Toowoomba rocks."

"That's where the aboriginals have their sacred initiations," Derek said.

"It always has infuriated Karl the way your father protected the abos. You know how Karl lets his bodyguards shoot them down like animals. It's terrible."

Cassandra frowned, but Becky suddenly began to glance around as if afraid. "I better go. They'll come looking for me if I'm gone too long."

"Who will?"

"My bodyguards. Karl ordered them not to let me out of their sight. I can usually sneak away long enough to come here, but Karl gets angry if he finds out."

"Why does he have you watched so closely?"

Becky mounted her horse, then looked down at him. "So I won't run away with you."

With that, she turned her horse's head back down the hill and spurred him into a hard gallop.

Cassandra turned questioning eyes on Derek. "Who is she?"

"She's an old friend. Her family owns a sheep station not far from here."

"She's more than that to you, isn't she?"

"If she can help me prove Strassman's guilt, she is. Come on, Cassie, let's go back before it gets dark."

Cassandra allowed him to lead her back to the

house, but they said little. With each footstep, she was gripped by an increasingly strong foreboding. Something awful was going to happen, and she didn't need Derek's intuition to know it. Suddenly she was more frightened than she had ever been in her life.

# Chapter 21

After darkness had fallen, Cassandra curled up in the soft cushions of a pink and green floral couch. They had eaten supper and retired to the parlor, and she watched silently as Derek fed a handful of dry kindling into the iron stove and then sat down at a small oak secretary. He quickly became absorbed in sorting through his father's correspondence, and she fought an internal battle over her fears concerning Becky Strassman.

Derek had been silent and reflective since the other woman's departure and because of his abrupt dismissal of the subject, Cassandra had not questioned him further. She realized the homecoming to Malmora had been hard on him emotionally, probably more so than he had anticipated. He seemed overwhelmed by memories, and perhaps guilt, too, because he had been so far away when his family had needed him.

Though she was trying very hard to be understanding, inside her heart where she was forced to face her own vulnerabilities, she quivered with every kind of doubt and insecurity. After a half hour of watching Derek absorb himself in work, her own good intentions were the losers.

"Are you going to tell me about her or not?"

Derek glanced up. "Who?"

"Please don't insult my intelligence."

Derek leaned back in his chair and gazed out the dark window.

"Like I said before, Becky and I are friends. We've been close ever since we were children. There's nothing between us now."

"I am not a fool, Derek. I saw your face when you first saw her. Whatever you shared with her is not over."

"I was taken by surprise. I haven't even seen her in nearly three years."

"What I saw was not surprise."

For the first time since they had become lovers, Derek's face creased into an annoyed frown. "Just what the hell do you think you saw, then?"

Cassandra hesitated. She didn't know exactly how to define his reaction to Becky's appearance, but she knew how sick inside she had felt when she had seen the expression on his face. "I'm not sure," she admitted, a thread of vulnerability detectable in her low words. "I only know it makes me feel afraid that what you feel for me isn't real."

Derek got to his feet and moved swiftly to her. He knelt on one knee before her chair and took both her hands. Bringing them quickly to his lips, he kissed one, then the other.

"Becky is a part of my past, Cassie. You are my future, and the only future I want."

Pleased and relieved by his sincerity, Cassandra welcomed his arms when he embraced her, but deep inside, a kernel of doubt clung stubbornly to her heart.

"Bear with me, sweetheart. Coming back here and facing Father's death is difficult. I have to handle things in my own way. You've just got to trust me."

"I do trust you," she said, and it was true.

Their lips met gently, and Derek lowered her back against the cushions and bent over her for a more thorough melding of their mouths. Cassandra slid her arms around his neck and submerged herself in the wonder of the deep, draining contentment he could create inside her. A moment later they both jumped and pulled apart when a door slammed loudly in the next room. Kapi and Rigi appeared in the doorway, breathless and excited. Big Roscoe was right behind them.

"Captain Derek, you must come quick!" Kapi cried. "Moolonga come to our cave and tell us Miss Becky be in bad trouble!"

Derek lunged to his feet. "What kind of trouble?"

Rigi gestured animatedly with the short wooden spear he held. "He say Captain must come quick. She have proof you want."

Derek snatched up his coat from where he had tossed it across the back of a chair. "Where is she?"

"She wait at river landing at Reeati," Kapi told him hastily. A look akin to fear passed over his face. "Moolonga say *mamu* fly in air over Reeati."

*Mamu* was Pitjantjatjara for an evil spirit; it was one of the first words Cassandra had learned from the boys. She stood up quickly as Derek turned to her. "I have to go. She's got what I need to see Strassman convicted."

"Let me come, too."

Derek shook his head. "Strassman's too dangerous. I don't know exactly what's going on yet. It could be some kind of trap. I don't want you to get hurt."

"I'm used to danger. I may be able to help."

"No. I won't be gone long, I promise. Big Roscoe and the boys will stay here with you." He slid open a drawer in the secretary and took out his gun belt. He looked at Cassandra as he buckled it around his waist, then strapped the black leather holster around his right thigh. "I probably won't have to use this, but Strassman's bodyguards tend to shoot at anything that moves."

"Please be careful," Cassandra whispered as he came back to her and enfolded her in his arms.

"I'll be back soon. Try not to worry."

When Derek strode rapidly from the room, the boys and Big Roscoe were at his heels. Cassandra walked to the veranda railing and watched until he had a horse saddled and ready. He mounted, then lifted his hand in farewell before he galloped off into the night. To Becky, she thought forlornly, into his past, where she had no part.

For several hours Cassandra paced, fidgeted, and peered in vain out the windows into the dark night. Against her wishes, Big Roscoe had quickly saddled a horse and ridden after Derek as his self-appointed bodyguard, but the boys had wrapped themselves in blankets and now lay sleeping in front of the stove. They kept their wooden spears and trusty boomerangs close by, however, in case of attack.

Cassandra told herself over and over that she was silly to be so nervous and edgy. Derek had tried his best to reassure her, had he not? But she kept seeing that awful, revealing look of pain on his face when he had seen Becky Strassman.

Nausea writhed in her stomach when she thought of them together on the Reeati landing, possibly locked in an embrace they had forgone earlier because she had been there. Perhaps that very moment Derek was kissing her, his hands sliding over her body until she moaned like Cassandra did.

No matter how much she scolded herself for such thoughts, her doubts nagged her endlessly. She knew only too well what Derek could do to women. She also knew he had enjoyed any number of women in his life before he had ever made love to her. What if he had used them all to forget Becky? What if he had been merely biding his time with Cassandra until he could return home to his first love? "Stop it," she whispered firmly. "Derek has asked you to marry him. He told Becky today that he was going to marry you."

Steadfastly trying to keep those points in mind, she walked over to the twins, tucked their blankets closer around them, then wandered restlessly into the bedroom she had looked forward to sharing with Derek. She picked up the shirt he had discarded when he had washed up and changed clothes. She held the white linen against her cheek and closed her eyes when she caught the lingering scent of him clinging to the soft material. Sighing, she lay down on the bed and stared at the ceiling. He would come back to her soon. Becky was his past. Cassandra was his future, just as he had said.

Regardless of her bone-deep fatigue, she lay wide awake for a long time, listening for hoofbeats that would announce Derek's return. Finally, when she could keep her eyes open no longer, she sank into troubled sleep in which Derek held Becky in his arms, his fingers tangled in her shiny russet-red hair.

The sound of horses awakened her. Derek was back! She leaped from bed. Misty gray light filtered through the lace curtains and cast patterns across the white chenille bedspread. She pulled on her silk wrap, realizing it was just past dawn as she ran to the front door and found it open, Kapi and Rigi already standing outside on the porch.

Startled to find the yard filled with riders, she

pulled her wrap together at the throat. The prancing horses were chopping up the grass and had already knocked down a length of the picket fence. One man dressed in tight tan breeches and a black shirt reined up at the base of the veranda steps. He wore a brown felt hat with the brim pinned up on one side, and he removed it with a flourish, uncovering long, tousled blond hair. He handled his skittish horse with expertise, and he had a long rifle propped across the saddle horn.

"G'day, miss. I'm afraid the blokes here have made a mess of the yard, but they're a bit roweled up."

He appeared somewhat civilized, his garments clean and neatly pressed, but his eyes didn't hesitate to take advantage of Cassandra's state of dishabille.

"What do you want?" she demanded coldly.

"Name's Clinton, miss. We work for Karl Strassman. If you'll forgive me, miss, you're trespassing on private property."

Cassandra raised her chin defiantly. "Derek Courtland owns Malmora, not Karl Strassman."

"Not anymore. Courtland killed a man last night, so Mr. Strassman is confiscating his property in the name of the law."

"I don't believe that. Now get off this property."

"Courtland shot down Miss Becky's bodyguard, Ray, in cold blood. She's run off with Courtland, but we'll catch'm soon enough, don't you worry 'bout that."

"That's a lie," Cassandra cried furiously.

Clinton shoved his hat back on his head and pushed it back off his forehead. "Better tell that to poor Ray so he can get up outa his coffin."

The other men laughed, and Cassandra turned to herd the boys back into the house.

"Sorry, miss, but you're gonna hafta come along with us. Mr. Strassman's orders was to bring back anyone we found hanging around the Courtland place." When she turned back, his eyes raked over her gown, this time with lewd disrespect. "You best get some clothes on or we'll have to cart you back wearin' just that thin little piece of fluff you got on right now."

All the riders were leering at her, so much so that Kapi and Rigi brandished their spears threateningly. The men laughed contemptuously, and when Cassandra remembered that Strassman's men bore no affection for the aboriginals, she quickly thrust the children behind her. "I'll go with you peaceable if you'll leave these boys here."

"Strassman wouldn't want no little abos on his place anyways. Hurry it up and we'll let you pack a few things."

Cassandra reentered the house, very frightened to go with them but determined not to let them witness her trepidation. Where was Derek? How could he just disappear like this and leave her to face Strassman alone?

# Chapter 22

During the ride through the bush to Reeati, Cassandra's contempt for her burly escorts intensified with each passing mile. Strassman's henchmen were crude and insulting. Derek had mentioned before that the whole bunch of them were convicted felons transported from England to serve their sentences on Australian soil—murderers now, hired by Strassman to do his killing.

While she rode silently in their midst, she tried to take note of the trail and memorize any distinguishable landmarks that could help her find her way back to Malmora. If she were at home in Virginia, she would have already attempted escape. Here, however, in a foreign land with a hostile, uninhabited environment unfamiliar to her, she felt she would be foolish to strike off on her own just yet.

On the other hand, when the time was right she was sure she could make it back to Malmora and Derek, and she meant to do so as soon as possible. She did not believe for a minute that Derek would run away with Becky and leave her to fend for herself even if he did still love the other woman. Derek would come for her as soon as he could, and if he had shot Strassman's man she was sure he had acted in self-defense.

After what seemed an interminable ride, Clinton led them out of a thick forest of white ghost gums. As they turned down a relatively passable dirt road, Cassandra stared in complete astonishment at the palatial house looming in the distance. The columned mansion seemed bizarrely out of place so far into the wilderness, and she thought it would seem more likely among Twin Pines and the other cotton plantations hugging the James River.

As they rode closer she looked out over the vast pastures that surrounded Strassman's estate. Seemingly thousands of sheep grazed on the rolling hills. Strassman obviously earned his living in wool and was successful enough to indulge any whim.

Wire fences acted as a barrier to keep the flocks distant from the main house, and at least a mile from the front portico a large iron gate affixed with an ornate S was manned by more vulgar-mouthed guards. There were many other men moving around among the ten or more long outbuildings.

When they halted at the grand mansion, Cassandra noticed yet another guard sat in a chair beside the front door. He stood and held his gun at readiness as Cassandra dismounted and was directed up the steps. Every man she had seen had carried at least one weapon, and she realized anew that she had walked into a veritable armed camp. Rebecca had intimated that she was watched constantly; now Cassandra understood the girl's plight. But Cassandra had just left a country torn by war and had slipped through armed enemy lines more times than she could count. Escape was never an impossibility, not if she used her wits.

The man posted at the entrance was big-boned and raw-faced with a misshapen nose that surely had been broken more than once. He doffed a sweat-stained, tan-colored hat and opened a massive door set with a leaded glass panel etched with a crown enveloped in fancy curlicues. Inside she found a plushly carpeted foyer decorated with tall mirrors and a white staircase winding gracefully to the second floor.

"The master say you go library."

Cassandra jumped at the unexpected voice and whirled around to find an elderly aboriginal man standing just behind her. He was dressed like an English butler in a staid black suit and white ruffled shirt. He said nothing else as he turned and led her to a room just down the hall. He opened the door and stood back silently as she entered. She glanced around a paneled library of gleaming cherry wood with bookcases lining every wall.

A fire crackled in a black marble fireplace, but the focal point of the room was a gigantic, life-size portrait hanging between two scarlet-draped windows. Becky Strassman had been younger when portrayed by the artist but just as beautiful, with her long auburn hair curled around her shoulders. Her sapphire eyes seemed to gaze sadly into the distance. Where was she now? What really had happened when Derek went looking for her last night?

"She's very beautiful, isn't she?" said a voice from the open doorway.

Cassandra turned slowly toward the man now standing in the threshold. He was tall and slenderly built with short sandy blond hair and a neatly trimmed mustache. Classically handsome with even features and soft cinnamon-brown eyes, he looked especially nice when he smiled. He did not fit her vision of Derek's black-hearted villain.

"Please allow me to introduce myself, madam. I am Karl Strassman. I welcome you with great pleasure into my home."

Cassandra contemplated him with an icy stare.

"I'm afraid I do owe you an apology. My bodyguards are so often oafish with cultured ladies such as yourself. Unfortunately, they are a necessary evil. I do hope they didn't offend you."

Cassandra's reply dripped disdain. "It's difficult not to be offended when one is arrested illegally and forced to travel in the midst of a ragged band of ruffians."

"Ah, you are provoked, I fear."

"Provoked does not come close to describing what I feel at this moment, Mr. Strassman."

Strassman smiled gently as if her remarks were particularly pleasing to him.

"May I inquire as to your name, madam?"

"I am Cassandra Delaney."

"An American, I would presume by your charming accent. The southern region would be my guess."

His good manners surprised her, but she remained unfriendly. "I was born in the state of Virginia."

"I am pleased to make your acquaintance, Miss Delaney. I have been following the progress of your civil conflict with great interest."

Cassandra did not respond to his absurd attempt at parlor talk, but fixed him with a haughty glare.

"I'm afraid I'm going to have to detain you here until Derek Courtland is captured." At last he got to the point. "Rest assured, however, that you will be treated as a valued guest while residing in my home. I intend to make your stay so pleasant that you'll forget the circumstances under which you were brought here."

"I rather doubt that I'll forget I'm an unlawfully held prisoner, Mr. Strassman."

"Then it will be my challenge to induce you to feel otherwise, but enough about that. It's nearly time for my midday meal to be served. Please, allow me?"

Strassman crooked his elbow in invitation, but Cassandra ignored his attempt to escort her and swept ahead of him into the adjoining dining room. The aboriginal butler came forward at once to hold her chair. As she was seated, Strassman moved to a more opulent armchair placed at the head of the long, polished dining table.

For the first time she realized that he walked with a slight limp. She watched him sit down and pick up a silver ring holding a white damask napkin. He smiled graciously as he removed it and arranged it upon his lap.

"I've ordered braised beef and honeyed yams for today. I do hope the fare is to your liking, but if you shouldn't care for my selections, my cook will prepare whatever you wish."

Cassandra unfolded her napkin. "You certainly take well to your wife running off with another man, and one who is a purported murderer, at that," she pointed out casually, thinking his nonchalant mien a bit out of place under the circumstances. "As a matter of fact, Mr. Strassman, one would think you were hardly concerned at all. Or that, perhaps, you know there's no truth to the story."

Strassman's face retained its pleasant expression. His answer was complacently polite. "Alas, I was expecting it once I heard my old friend Derek was back. Becky's always been in love with him, and I knew she would find a way to join him sooner or later. Every two or three years he comes back to see her, then breaks her heart by going off again."

Sighing, Strassman shook his head. "This time, however, she seemed to go a little crazy, probably because Derek brought you along with him. He's never brought a woman home before, you see. Even so, I hadn't expected her to run off with him quite this soon."

He flourished a hand in an expansive gesture that

encompassed the lovely room and its rich furnishings and expensive porcelains. "I'd hoped I could win her affection by giving her all this. I even built this house to please her, but she never got over him. Moolonga," he murmured aside to the butler, "we're ready for tea to be served."

Cassandra looked quickly at the servant. Moolonga was the name of the person who had sent Kapi and Rigi after Derek the night before. She hoped he would be an ally who might help her escape from Strassman's house.

"I suspect you're in love with Courtland, too, aren't you, Miss Delaney?"

Cassandra put her full attention back on Strassman. She could see the sympathy in his eyes, and she resented the implication. "I don't think that's any of your business."

Strassman watched Moolonga pour tea into her gold-rimmed white china cup. "Derek has always affected women in a way most men can only dream of. I used to envy him that knack when we were younger. We were great friends once, you know, absolutely inseparable."

"How is it, then, that Derek detests you so much now?"

Strassman fastidiously dabbed the corners of his mouth with his napkin. "You're quite blunt, aren't you, Miss Delaney?"

"I don't quibble over the truth."

"My falling out with Derek was unfortunate. Becky was the cause, of course. We both loved her to distraction. If Derek had not elected to leave her and go to sea, I would never have had even a remote chance of wedding her. But after years went by without even a letter from Derek, she decided he was never coming back. I'm a very patient man, Miss Delaney. I was content to bide my time until she decided to accept my proposal of marriage."

"Derek and I are in love, and we're planning to be married. If you're trying to turn me against him, you're wasting your time."

"You haven't known him long, I'll wager, or you'd know that he uses that same story with every woman he takes as his lover. Believe me, Miss Delaney, he'll never marry anyone except Becky."

Cassandra stiffened under his insult, but Strassman continued in his soft voice, a faintly compassionate smile curving his mouth.

"He came home to Australia for one reason only, and that was to take up with Becky again. As lovely as you are, I'm sure you were quite a pleasant diversion on the long voyage down under, but he loves my Becky. He always has, and he always will. I wish it weren't true, believe me. I love her as much as you love him."

For a brief instant she caught a glimmer of the hurt his wife's desertion had dealt him, but he covered his emotions at once.

"Derek went too far when he gunned down one of my men. Since I am the constable in this district of Victoria, I'm required to bring him to justice. But that's no reason for you and me to be at odds. We have a lot in common, you know."

Karl Strassman was very suave, very persuasive, but Cassandra had been associated with such men while working undercover in Washington. He was eager to discredit Derek in her eyes. Why? Perhaps she should dupe him into believing he could turn her against Derek until she could steal away from Reeati. She couldn't let him suspect her motives.

"Virginia's a beautiful place," Strassman continued. "I visited Richmond once before your war commenced. The people there are most genteel and accommodating. That's why I support the Confederate war effort."

Cassandra hid her surprise. "Indeed?"

"I have already sent nearly twenty thousand English pounds through my family members residing in London. You can see that we have need of servants here on Reeati, too." He glanced at Moolonga. "Our coloreds are even less intelligent and more primitive than your Negro slaves."

Moolonga looked straight ahead as if he did not hear Strassman's denigrating remarks, and Cassandra thought of Kapi and Rigi and how quickly they had picked up reading and the other subjects she had taught to them aboard the ship. They were as intelligent as anyone and certainly could do more than menial labor, she thought, but even as it crossed her mind, she realized that her own mother had often voiced the same opinion of negro intellect when discussing the slaves of Twin Pines. She was appalled that the unfairness had never occurred to her until seeing it in a different setting, a foreign country.

"You have no right to hold me here. I've done nothing wrong."

"Perhaps, except that Derek won't like you being here in my house, regardless of the fact that he now has Becky with him again. You're a nice pawn that I can use to capture him. Perhaps he'll even do the honorable thing and turn himself over to me in return for your freedom. Knowing him as I do, I doubt he'll do that. He uses people to gratify his own needs. He has always done so. But the truth is, he's a murderer and has to be punished."

"You'll never make me believe that. You're the one who killed his father. Or perhaps you had those cretins outside do it for you."

She watched Strassman closely for any indication of his guilt but saw nothing untoward in his manner. "I didn't do either of those things, my dear. You'll realize that in time." He smiled. "Derek was last home nearly three years ago. He seduced my wife then and he's doing it again now."

"Perhaps that was true before he met me, but now Becky is part of his past. He said so himself after he saw her again last night."

Strassman examined her face for a long moment. "Poor Cassandra, I do sympathize with your position, but Becky's more a part of him now than ever before. I can prove that to you, if you wish."

This time Cassandra smiled. "I'd be interested in seeing such proof, Mr. Strassman."

"All right. Come with me."

Strassman rose and waited for her to join him at the door. He led her across the entrance hall and up the staircase to the second-story corridor, then eventually stopped before a closed door at the back of the house.

"You'll find the proof I'm talking about inside this room, Miss Delaney. The guest room you'll be occupying while you're here is just across the hall. If you should need anything, just ring for Moolonga. Now if you'll excuse me, I have some important papers I must attend to this afternoon."

As Strassman strode away, Cassandra stared after him, perplexed by his behavior. Once he had disappeared down the stairs, she turned the brass knob and pushed the door ajar. The interior of the room was so dark that she could barely make out the furnishings. The drapes were drawn tight across the single window, and she quickly crossed the room and jerked the curtains apart.

She turned and looked at the pictures of baby ducks and rabbits decorating the white walls. Every sort of toy and childish plaything was set about on the floor. When her eyes found the small bed placed against the corner, she saw tiny hands grasp the top rail. A moment later a child who looked to be around two years old pulled himself up and stared forlornly at her. Cassandra's heart lurched when the toddler whimpered and caught hold of his black curls. Tears shone brightly in his large dark eyes.

*Oh, God, Becky has given Derek a child,* Cassandra realized, something she could never do. She bit her lip, an awful pain of despair crushing her heart. When the child began to sob, Cassandra hurried forth to take him into her arms. Tiny arms clutched tightly around her neck as if he would never let go, and she was appalled when she found his sleeping gown and diaper wet and cold as if his needs had been neglected for a very long time.

"You poor little thing," she whispered, looking around and finding a bureau stacked with clean infant diapers. She carried the child there and quickly changed his soiled garments. "So you're Derek's beautiful little son," she murmured.

Tears burned and threatened to fall, but when he reached out his arms to her, she picked him up again and cuddled him close. She sat down in a cushioned chair near the bed and began to rock him. Derek loved children. He would never desert his son or the woman who had borne him. Could Strassman be right? Would the child change everything between Derek and her?

# Chapter 23

Several days later Cassandra found herself still on Reeati with no word from Derek. With each passing hour her desire to leave Strassman's compound became stronger, and one afternoon she sat on the back steps of the veranda contemplating various escape plans as she watched little Joey romp and roll about in the grass with three feisty brown puppies. While she was thus employed, Karl Strassman moved down the veranda and stood at the porch rail behind them. She glanced up at him where he stood slapping his leather gloves against a thigh encased in tight black riding breeches. He carried a suede saddle bag in his other hand.

"You certainly have taken to the boy," was his greeting. "One would think Joey was your own child, instead of the ill-begotten by-blow of Derek and Becky."

"I don't consider beautiful little children in those distasteful terms, Mr. Strassman. If I hadn't decided to look after him, he'd probably still be lying in his baby bed, soiled and crying, wouldn't he?"

"He had both a mother and an aboriginal nurse-maid to care for him. It's not my fault they chose to run away and leave him behind. I haven't touched him since I found out he wasn't mine." He hesitated briefly while he watched the child play. "I was thrilled the day Becky told me she had conceived. I thought having my child would make her forget about Derek, but Derek had the last laugh. I didn't even realize they'd been together when he was last here until Joey was about six months old and I saw the resemblance."

Despite her dislike of the man, Cassandra clearly heard the pain permeating his voice. When she looked at him again, he was gazing longingly at Joey, as if he wanted to hold him. How could Strassman resist such a darling little boy? *How could Derek?* she thought morosely as Joey laboriously climbed the tall steps on his short legs, one of the puppies hanging over his shoulder. He threw himself into Cassandra's waiting arms.

"See doggy, Mama," he gurgled happily, both his small arms entwined around her neck.

Regret such as she had never felt before pierced her heart, intense and awful, an agony she suspected every barren woman felt when holding another woman's adorable child. But Cassandra's pain was a thousandfold worse because Joey was also Derek's child. Joey was the son of the man she loved and wanted to wed but to whom she could never give children. She fought her desire to weep as she hugged the affectionate little boy and pressed a kiss atop his dark curls.

To her surprise Karl Strassman sat down on the top step and leaned a shoulder against the banister. He watched her settle the baby more comfortably on her lap. "He likes you better than he does his own mother. Becky isn't one to cuddle him. She can be quite cruel and heartless to those around her when she wants to be."

Cassandra was startled by his less than complimentary remarks concerning his wife, but she didn't reply or necessarily believe him. He no doubt held a grudge against Becky as well as against Derek.

"I was quite a scholar in my youth," he ventured a few moments later as she took Joey's tiny hands and guided him in a game of pit-a-pat. "I attended several different colleges in Sydney before my father died and I took over here at Reeati. You're interested in books and learning, too, aren't you, Miss Delaney?"

Cassandra shot him a surprised look. "How did you know that?"

"I saw you perusing the books in my library the other night."

Actually she had been snooping around trying to discover his safe and any incriminating evidence therein which Derek could use against him. She had not been successful in that pursuit, but she had been impressed with his reference books, especially those dealing with Australia and the aboriginals.

"I've studied with Dr. Joseph Henry of the Smithsonian Institution in Washington, D.C. I worked there until the war began."

"Indeed?" he said, obviously impressed by her credentials. "I've read about the place. It was built to resemble a castle, was it not?"

Cassandra nodded, but she was reluctant to get into a civil conversation with him. The appalling truth was that she found him both friendly and polite. In truth she felt rather sorry for him and probably would have liked him if they had met under better circumstances.

"I'm afraid I have some bad news to share with you, Cassandra."

Something in the subdued tone alerted her. Her heart seemed to clog the back of her throat. "Is it Derek? Is he all right?"

Strassman shrugged. "All I can tell you at the moment is that he's riding with a band of bushrangers. Becky's with them, too, but I'm not surprised. She's always had a wild, uncontrollable streak, especially when Derek's around. Sometimes I think she would stop at nothing to get him back."

Again he was insulting his wife. She wondered why he continued to do so, but at the moment she was more interested in Derek's whereabouts. "Who are the bushrangers?"

"They're outlaws who live in the bush and rob from honest people such as myself. I know some of them personally. They rode with Derek and me in the old days. They always looked up to him, so I'm not surprised he's assumed command of their ranks.

I've heard something else, too, but I don't think you'll welcome the news."

"I'll welcome any word concerning Derek."

"He and Becky have become lovers again. In fact, they're blatantly flaunting their affair to those who have seen them, probably in order to humiliate me."

"I don't believe that." Cassandra looked coldly away, but the thought of Derek being with Becky, riding with her, living with her, perhaps even sleeping with her upset her more than she liked to admit.

"That's not even the worst of the tidings I have for you, I'm afraid." Strassman's voice had become more gentle now. He was probably sensing her doubts about Derek and Becky, she thought. Had he seen the fear in her eyes? She silently cursed herself for her lack of control when it came to Derek. She set her chin atop Joey's head and snuggled the toddler closer.

"I have daily newspapers brought out from Melbourne once a week so I can keep abreast of what's happening in the rest of the world."

"Do you have news of the war back home?" she asked quickly. She had heard nothing of the status of the fighting since they had left Nassau months ago.

The somber expression on Strassman's face warned her, but she was in no way prepared for his next statement. "There's no easy way to tell you this, Cassandra, so I'll just say it. The Confederacy has fallen. General Lee surrendered to the Union command sometime in early April. I was told that the

American papers carrying the news arrived a few days ago on a British steamer which apparently sailed from New York right after the surrender took place in someplace called Appomattox."

The bottom dropped out of Cassandra's world. She was so stunned by his quiet revelations that she had to grab hold of the porch railing to right her dizzied sensations. "No," she whispered hoarsely, "that can't be true."

"I know it's a shock, dear, but I have the newspapers right here, both New York and Boston editions. Would you like to read the accounts for yourself?"

When Cassandra nodded numbly, he took several newspapers out of the saddle bag. Joey fussed and tried to climb back into her lap, but she set him aside and unfolded the first newspaper with shaking hands. The first headline glared out at her: LINCOLN VICTORIOUS! SECESSIONISTS CRUSHED!

"I'm truly sorry, Miss Delaney."

Cassandra hardly heard Strassman's sympathetic words. She stared blindly at the newsprint, having trouble comprehending the ramifications of the war's end.

"Would you prefer to be alone?" Strassman asked quietly.

Gratified by his thoughtfulness, Cassandra nodded mutely. Once he had reentered the house, she pored over every word describing the cessation of the war. Though she had tried to prepare herself for a possible defeat during the weeks at sea, tears burned and began to fall before she was through the first column. The Yankees had taken Richmond and burned most of it to the ground. Jefferson Davis and the rest of the Confederate government had fled and were in hiding. *Oh, my God,* she thought in horror, *Twin Pines is just down the river. Have they torched my home, too?*

Despair hit her full force. For the first time she could ever remember, she felt as if her life were over, all her hopes and dreams destroyed. A sob escaped her. Joey looked up and saw the tears running down her cheeks, then puckered up himself. Cassandra pulled him close, but she could hold back her grief no longer. Her heart full of pain and hopelessness, she clutched Derek's son tightly in her arms, and the two of them wept together.

Later that evening when she sat once again on the rear veranda, Cassandra had begun to come to terms with the loss of the war. She had wept all the tears over the defeat that she intended to, and she would no longer sit idle and wait for Derek to show up. Strassman had invited her to dine with him, and she had agreed in order to throw him off her real intentions. She would be polite and attentive to him; then, as soon as he retired for the night, she would flee Reeati and find her way back to Malmora.

Earlier, after she had rocked Joey to sleep, she had come downstairs and found the veranda table set with fine china, glittering crystal, and a romantic five-prong silver candelabra.

The night air was cool and fresh, and the darkness closed comfortingly around the breezy porch as Strassman tried very hard to console her melancholy about the outcome of the war.

"I'm glad you decided to join me," Strassman murmured as he poured champagne into her fluted goblet. "I've been saving this bottle for a special occasion."

The champagne reminded her of Kahlel and the first night Derek had made love to her, but she shook such thoughts away. She didn't want to think about him, or Becky, or anything else. She would concentrate on her escape and throwing Strassman off guard.

"I noticed in the newspaper accounts that Richmond was burned," continued Strassman. "I do hope your family wasn't there?"

"We have a plantation on the James River, not far from Richmond, so I am worried. Twin Pines is the only legacy I have left. My parents are dead, and my brothers fought on opposite sides of the war, so I'm not sure where they are."

"Their different allegiances must have been difficult for you." Strassman's brown eyes brimmed with kindness and concern. "When I was twelve I saw my own parents massacred by the aboriginals."

"Massacred?" she repeated in surprise. "But aren't the aboriginals a peaceful people?"

"They are now, for the most part. This happened a decade or so ago when the tribes were still attacking the settlements in the outback. My father cut down an ancient tree which they considered to be one of their primary dreaming sites. They retaliated viciously, and I hated them for it for a long time. As I've grown older, I've begun to come to terms with what happened."

Cassandra wasn't sure she wanted to be privy to the intimate details of his past or his family tragedies. She did not want to reevaluate her feelings for Karl Strassman. From the beginning he had not fit the image of the monster Derek had described to her, but she also knew that the most despicable among men learned to hide their villainy behind gentle smiles. Nevertheless, Karl Strassman did seem erudite and well-read, the kind of man she had enjoyed having as colleagues while at the Smithsonian Institution.

"What are your plans now that the war has ended, my dear?" Strassman asked as Moolonga sliced him a portion of roasted lamb.

"When Derek returns for me I intend to go home to America and claim Twin Pines, if it's still standing."

"So you haven't given up on Derek yet?"

"I still believe he'll come back for me, if that's what you mean."

"For you, or for his son?"

Strassman's words pierced the soft underside of her worst fear, where she was most vulnerable. At that moment she was forced to admit that Joey's existence could very well end forever her relationship with Derek.

"I have begun to feel as if I made a terrible mistake by bringing you here and holding you against your wishes. I now consider you as much a victim of Derek's and Becky's love affair as I am. If you wish, I will immediately arrange passage back to Virginia for you. Steam sloops sail regularly out of Melbourne. I daresay you could be ready to leave in two or three days, if you like."

Cassandra stood and leaned against the veranda railing in order to consider his unexpected offer. Perhaps she should agree. If he thought she wanted to leave Australia, he would never expect her to try to get away that night.

"I think perhaps I will go home," she said at last, turning and finding that Strassman was standing very close behind her. "I think Twin Pines is where I belong now."

"I'll see to it for you at once, Cassie, but I must tell you that I'll miss you. In the short time you've been my guest, I've recognized just how special you really are." To her surprise, Strassman reached out and brushed his fingertips down her cheek in a particularly intimate caress. Not liking him to touch her, she jerked quickly away, inadvertently knocking into the table and overturning her wineglass.

"That's quite all right, my dear," Strassman said solicitously as he dabbed at the stain with his napkin. "Moolonga, come!"

When his servant did not appear, he straightened and looked toward the house. "I'll have to fetch him, I suppose. Will you excuse me for a moment?"

Cassandra nodded, but the moment he left the veranda, she followed him into the house, wanting to avoid more advances from him. He had obviously taken her willingness to dine in the wrong way, and she wasn't about to let him be familiar with her.

Inside the side hallway she hesitated and listened to him calling for Moolonga somewhere in the back of the house. She took a step toward the stairs, then gasped when someone grabbed her from behind. A hand clamped hard over her mouth, and she was dragged backward into the darkened dining room.

"That was a goddamn touching little scene I just witnessed, Cassie."

*Derek,* she thought in joy, but then she realized how his voice was hoarse with anger.

"It's obvious that you've grown rather fond of Strassman since you've been at Reeati."

When she struggled against his hold, his grip tightened. He removed his hand, and she whispered quickly, "My God, Derek, you shouldn't be in here! How did you get through the guards?"

"Moolonga helped me get in through the kitchen. But what's the matter, luv, disappointed I came and interrupted your little tryst with Strassman?"

"What the devil are you talking about? It's dangerous for you to come in the house! Karl's just down the hall!" she warned softly, shocked that he had been so reckless. "Besides, you're the one who went off and left me here with him—" she added breathlessly, angered by his ridiculous accusations, but he cut off her words, his mouth attacking her lips so hard and punishingly that she could barely think. Almost as quick as the brutal kiss had begun, Derek pulled back and bracketed her head tightly between his hands.

"I came back for you, didn't I?"

"Did you come back for me or did Becky send you back for your son?"

Derek's muscles tensed, and Cassandra knew then that Becky had indeed told him about Joey. His grip lessened a degree, and he tangled his hands in her hair. "Strassman's been using the boy to turn you against me, hasn't he?"

"I didn't have to, Courtland," came Strassman's low voice from the doorway. "You and Becky alienated her for me."

Cassandra gasped and swung around to find Karl's figure silhouetted in the threshold. The light from the hall lamp illuminated the gun he had trained on them, and Derek pushed Cassandra behind him.

"So we meet again," Derek said, his voice low and almost conversational. "It's been a long time, Karl."

"That's right, but I knew you'd come sooner or later because you wouldn't be able to stand Cassie being here with me. I've found her to be a wonderful woman in the last few days. She deserves better than you're giving her."

"From a fine, upstanding man like you, maybe?" Derek responded, taking a step toward Strassman.

"Hold it right there, Derek," Strassman said, holding the gun steady on him. "I have every right to shoot you. You're wanted for murder."

"Then I don't have a lot to lose, do I, Karl? Maybe I should just draw on you and be done with it. I've spent enough time in prison. I don't think I really want to go back."

"Don't be stupid. Take the gun out of your holster, drop it, then kick it across to me. Cassandra, get out of the way. There's no need for you to get hurt."

Cassandra stood still, not sure what she should do. She considered lunging at Strassman so Derek could pull his weapon, then changed her mind when she saw a movement behind Strassman. Moolonga was creeping up behind his master, a rolling pin clutched in his hand.

"Karl, please don't hurt him," she begged, trying not to look at the aboriginal as he raised the heavy wooden club high into the air. He brought it down swiftly on the back of Strassman's head. The blow landed with a sickening thud, and Karl collapsed forward, overturning a table set with porcelain. The dishes and bowls shattered with a great tinkling and smashing of glass, and Derek grabbed her arm and pulled his gun.

"Shh, stay still. The guard at the front door might have heard."

"I put drug in coffee. He sleep," Moolonga told them in his quiet way. "Go now before it wear off."

"All right, let's go," Derek said urgently to Cassandra. "Where's the boy?"

"This way," Cassandra told him. She ran for the staircase, and Derek paused to speak a few words to the aboriginal before he followed her. Moolonga doused the hall light as they reached the upper balcony. Elated to finally be escaping the confines of Reeati, she headed straight for Joey's room and found the boy sleeping in peaceful oblivion, his thumb in his mouth.

"Moolonga says if we dress like servants we'll have a better chance of getting Joey off the compound. He said there's a trunk at the foot of the bed where the nursemaid keeps her uniforms," Derek whispered as soon as he entered the room behind her. "Quick, put them on and let's get the hell out of here."

Cassandra obediently moved across the room to the narrow cot and lifted the lid of the chest. Inside she found a gown of plain black cotton and several long white aprons. She quickly unbuttoned her silk dress and stepped out of it. As she donned the servant attire, Derek was pulling on Moolonga's long-tailed butler's coat over his shirt and pants. She quickly stuffed her bright hair in the white mobcap she had found with the other clothes, then hesitated momentarily when she realized that Derek had moved to Joey's bed. *He's seeing his son for the first time,* she thought, pain squeezing her heart, but she shook off her feelings, knowing she had no time to think about that now. Instead she hurriedly stuffed a pillowcase with some of Joey's extra clothes and supplies.

"Come on, Cassie, we don't have time for that. Get him and let's go," Derek was ordering, and she went to the child's bed and carefully lifted Joey into her arms. He whimpered softly, then settled quietly against her shoulder.

"Do you think he'll cry?"

"Probably not, unless something frightens him."

"Try to keep him quiet. Moolonga said we should go out the back in case the drug wears off the front guard."

She quickly followed him across the upstairs landing then descended the servants' stairs that led down to the rear of the house. Moving through the dark kitchen, they gained the backyard and crept across the grass in the shadows of the trees. Clutching Joey tightly to her breast, she followed Derek's rapid strides toward the main road that led off Reeati.

"We're going to walk out of here like we have every right to. Servants go in and out of the main gate all the time, and Moolonga says most of the hired hands are drinking and gambling in their quarters."

Cassandra thought it sounded too risky to be a good idea, but Moolonga would know how the guards operated better than she. He had proved his trustworthiness, and Derek had his gun in his hand, cocked and ready to fire.

"Keep your head down and walk fast," Derek whispered, leading her by the arm.

The entrance road was deserted, and she could

hear faraway shouts and laughter coming from the bunkhouses. Derek kept them moving at a rapid pace, and she had just begun to believe that they were going to make it when she heard the sound of galloping horses. Two men rode into the pasture just to their right, and Derek slowed down. He kept his voice low.

"They're coming off guard duty. Just keep walking, and maybe they won't notice us."

Unfortunately, the riders reined up on the other side of the fence.

"Hey, who's walking there?"

"Moolonga and my woman," Derek answered in the guttural speech of the aboriginals.

An amused voice came out of the darkness. "You're too old for that sort of thing, Moolonga. Why don't ya give 'er to us tonight?"

The other guard laughed. "Let him be, Johnny. A man's never too old if the tart's willing enough."

Cassandra breathed easier as the two men laughed together, then spurred their mounts toward the bunkhouses. Derek pulled her with him again, and within minutes they had reached the ornamental iron gate where only one man stood guard. He had been sitting on the ground with his back against the side of the arched gate, but he stood up as they approached.

"Hold up there," he said, peering through the darkness at them. "Is that you, Moolonga?"

"Me and my woman."

The man walked closer. "What's that she's carrying?"

"Son. He sleep."

Cassandra tensed in dread but kept her head down as he approached them. She gasped when he suddenly grabbed off her cap.

"You ain't no abo. What the hell's going on—".

Derek moved as the man grabbed Cassandra's arm. He slammed his pistol butt hard into the man's temple, and when the guard grunted and fell, he thrust open the gate.

"The shearing sheds are on the other side of this field," Derek whispered. "Hurry, we don't have much time before someone finds him."

Cassandra hurried to keep up with him as he pushed his way through the tall grasses that edged the road. Her labored breathing alarmed Joey, and the boy was crying by the time they reached the deserted shed. Derek led her through the dark interior to where he had secreted his horse in one of the stalls. He took the fussy, squirming child out of her arms and boosted her into the saddle, then handed the boy up to her before swinging onto the horse's back.

Neither spoke again, and Cassandra held on tightly to Joey as Derek walked his horse quietly under the long iron-roof and into the wooded area beyond. They were a good distance from the main house now, and once they had attained the open road, he spurred the horse into a swift flight toward safety.

For a long time he kept up a grueling pace as he pressed hard north toward the outback. She wondered where he was taking her and whether Becky would be there when they arrived. After what seemed like a very long time, he finally slowed his horse as they neared a series of limestone boulders and cliffs, barely visible in the faint moonlight.

"Hold on, luv, we're almost there," he whispered softly against her ear.

Cassandra shut her eyes at his endearment and wearily lay her head back against his shoulder. He urged the horse into a small gully that meandered through the high rock formations. Not long afterward, he gave a low whistle that echoed slightly off the walls of the stone gorge. A man's voice called out in answer, and Derek quickly spurred the horse through a second narrow fissure into a large canyon.

Far away, high above them, she could see the glimmer of several sentry campfires, but otherwise the place was dark and quiet except for the moan of the wind through the steep boulders. Derek walked his horse forward, and she detected several small cabins hugging the base of the rock wall.

Derek dismounted and looked up at her. When he reached for Joey, she handed the child down to him, then slid off the horse without Derek's assistance. Without comment, Derek took her elbow and led her toward one of the cabins. He opened the door and allowed Cassandra to precede him inside. Her eyes swept over the room with its clean-swept floor and a welcoming fire crackling inside the belly of a small iron stove. A round table set with an oil lamp had been placed in the center of the room. Through an open door, she could see an iron bed and nightstand.

"Derek? Is that you?"

Cassandra turned at the sound of Becky's voice and found the other woman rising from a cushioned chair next to the stove. They stared at each other without speaking.

The tension was thick until Derek put a hand on Cassandra's shoulder. "Cassie, go into the bedroom. I'll be there in a minute."

Certainly unwilling to watch Derek return his son to his lover, Cassandra walked quickly away as Becky hurried forward to claim her child. She glanced back as she reached the threshold and found Becky smiling up at Derek as she took the child from his arms. Cassandra shut the door and leaned against it. She shut her eyes, not wanting to hear what they said.

# Chapter 24

After Becky had taken her baby to the cabin next door, Derek paused outside the bedroom where Cassandra awaited him, loath to step inside and face her. She was no doubt angry and hurt that he had left her alone at Malmora to be captured, and she had every right to be. The fact that Becky had been waiting in Derek's quarters couldn't have helped.

Fortifying himself with a deep breath, Derek turned the knob and entered the room. Cassandra sat on the bed, her back to him. She didn't look up, and she didn't speak.

Derek shut the door and leaned against it. "We have to talk, Cassie."

Cassandra turned to face him, and she wore the calm, resolute expression he had seen on her face in the past when she had made up her mind to do something dangerous. She had not been crying, but he wasn't sure if that was a good sign or a bad one.

"I want to go home as soon as possible. If you're not willing to help me do that, then I'll find a way to get there on my own."

The casual way she voiced her decision to leave him sent anger whipping through his blood, but he imposed enough self-control to maintain his calm. He did not want to fight with Cassie; that was the last thing they needed. "So you've decided to run back home without even giving me a chance to explain where I've been and what I've been doing since I left you at Malmora?"

"I think what you've been doing is fairly obvious. That, and a lot of other things."

"Why are you treating me like this, Cassie?" he asked quietly, trying to search past the cold expression glazing her aquamarine eyes. "I came for you as soon as Moolonga got word to me that you were on Reeati. I didn't plan for things to happen this way. You have to know that, dammit, after all we've been through together."

Frustrated, he raked impatient fingers through his hair and strove to regain his composure. "Becky summoned me that night because Strassman found out that she had been to Malmora. She thinks her bodyguard told him. When Karl heard she had seen me again, he went into a rage. She was frightened and afraid for the little boy—"

"Karl wouldn't hurt Joey."

"How the hell do you know what he's capable of?" Derek demanded, infuriated by her loyalty to Strassman. "Are the two of you so close now that you know him better than his own wife does? Is that why you were letting him put his hands all over you out on the porch?"

For the first time the frigid mask dropped away from Cassandra's face. "How dare you accuse me of anything when you left me alone for days while you ran off with your lover!" she cried, spots of angry color flushing her cheeks.

Derek swallowed his ire. He took another deep breath to avoid losing complete control of his temper. Cassandra had a right to be furious, he told himself again, a lot more reason than he did. He tried hard to calm himself, but every time he thought about Karl touching Cassandra, even in the most innocent way, his jaw clamped hard and jealousy raged through his blood.

"Before we could get Joey," he went on tightly, "Becky's bodyguard showed up at the dock where we were talking. He drew on me before asking any questions, and I had to fire in self-defense. It wasn't murder, the way Strassman's been telling everyone."

"You could have come back for me that first night," Cassandra accused, bitterness coloring each word. "Instead you left me alone to fend for myself while you protected Becky. Didn't it occur to you that I would be worried when you didn't return to Malmora? I had no idea where you were or what was happening to you!"

"I didn't have any choice, Cassie, you've got to believe me. The only reason I didn't come back home that night was because they were tracking us. I didn't want to lead them straight to you. Becky knew where the bushrangers were holed up, and she brought me up here into the canyons. It never occurred to me that Karl would arrest you and take you to Reeati. I was going to come back for you later when I was sure it would be safe for you. I've thought of nothing but getting you back, sweetheart, you have to know that. I hated the thought of your being in Strassman's house with him."

Derek took a step toward her, wanting to touch her, to hold her in his arms, but she backed away as if he were the devil incarnate coming forth to snatch her soul.

"What in God's name did Karl tell you that could turn you against me so quickly?"

Cassandra's eyes narrowed. "He told me you loved Becky, that you always had and always would. He told me you had taken his wife as your lover again, just like you do every time you return to Australia. He told me that you'd been using me as a convenient substitute for her like you've done with lots of women since you fell in love with Becky years ago."

"And, of course, you believed every damned lie he told you?"

Cassandra's stare was defiant. "I believed that Joey was a pretty good indication that what he said was true."

For the first time, Derek felt fear constrict his chest like a tightly cinched belt. She believed Strassman. She was going to leave him if he didn't convince her of the truth. "Joey's not my son, Cassie," he said quietly.

First she looked astonished, then she said, "Then how is it that he looks just like you?"

"He also looks just like Becky's bodyguard, Ray, with whom she's been having an affair for the last four years."

"How do you know that?"

"Some of my friends here told me. They say that's why the man drew on me the way he did, out of jealousy."

Cassandra did not look convinced. "What does Becky say?"

"She says she thinks he's mine."

"Then he could be?"

Derek hesitated, reluctant to answer. He had to tell her the truth; she would never forgive him if he didn't. "I was with her once the last time I was home. She came aboard the *Mumu* to see me, but that was three years ago in April. Don't you see? In order to be mine Joey would've had to have been born by that following January but Moolonga swears that Becky gave birth in March. I hadn't been home in years, and I didn't find out that she was married to Strassman until I got to Malmora several weeks later. Even then my father mentioned that he had heard rumors about Ray Jenson and her. I didn't see her again after that, I swear. I did love her once, but it's over, Cassie. It was over the first time I ever laid eyes on you, I think."

As Derek moved closer, Cassandra retreated until he braced his hands on the wall and trapped her between them. He leaned closer and held her gaze as he spoke low and urgently. "I've missed you, darlin'. Don't do this to me, not when we've been apart for so long."

Cassandra was breathing hard now, her body trembling a hand's breadth away, her lips quivering only inches from his mouth.

"I love you, Cassie," he breathed hoarsely. "I want to spend my life with you."

"I don't know what to believe."

"I can prove how I feel. Marry me, Cassie, to-night, right here. All you have to do is say the word."

Cassandra raised her eyes to his face, and Derek could read the shock in them. He pulled her into his embrace, held her tight, pleased when she didn't pull away. "I never felt this way about Becky. I left her behind a long time ago, and she married some-one else. I haven't even thought about her since I met you. Hell, I haven't thought about anything else since I met you." He paused, then went on softly. "Marry me, darlin', and let me take you back to Twin Pines. We'll have our own family. I want lots of children—"

Inside the circle of his arms, Cassandra suddenly went rigid. She twisted blindly away and stumbled to the end of the bed. Derek frowned as he watched her clutch the rails of the iron footboard until her knuckles went white.

"There are things you don't know about me." Her whisper was nearly inaudible. "You'd be better off with Becky."

Derek knew he had to be careful. There was the most terrible expression in her eyes, one he had never seen before. "What are you talking about, Cassie?"

When she turned around again, she seemed to have regained control. "I can't marry you or anyone else, ever. All I want is to go home to America. Becky wants you here with her. Joey could possibly be your son—" she stopped and tears filled her eyes.

"Aren't you forgetting that I don't love Becky and don't want to marry her? You're the one I want."

"You don't understand." Her teeth caught at her bottom lip.

"No, I don't. Explain it to me."

Derek had never seen Cassandra look afraid, but she did now. She was wringing her hands compulsively, so agitated that he knew something horrible was haunting her.

"I can't marry you," she began in a shaky voice. She sank down on the bed, not looking at him. "I can't because—" she hesitated again, then finished in a rush, "because I can never give you a child."

Derek sat down beside her, trying to understand. "Only God knows if we'll be blessed with children, Cassie."

"I can't conceive—I know I can't. I did a terrible thing once, Derek. I committed the most awful sin—" she choked on her words.

A cold chill undulated slowly up Derek's spine as he was gripped with an awful sense of foreboding.

"What did you do?" he asked gently.

Cassandra hesitated for a long time. She sighed

heavily, then answered so softly that he could barely hear her. "I took a drug. It made me barren."

"A drug? Was it administered to you when you were ill?"

"No," she whispered, watching his face. "I took it on purpose so I'd never beget a child."

Derek attempted to hide the shock he felt, but he couldn't stop the initial flood of disbelief and disappointment. When she saw his expression, Cassandra looked as if she had been stabbed through the heart. She dropped her face into her hands, and Derek quickly put his arm around her shoulders. She grasped hold of the front of his shirt and sobbed. Derek stroked her soft hair, fighting an internal battle to come to terms with what she had said. His own voice sounded unnatural. "Why, Cassie? Why would you do such a thing?"

"Because of the quinine," she whispered against his shoulder.

"The quinine prevents you from conceiving?"

She shook her head. "No, but I have to take it for my malaria. I have to, Derek. I don't have any choice."

"I know," he whispered soothingly, confused by the things she was saying. "I saw how it helped you when I tended to you."

Cassandra sat up and wiped her tears away with her fingertips, but she stared down at her lap as she began to explain in low, tormented tones. "When I was in Peru with Dr. Henry, I helped him deliver a baby." She swallowed hard, then put her palm over her mouth. "It was horribly deformed, Derek. It was a little boy, and his body was all twisted up and shriveled. He didn't have arms and his legs were grotesquely misshapen. I can still hear Cheopi's screams of horror when she saw him—" Cassandra's face crumpled with the memory, more tears welling and rolling down her cheeks. "Cheopi had suffered from malaria, too, Derek. The shaman gave her the bark of quinine during her pregnancy. That's what caused the defects in the baby. He told me so—"

Derek remembered Cassandra's nightmares about a baby during her delirium, remembered the name Cheopi, and he began to understand her motives even before she completed the painful revelations in a halting, sob-choked voice.

"Then I succumbed to malaria while we were down there, too, and it began to recur just like Cheopi's had. I told the shaman that I was frightened about having a baby, and he told me about a plant he knew, one whose leaves the Indian women chew when they want no more children."

Her voice caught pitiably. "So I did it, Derek—I shouldn't have, I know that now, but I knew I would continue to have relapses of malaria and I was terrified to think of having such a child. At the time I never planned to marry, anyway. I only wanted to be a scientist and continue my studies. I didn't know I'd meet you and want so desperately to give you a child. Oh, God, can't you see what a terrible mistake I made? Can't you see why I can't marry you—"

"Hush, sweetheart, you were young and afraid. I

understand why you did what you did." Derek held her tightly. "We don't have to have children, Cassie. I'd rather have you with me as my wife than to have a dozen children by Becky or any other woman."

Cassandra slowly raised her eyes, and he could actually see the relief dawning behind the tears in her eyes. "Do you mean it, Derek? Do you really want to marry me anyway?"

Derek realized then what a terrible burden of guilt she had been carrying, but now the time had come for her to put it aside. "I only want you," he murmured, kissing her forehead, then her tear-damp cheeks. "I've missed you. I want us to be together. Say you'll marry me, right here, right now, tonight."

He found her trembling mouth, and she clung to him, her body so eager and warm and familiar that his own passion roared alive. She pulled his head down, kissing him with all the passion he had been denied since he had last seen her at Malmora.

"There's a man outside, an old friend who rides with the bushrangers now. His name is John Newport and he's an ordained minister, Cassie. He can marry us," he murmured against her mouth, then was lost in deep, draining kisses as they fell back on the bed, limbs entwined, breaths mingled, bodies molded.

"I'm going to go get John now," he managed at length. Then he pushed her onto her back and lay atop her, his fingers tangled in her hair. "In just a minute, woman, I'm going to go get him." His mouth attacked hers again.

"What about Becky? What will you tell her?" she asked breathlessly, her words muffled under his lips.

"I told her I was going to marry you as soon as I got you back. I told everyone here how much I love you—"

Cassandra moaned with pleasure, and their mouths touched, tasted, lingeringly, tenderly.

"All right, I'm going to get him now," he muttered, drawing away, but she pulled him back and their passion flared again as their lips met and caught fire.

"I'm beginning to think you're trying to put off the wedding," he said at length when she continued to clutch him tightly each time he tried to leave.

"I can't help it," she whispered next to his cheek. "I've missed you so much. I've lain in bed thinking about you and about the way you touch me—"

Their lips mingled more gently, but their breathing was hard and impassioned when Derek finally thrust himself to his knees and staggered out of the bed. He sucked in a steadying breath. "John's been waiting in the other room, and I have a feeling he's going to know what we've been doing in here," he muttered as he tucked in his shirttail. "I sure as hell can't hide how much I want you at the moment."

He pulled Cassandra up and helped her straighten her skirt, but he was absolutely, unquestioningly on fire for her. She patted her hair and wiped away any lingering traces of her tears as he pulled her into the front room. John jumped up from where he had been waiting by the warm stove.

"We better make this quick and to the point, John, if you know what I mean," Derek told his old friend, smiling at Cassandra's flushed face. "Before she changes her mind."

"I understand, Captain. Any man would be eager, with such a beautiful bride standin' at his side." John grinned at Cassandra, then launched into a shortened version of the wedding ceremony, barely waiting for them to repeat the vows before he barreled on to the next one.

"You're now man and wife, congratulations, and a long and happy life to the both of you," he ended, nearly running his words together in his haste to take his leave. Before the door could bang behind him, Derek had Cassandra on the bed again, his lips on hers, his fingers tangled in her hair.

"I don't think I could stand to be away from you this long again," he whispered, and then he lost himself in the feel of her skin and the silkiness of her hair. She was his wife now, his own, forever. She cried out and arched her body as he entered her, and he held her waist and groaned aloud as his own pleasure expanded inside him.

Cassandra grabbed his hair and brought his mouth back to hers, and he swam through a sea of sweet sensation, his lips seeming to burn with heat until they reached a fever pitch of excitement that sent them over the edge of desire with great, wracking, wonderful waves of ecstasy. He groaned, clutching his wife fiercely against him as the release came, and he lay with her sated, content, and never in his life more happy than he was in that moment.

# Chapter 25

"G'day to you, Mrs. Derek Courtland," whispered a voice close to Cassandra's ear.

Cassandra smiled sleepily and snuggled closer into Derek's warmth. She laid her palm on the hard muscles of his chest. "This marriage had better be legal, Captain Courtland. Who is this John Newport, anyway? Is he really a minister?"

"He's an old friend who went wrong and became a preacher instead of a rogue like the rest of us."

"I like rogues like you."

Their lips touched softly, and Derek smiled into her eyes. "And I like having you in my bed again."

"Not as much as I like it."

Derek reached out and pushed a silky lock off her cheek. "I should have given you a more formal wedding, since you're a Virginia blue blood and all."

"I got what I wanted," she whispered, her fingertips tracing through the crisp black hair covering his chest.

"I should have taken you back to Melbourne last

night instead of bringing you out here, but I couldn't bring myself to leave you again so soon."

"I wouldn't have stayed without you."

"You'll have to go soon, sweetheart. Strassman will come after us now that you aren't at his house to distract him. He'll probably start hunting for us again and attacking the Pitjantjatjara."

"It's just hard to believe that he's so cruel. He seems gentle and kind, and he told the story about his parents being murdered by the aboriginals. He said he had come to terms with their massacre."

She watched Derek's mouth constrict into a thin line. "He's ruthless. You wouldn't believe the things Becky told me she suffered all these years while under his roof."

Cassandra put her fingers against the lean contour of his bearded cheek. "Then I'm glad you got her away from him."

When she slid her forefinger over his bottom lip, he took her fingertip in his mouth and her erotic response shot all the way to her toes. "I want you out of here before he finds out where we are. George and the crew can watch over you on the ship until I can get enough evidence to hang Strassman."

"That doesn't sound like much of a honeymoon."

Derek grinned. "After I'm finished here, I'll give you a wedding trip you'll never forget."

Cassandra sobered when she thought about being sent away. "Please don't ask me to leave here."

"Cassie, be sensible—"

"I *won't* leave here without you," she decided firmly and emphatically.

"It's too dangerous for you to stay."

"I'm used to danger, and you know it. I'll do what you tell me to, I promise. It seems safe enough here in the canyon."

"For a while, maybe, but they'll track us here eventually. There's a warrant out on me."

"Then we'll move somewhere else, but we'll stay together."

Derek leaned down and kissed her, then raised his head as a shout filtered in from outside the cabin, followed by a burst of male laughter. He laughed. "My mates want to meet you, darlin'."

"The notorious bushrangers of Victoria? Should I be frightened?"

"They're good men," Derek answered, his eyes growing serious. "Honest men who owned small sheep or cattle stations around here until Strassman began driving them off their property with his so-called legal evictions. They turned to thievery to survive, but they usually confine their stealing to Karl's properties and leave the other landowners in peace. Believe it or not, I think they've put together some sort of wedding reception for us."

"John told them we were married?"

"I told them I was going to ask you before I ever left for Reeati. Big Roscoe and Kapi and Rigi are ecstatic, since they think you're the perfect woman for me."

"They're here? Thank goodness, I've been worried about them."

"These hills and canyons are sacred to the aboriginals, but the tribal elders know we're trying to help them, so they've allowed the bushrangers to make camp here."

"Kapi and Rigi must be happy now that they've returned to their dreaming. Do you think the aboriginals would object to my interviewing them while I'm here?"

"I think they'll love you, just like everyone else does," Derek answered, rolling over and sitting up. "Now come on, the men are getting restless for a good reason to eat and drink whiskey. They even went to the trouble of lugging fresh water from the spring for your morning bath. I heard them pouring it just before I woke you. Believe me, a bath's a luxury in these canyons." He raised a suggestive brow. "Therefore, I feel I ought to join you, to conserve the water, you understand."

"I think that's an admirable decision," Cassandra murmured, laughing as he swung her naked from the bed and carried her to the next room, where the tub of lukewarm water was waiting near the stove. He climbed in beside her, and Cassandra closed her eyes as he rubbed the bar of soap slowly over the top of one breast, then up over the other.

"Did they provide this lovely scented soap, too?" she asked, sighing. "Or did Becky leave it here?"

"Becky has her own cabin. She's an old friend, nothing else, so let's just not mention her anymore," he murmured as he pulled her atop his lap. "She understands how I feel about you. Just think about me and what I'm getting ready to do to you."

It didn't take long for Cassandra to forget Becky, or the men waiting outside to meet her as her husband pulled her flat against his chest, their warm, wet bodies sliding together, their lips fusing until she felt she was a part of him, and he a part of her.

After a bath that took a lot longer than necessary, Derek opened the door and presented his bride to his friends. Cassandra felt at a distinct disadvantage, mindful of the fact that Derek's hair was as damp as her own. It wouldn't take a genius to figure out they had enjoyed the tub together, but even as she stepped outside, she didn't care who knew how happy they were. She had never felt so wonderfully content in her entire life.

"Cassandra, you've already met John, of course. This is Robin Oates, who worked for Father on Malmora until Lily left last year."

Robin was the first person in a receiving line containing ten smiling men, and Cassandra was relieved to see that Becky Strassman was not among them. The bushrangers gathered around her, and she found them to be leanly built with rugged, weathered faces, despite the fact that nearly all of them wore wide-brimmed hats to protect their skin from the harsh sun.

Most were dressed simply in plain white linen shirts atop brown or tan riding breeches, and the knee-high riding boots which Derek preferred. Each bushranger politely shook her hand as Derek introduced her as his wife. In no way did they resemble the band of bloodthirsty murderers Strassman had described to her.

Greeting each man in turn, she watched as they cheerfully raised mugs of beer and toasted Derek and her. Two places of honor had been set near a table spread with bread, cheese, and roasted beef, and she sat in one of the straight chairs while Derek was slapped heartily on the back by his friends and teased relentlessly about his wet hair and hasty wedding. One of the men took up a fiddle and commenced a lively tune, and Cassandra smiled to herself as she thought how very different her wedding party was from the elaborate marriage fetes held on the plantations of Virginia.

The towering canyon walls of yellow rock bore little resemblance to the emerald grass of Twin Pines, where the velvety lawn swept all the way to the banks of the beautiful James River. The image of the stately mansion with its twelve white columns rose, splendid and beloved, in her mind's eye, and her heart clutched with fear when she imagined the Yankees burning it to the ground. She blinked back her emotion, not wanting to ruin her wedding day, but not before Derek had noticed the anguish in her eyes.

"What is it, Cassie?" he asked, sitting down and taking her hand.

"I was thinking about Virginia. The Confederacy

fell in April. Karl brought me newspapers from America with the news of the surrender."

"I'm sorry, Cassie. I was afraid your defeat was inevitable. That's one reason I brought you with me when Harte requested me to. You're better off here during the immediate aftermath. Things are bound to be ugly for a while."

"I've been thinking about Harte a lot lately," she admitted slowly. "I really don't know him at all, and he's my own brother." She searched Derek's face. "I think I'd like to change that when we go home."

Derek took her hand and squeezed her fingers. "You will. And I'm just as eager to make sure Lily's well and happy there. I hope they've gotten married. Lily predicted they would, and her visions always come true."

"Captain, look here what I done got," came a voice nearby, and Cassandra turned to find Big Roscoe standing there beside them with Joey in his arms. The minute the little boy saw Cassandra, however, he stretched out his arms to come to her. Big Roscoe handed him over, and the moment Cassandra took him, he wrapped his chubby arms around her neck.

"Big Roscoe," she said, "I'm so glad to see you. I've missed you."

"I be glad you marry up wid de captain," he said solemnly.

"Where's Becky?" Derek asked him, glancing around.

"Her ride off early dis mornin' and say for Big Roscoe to watch baby till she come back."

"Where do you think she's gone?" Cassandra asked Derek in surprise.

"I told her last night I was going to marry you if you'd still have me. She was afraid that she'd ruin our wedding day if she hung about. She'll be all right, because she knows every inch of these canyons. We used to explore out here when we were children. I'm surprised she didn't take Joey with her."

"He be a sweet li'l baby," Big Roscoe interjected eagerly. "I been playin' wid him all mornin' long, and now I gonna up and show him to Kapi and Rigi. Dey like babies, too."

"Where are Kapi and Rigi?" Cassandra asked Derek. "I thought they were here in the camp, too."

"They stay pretty much with the Pitjantjatjaras where they live up in the caves at the rear of the canyon. It's down close to the spring. Would you like to go see them?"

Cassandra nodded. "I've missed them. Have the boys built themselves a *wiltja* yet? They told me how they were going to build themselves a shelter out of branches and leaves when they got here."

"Most of the tribe lives in the caves that crisscross these canyons."

"I sure would like to hold dat baby some more," Big Roscoe was saying now as he gazed longingly at the toddler. "He be too heavy for you to carry, Miss

Cassie, 'cuz it be a long walk to de cliffs. I surely would be pleased to tote li'l Joey for you."

"All right." Cassandra smiled and handed the boy back to the huge man. The baby looked very small as Big Roscoe settled him in the crook of his arm.

"I know de way fine. Jus' follow after me," Big Roscoe told them, then strode off ahead with Joey's tiny fist clutching the back of his collar.

Derek and Cassandra followed, smiling and nodding to the men who were enjoying the food and drink set out for the celebration. As they walked along together, Derek took her hand and laced her fingers through his own. "I'm going to have to ride out tomorrow, Cassie. Becky couldn't get any kind of proof for me, so we're still trying to find someone who might be able to link Strassman to my father's death. There's been talk of a vein of gold somewhere on Malmora that Strassman's been mining. If we can find it, I'll have a legal charge of trespassing. If we can get him up on those charges, we can probably encourage some of his bodyguards to testify against him."

"How long will you be gone?"

"A day or two, probably, but I'll try to get back as soon as I can. I'll post guards on the cliffs and the Pitjantjatjaras know safe places to hide if you should be attacked. Maybe you can get started on that dissertation on the aboriginals that you wanted to write."

"That's exactly what I intend to do. The scientific community in Washington knows very little about the aboriginals, so what I can discover will be invaluable. Perhaps I'll even make a name for myself with this study."

"You already have made a name for yourself. Ask your brother or any other man in the Yankee Secret Service."

Cassandra laughed, half surprised she could do so. But here in the wilds of Australia, America seemed very far away. The war there was over, but Derek was fighting a different kind of battle, one that was very important to him. She would stay and help him, then would return to her own country and whatever fate awaited her there.

Thick vegetation covered portions of the canyon floor, and once they had made their way through it, Derek took her hand and pulled her up graduating levels of stone outcroppings until they came out atop a cliff that overlooked a different, smaller canyon. There, a large pool of dark blue water was captured in the rocks, its moisture sustaining a few scraggly trees alongside its banks. Several other crevices had filled with water, creating shallow reservoirs, and Cassandra could see groups of aboriginals moving around the water and among the cave openings dotting the cliffs.

"The water comes from an underground basin," Derek told her. "During some parts of the year it's diverted and the Pitjantjatjaras have to move on to other places. This year has been better than usual, and it's a good thing now that Strassman has resumed his hunts."

Cassandra still couldn't imagine Karl hunting the aboriginals and killing them in cold blood, but she didn't contradict Derek because she had heard the bitterness in his voice. Her attention was diverted by a shout, and she turned her gaze down to the bushes below where they stood.

"Miss Cassie!"

"You come at last!"

The voices belonged to Kapi and Rigi, and Cassandra laughed with pleasure as she saw the twins balancing together on top of a high boulder. Big Roscoe and Joey already stood with them, and all three were waving their arms wildly and motioning her down.

"It looks like they missed you as much as I did," Derek said with a smile.

"How do we get down from here?"

"Follow me. It's steep. Hold on to my hand."

Cassandra did so, deciding she would have to don shirt and pants if she stayed long in the lair of the bushrangers. The gown she wore was not made for sliding down rock formations. By the time her feet touched the ground, the boys burst forth to meet her, their small brown faces alight with wide, happy smiles.

"Welcome to the dreaming," Kapi cried, taking her hand and jumping up and down with it.

"We want come for you at Reeati, but Captain Derek say only him go," Rigi added, looking apologetic for not being a part of her rescue.

"We miss you," they said in unison.

Truly happy to see them, Cassandra put her arms around their shoulders and both boys eagerly pressed themselves closer. "I missed you, too," she said.

"We never leave the land of Pitjantjatjaras again," Rigi stated emphatically.

"We are home and soon we will be great hunters. And Big Roscoe be warrior with us!"

Cassandra looked at the little boys fondly, glad they had finally returned to their homeland.

"Come and meet the tribal elders," Rigi said, pointing through the trees to where the largest water hole could be glimpsed. "We have told them how wise you be, how you taught us many things about the stars and the sea. Perhaps you can be elder, too."

Cassandra laughed and glanced at Derek, who shrugged. "I wouldn't be surprised, knowing you the way I do."

The boys pulled her with them by the hand, and Derek and Big Roscoe followed behind. Soon they reached the deep pool, where thirty or more aboriginals worked at various tasks along the edge. None of the natives, men or women, wore anything more than a brief loincloth made of brown leather, and they quickly gathered around the newcomers.

"This be Tjilkamata. He adopt Kapi and me," Rigi announced proudly. "Soon we go with elders and learn the Way of the Law. Then we be men."

Cassandra looked down at the two small boys, thinking how different the aboriginal culture was from her own. In Virginia, Kapi and Rigi would still be in knee britches and coddled by their mother, but here in the wilds of the outback, they were considered men before they even had an opportunity to experience boyhood.

Derek moved among the aboriginals, shaking hands and speaking with them in their own tongue. He was obviously accepted among them as a man they respected and admired. She wondered how he had acquired such a close kinship with the tribe, but as the twins introduced her to each man, woman, and child, she found herself growing excited to learn more about their primitive way of life.

Even the Indians of Peru had been more advanced in their culture, with well-structured villages and techniques of farming and commerce. And as Kapi and Rigi continued to show her about, she wondered if she'd ever become comfortable with the fact that nearly everyone was practically naked.

Some of the smallest children ran and played; the older ones helped with the cooking or fed sticks to the fires. All were friendly and welcomed her readily into their midst, and though she knew many of their words and tried to master the Pitjantjatjara's pronunciation, she caused laughter among them when she tried to communicate in their own language.

After a time the men gathered for a hunt, and both Kapi and Rigi raced to be included. As the women busied themselves gathering roots and berries, Cassandra and Derek sat together under a stunted gum tree, dangling their feet in the water as Big Roscoe played with Joey on a rock across the spring.

"What do you think of the Pitjantjatjaras?" Derek asked.

"I think they're fascinating. And very gentle and kind."

"They're peaceful people. They don't kill anything but the food they eat. They only kill men when their land is desecrated or their songlines disrupted."

"You seem very close to them, especially the man named Tjilkamata, yet they live far away from Malmora. How did you become so friendly with them?"

Derek looked out over the canyon. "I took a walk-about once before I went to sea. I lived with them for a time. They accepted me and taught me their ways."

"What's a walkabout?"

"That's what we call it down here when a man goes off on a trek in the outback and comes to terms with his existence."

His voice had roughened and lowered in pitch, and Cassandra knew something dire must have caused him to take such a walkabout.

"Is that when you decided to go to sea?"

"Yes."

"And when you broke off your friendship with Karl?"

He nodded without speaking.

"Something terrible happened between you, didn't

it? I've sensed it in you, and in Strassman, when I commented once on his lameness."

"He limps because I put a bullet in his knee. Sometimes I wish I'd put it between his eyes."

Cassandra was shocked at his sudden anger. "You shot him? Why?"

"What difference does it make? I've seen him do things to the Pitjantjatjaras that only a devil could do."

"He told me he hated the aboriginals because they killed his parents, but that now he's gotten over those feelings."

"I don't believe that. I know him too well."

"He said the two of you were very good friends when you were young," she probed, not letting him shut her out.

"That was before I knew what he was capable of."

Cassandra hesitated. "He also intimated that you came to odds because you stole Becky away from him."

"We both wanted Becky then, but it wasn't that."

"What was it?"

Derek grimaced. "I don't want to talk about it, Cassie."

Cassandra splashed her toes in the cool water, contemplating what could have happened between the two men. Derek was clenching and unclenching his fists, and Cassandra knew he was very upset, so she kept quiet. A muscle jumped spasmodically along Derek's lean jaw as he kept gritting his teeth. He picked up a rock and tossed it out into the water, then turned slightly, and she could see the terrible expression on his face.

"Maybe I should tell you. Maybe then you'd see Strassman for what he really is."

Cassandra didn't press him for answers. Never before had she seen Derek quite so tense and angry, not even after the incident in Rio. Somehow she felt she should know, that he would feel better if he told her—just as she had when she had admitted to him her guilt over ingesting the sterilizing leaves in Peru—but only when he was ready to share his feelings with her.

"Like he told you, we were good friends. We rode together with Robin and some of the other bushrangers. Karl was a few years older and had already inherited Reeati from his father. He was rich and powerful and could do whatever he wanted, and the rest of us looked up to him. My father tried to keep me away from him, but I was young and wild and I did what I wanted." He stood and took a few steps away, his back to her. "His idea of having a good time was going out and using the aboriginals for target practice."

"It's hard to believe that anyone could be so cruel," she said softly.

Derek whirled to face her. "Well, he did it," he ground out between clenched teeth. "I never could bring myself to shoot them, but I'll hate myself until the day I die for standing by and watching him do it."

Silence descended, and Cassandra felt frozen

with dread as he went on in a low, tightly reined voice. "One day we were hunting crocodiles up north, just Karl and me, and we came upon a family of aboriginals on the riverbank. A mother and father with a baby and two little toddlers about Joey's age. They were fishing, but when they saw us, they started to run." He forced down a convulsive swallow. "Karl gave chase. He shot the man dead with his pistol, then he caught the woman. She had the baby in her arms, a tiny little girl, not even old enough to crawl."

A terrible presentiment of dread paralyzed Cassandra. "Derek, please—"

"And oh, God, Cassie," he muttered hoarsely, rubbing his hand across his eyes, "he grabbed that baby girl out of her mother's arms—" he stopped again and his throat seemed to close up, "and he threw her to the crocs, way out in the river where they were hiding and waiting—"

"Oh, my God, Derek, no," Cassandra breathed out in absolute horror.

"The mother went after her child, but it was too late. The crocs already had the baby. I tried to shoot them before they could get the mother, too, but they pulled her under. When Strassman grabbed the other two children, I shot him in the leg to stop it. I should have killed him then, but that was the last time I ever saw him until I went to Reeati to get you out."

Sickened by his revelation, Cassandra couldn't speak. Derek looked at her, his face set in hard, angry lines. "Those two boys I saved were Kapi and Rigi, Cassie. That day I took them back to Malmora to live with my family. They were barely two years old when it happened."

"Oh, Derek, how could Strassman do such a terrible thing?"

"Because he blamed them for the deaths of his parents, and Becky said he's still hunting them down like animals. She said that's why he turned on my father—for giving them sanctuary on Malmora land. She says Father threatened to have Strassman arrested if he trespassed to pursue them."

Cassandra went to him and took his hands in hers. "What happened to Kapi and Rigi's family wasn't your fault. You did what you could to stop it."

"No, I didn't. I ran away instead of staying here and making sure Karl stopped his murdering. Apparently it's only gotten worse since I left. That's why I have to get him up on charges and put him in jail, where he won't be able to buy his way out."

Cassandra nodded, aware of the pain still lurking in his dark eyes, but deep inside she was very afraid for him. She had seen Strassman's men, a veritable army of hooligans who were ready to obey any order their employer gave them. How could Derek's small group of bushrangers ever succeed against them?

# Chapter 26

*After close observation for nearly twenty-four hours, this scientist has found the Pitjantjatjara tribe of Australian aboriginals composed predominantly of close-knit family units. The social roles among these primitive bushmen are strictly divided by gender. The men spend their days hunting the kangaroo and wallabies which abound in the bush, or travel by foot to nearby rivers to fish by spear.*

*As in many primitive cultures, the women are the primary nurturers and gatherers of firewood and other forms of sustenance such as berries, edible grubs, and small game that can be trapped. The children are happy and lively but taught from birth the role they will assume when adulthood is reached. The males are initiated into tribal law at a very early age, and the men often join together at important dreaming sites for ceremonies known as corroborees . . .*

Cassandra laid down her pen and massaged her weary eyes. She had been setting down her early findings for her dissertation under the flickering light of an oil lamp using a makeshift desk Derek had constructed by balancing a wooden plank on two empty beer casks. Tonight he had joined the Pitjantjatjaras at a corroboree welcoming Kapi and Rigi home to the dreaming time, and more than anything she longed to observe the secret ritual. No females were allowed to witness the dances or songs, so she had no choice but to wait for Derek to describe the ceremony to her.

Across the room Big Roscoe was playing with Joey, as he had done all day long. She smiled as Big Roscoe balanced the child on his foot, then jiggled him up and down in a wild horsey ride. Joey squealed with delight and clung tightly to the big man's trousers leg.

"May I come in, Cassandra?"

Cassandra turned and found Becky Strassman standing in the open doorway. Though she felt extremely uncomfortable in the other woman's presence, she stood and tried to behave graciously toward the woman Derek had once loved. "Of course, please come in, Becky."

Appearing a bit nervous herself, Becky stepped inside, and when she saw her son, she smiled and walked quickly to him. Scooping him out of Big Roscoe's arms, she cuddled him affectionately. "There you are, my little sweetie. Mummie has missed you."

She shifted the child in her arm and carried him to Cassandra. "I didn't want to leave Joey here this morning, but he was terrified when I tried to hold him in the saddle in front of me." She hesitated as if embarrassed. "Derek told me last night that he was going to ask you to marry him. He also said that you thought the two of us, well, you know, had gotten together again while you were kept at Reeati. I want to tell you myself that nothing like that happened between us. I stayed in another cabin, and he used this one. I was only here last night because I was so anxious to get Joey back."

"Derek has explained everything to me now, but I do appreciate your telling me yourself."

"I know you'll be pleased to hear that Derek spoke of nothing but you and how anxious he was to get you back." She gave an odd little smile that somehow didn't seem pleased at all.

"Actually, I knew the moment I saw you with him at Malmora that he was very much in love with you," Becky went on quickly. "Something in the way he looked at you, I guess. I'd never seen him look at anyone else like that." Her words trailed off before she began hurriedly again. "I felt especially bad about Karl taking you to Reeati, since Derek was trying to help me when all this started. In any case, I thought the least I could do this morning was make the wedding celebration less awkward for you by making myself scarce for a while. When Derek's black slave there" —she gestured at Big Roscoe— "seemed so eager to take care of Joey for me, I felt it would be all right to leave him in his care until I returned."

Although Becky had seemed rather nice so far, the Australian girl's patronizing air toward Big Roscoe irked Cassandra. "Big Roscoe's not a slave anymore, Becky. Derek gave him his freedom."

Becky seemed taken aback by the annoyance in Cassandra's tone. "I didn't mean to offend you, Cassandra. I understood from what Derek told me that you're from the southern part of the United States. They're the ones fighting to sustain slavery in America, aren't they?"

Cassandra felt suddenly ashamed and tried to defend herself. "My family has always owned slaves, but we treat our people with kindness. Some southerners, such as Roscoe's former owner, do not. In any case, the war's over. I recently learned that our side has been defeated. Slavery in America has been abolished." It seemed strange to say the words out loud, and for the first time she wondered how the freed slaves could possibly survive in the hostile environment of the South.

Becky placed a comforting hand on Cassandra's shoulder. "I'm so sorry, Cassandra. I know you must be very disappointed and upset."

"I was at first, but the war seems very far away since I've come here with Derek."

Becky glanced at a nearby armchair. "May I sit down and visit with you until Derek returns? Robin told me he's dancing at the corroboree. I'd like for us to become friends, if you think it's possible."

"I'd like that, too," Cassandra answered, gratified that Becky was being so sociable, but surprised, too.

She wasn't sure that if their roles were reversed she would wish to spend time with the woman Derek chose instead of her. Why on earth would Becky want to put herself through such pain?

"I want to thank you, too, for bringing Joey out here to me. I was afraid to go back for him, but I've missed him desperately. He's a good little boy."

Cassandra smiled down at the chubby toddler. "Yes, he's very sweet."

Karl Strassman had hinted frequently that his wife was not a good mother, but at the moment Becky was hugging and kissing her young son as if she loved him very much. Derek was adamant that Joey could not be his son, and if that were true, the poor little boy had no father. Ray Jensen was dead, and Karl Strassman did not want him. She was beginning to feel sorry for both Becky and her child.

"I am glad for you and Derek," Becky told her then, leaning forward to accentuate her earnestness. "I wish the two of you every happiness in your marriage, I really do."

"Thank you."

"He never forgave me for marrying Karl. He hates him, you know."

"Derek told me that you've suffered a lot during your marriage."

The girl avoided Cassandra's eyes. She seemed evasive, but perhaps she was only embarrassed to be speaking of her personal life. At times Cassandra sensed something peculiar in the way Becky acted, but she had obviously been through quite a lot.

"Yes, he became very cruel after Joey was born. I was afraid of him." Becky looked up, smiled, and changed the subject. "Derek tells me you're quite a scholar. He says you know just about everything about everything. I envy you that because I never had the opportunity to go to school at all."

Cassandra had to laugh. "I hardly know everything. As a matter of fact, I'm quite uninformed about your country. I intend to study the aboriginal culture while I'm here. I was just working on a thesis about the Pitjantjatjaras when you came to the door." She gestured at her pen and paper lying on the desk.

"Then I bet you'd like to see the corroboree for yourself, wouldn't you?"

"Oh, yes, I'd love to, but Derek told me it was taboo for women to watch."

"Yes, but I know a place where we can hide and watch them dance without being seen. I've done it before on several occasions. If you want to go, I can show you the way."

Cassandra was very tempted. "Is it far?"

"Oh, no. I can easily find my way there, even in the dark. Derek used to play hide and seek with Lily and me out here when we were small. The corroborees are really fascinating to watch, and you could describe it so much better in your paper if you observed it firsthand. Come outside, and you can hear their drums from here."

Cassandra followed Becky outdoors, where a tiny sliver of the new moon had risen high in the night sky. As she looked into the sky, she marveled again at how very different the constellations appeared from the southern hemisphere.

"Listen," Becky whispered. "Can you hear them?"

Far away, probably well past the water hole, Cassandra could hear the strange, haunting sounds that the aboriginals make by swinging some kind of strange stringed instrument around in the air. The music moaned like a ghostly entity calling to the living, and she looked longingly into the night, wanting very much to take Becky up on her offer.

"Are you sure they won't see us? I wouldn't want to offend the elders of the tribe by ignoring their taboos."

"I've watched many times this past year since the aboriginals allowed the bushrangers to camp in their sacred canyons. They've never known I was there."

Cassandra hesitated briefly, but she was well aware that such personal observations of the tribal ceremonies would be invaluable to Dr. Henry and the other scientists at the Smithsonian Institution.

"All right, I'll go with you, but only if you're positive they won't be able to see us."

"Follow me, but you must be very quiet. Do you think Big Roscoe will watch Joey until we get back?"

Big Roscoe came forward, smiling eagerly. "I like dat baby and he like me."

Becky handed the toddler over to him, and Cassandra took a moment to pull on one of Derek's shirts for extra warmth. Becky led her into the night, and after they had made their way past the cabins and fires of the camp, they hurried along with little conversation passing between them.

In time they passed the ledge Cassandra and Derek had climbed to reach the water hole, then walked a good distance more before Becky climbed a steep rocky outcropping where Cassandra could make out a faraway fire that glimmered like a red-orange jewel in the darkness. After about ten minutes of squeezing through narrow fissures and climbing boulders, Becky finally brought her out atop a flat ledge. She hunkered down behind a thick stand of scraggly bushes.

Peering through the branches, Cassandra had a wonderful view of the clearing below the cliff. The corroboree was being held in a box canyon protected on three sides by steep rock walls, with a brush fire guarding the entrance. Some of the men were dancing around the roaring flames, while others sat on the ground watching the ceremony. Cassandra felt a twinge of guilt for breaking such an important tribal taboo, but on the other hand, Becky was providing her an opportunity few other scientists would ever enjoy.

"Go ahead, lie down in front of me where you can see them better," Becky whispered.

As Cassandra lay on her stomach and watched the aboriginals lunge and bend, she was struck by the realization that the primitive Pitjantjatjaras were little different than the males of her own more civilized culture in the United States. There, too, the men controlled the power structure of the government and the family, with women excluded for the most part from the important decisions of human existence.

Her attention was piqued when she saw Kapi and Rigi being brought forward. In the flickering light she could see them being painted white by the old men. Red stripes and dots were added across the bridge of their noses and across their foreheads as well as down each arm and leg. After they were appropriately adorned they joined the others in the strange gyrations that seemed to mimic a hunt for game. All participants in the circle carried a spear, with which they lunged and postured in time to the wailing music, as if attacking animals of prey. Kapi and Rigi danced in the same fashion, and she knew how proud they must be now that they were considered one with the men of their tribe.

The music suddenly changed to a different cadence and the older boys to be initiated were brought into the light. They sat on their heels while one of the elders, an old man who wore a long white beard and a black band around his forehead, moved slowly from one initiate to the next, whispering at length into their ears.

Dr. Henry had told Cassandra about some of the aboriginal rites of passage, but even he did not know the exact procedures. Intrigued to be the first to observe the initiation ceremony, she turned to ask Becky how long the ceremony would last and was startled to see the girl squatting very close behind her. The firelight from below glinted on the long, wicked blade she held in her hand. Becky was staring at her with an almost glazed look in her eyes. For one awful second Cassandra was frozen with dread, then quickly berated herself for being silly when Becky merely used the knife to cut away a branch that impeded her view.

"Look, there's Derek," Becky said softly, and Cassandra focused her attention on the dancers again as Derek emerged from the shadows. He absolutely towered over the aboriginals when he entered their circle and went down on one knee beside a large kettle. With one swift motion, he stripped his shirt off over his head.

Cassandra was surprised to see him dip a handful of the white paint and spread it across the sculpted muscles of his chest. He was accepted as one of the tribe, she realized, and she watched as he dotted the paint over his neck and face. Suddenly he looked straight up at her hiding place as if something had caught his attention. Dismayed, she ducked.

"I think Derek might have seen us," Becky hissed softly from behind her.

"We better get going, then," Cassandra answered, already inching backward away from the ledge. But she could not stop herself from venturing one last look. Derek now wore the brief loincloth of the aboriginal dancers, his long, muscular legs decorated with white paint. Her body reacted to the sheer power of his masculinity adorned in such primitive garb. He resembled some huge, magnificent god who had descended to earth to join the mortals. Her eyes riveted on him as he joined the shuffling spear dance. His molded muscles rippled with each thrust he made with the weapon, and she had to drag her eyes off him in order to turn away and follow Becky back to the camp.

"He's not going to like us coming here," Becky predicted as they made their way down the rocks.

"Do you think he'll be angry? We did nothing to disrupt the corroboree." Cassandra sounded more confident than she felt.

"I hope not, but I'm pretty sure he saw me."

At Derek's cabin, Becky fetched Joey from Big Roscoe's arms, then held the sleeping boy as she spoke again to Cassandra.

"If you like, tomorrow I can show you the caves where the aboriginals have done their artwork since time began. It's a wonderful place to explore. The paintings tell the stories of the creation."

Too intrigued to refuse, Cassandra nodded. "I'd like to go very much, Becky. Thank you."

She bade Becky good night, and as soon as the other girl was gone, Cassandra returned to her desk and hastily scribbled down her impressions of the corroboree. A short time later some instinct made her look up, and she was startled to find Derek standing in the doorway. His entire body was still painted white, and he still wore the brief brown loincloth.

"What the bloody hell do you think you're doing spying on the corroboree?" he demanded furiously. "Good God, you're an educated woman. I thought you'd have more sense. I told you flat out it was taboo for women!"

Startled by the extent of his anger, she rose in alarm. "I'm sorry. Becky thought it would be all right if no one saw us."

Derek's lean jaw worked with anger. "Then why the hell did she stand up where the dancers could see her? She knows good and well how strongly I feel about honoring tribal taboos, especially at the corroborces!"

"She stood up? I didn't know that. I guess she thought she was hidden from view."

His features still carved in a dark, forbidding scowl, Derek crossed the room with long, angry strides. He stopped in front of the washstand, poured water into the bowl, then splashed it over his face.

"I'm sorry. I really didn't mean to offend anyone," Cassandra offered quietly after a moment had passed.

"Well, you did, dammit. Don't break a taboo again, Cassie. I mean it, not for your thesis or any other reason."

"I won't. I promise." Cassandra hesitated, truly regretful. "Becky was going to take me to some caves tomorrow to view ancient paintings, but I won't go there if you think I shouldn't."

Derek turned from the washbowl, still holding a towel in his hand. It appeared that his burst of anger had dissipated somewhat, and Cassandra was distinctly relieved.

"The domed outer chamber isn't off limits," he told her, the hard edge gone from his voice, "but there are holy sites down some of the other passages that are strictly taboo. It's dangerous to go deeper into the mountain anyway because of sinkholes and quicksand traps, but Becky knows that."

He toweled off his chest as he finished, and Cassandra's gaze was drawn inexorably to the tiny scrap of leather covering his loins.

"I must say you look rather nice dressed like a Pitjantjatjara," she admitted, wetting dry lips.

Derek gave the slow grin that never failed to evoke tingling erotic responses deep inside her. "Would you like for me to wear it all the time?"

Amused at such an idea, Cassandra pretended to ponder his question. "I think maybe I would."

Derek came across the room and pulled her up from her chair.

"I will if you will," he muttered hoarsely in her ear, and Cassandra melted into his arms, acutely aware of his nakedness pressed so intimately against the front of her body. It had always been that way with him, from the very first time they had met. But now she knew how it felt when he touched her, when he was inside her. Already her body burned for him, as out of control as a wind-driven fire. She felt him lift her in his arms and carry her away to their bed, and she let him take charge of her senses, reeling under her love for him until she could think of nothing else.

# Chapter 27

The following afternoon Cassandra followed Becky up the rocky incline, glad she had worn her leather riding skirt and comfortable boots. Just after lunch they had left Joey once again in Big Roscoe's care and struck out on horseback for the caves. Derek had left earlier that morning when Kapi and Rigi had run into camp with a message from Moolonga, and she hoped he would be back by the time she and Becky had finished exploring the caves.

"We're almost there, Cassie," Becky called back to her. "It's just over this ridge."

Pausing momentarily to wipe her brow, Cassandra looked up at the bright blue sky. It was a wonderful day to get out in the sunshine and fresh air, and she was finding Becky to be a pleasant companion. Earlier, when they had stopped beside a small creek to rest and let their mounts drink, Becky had told her about growing up in Australia and some of the stories she knew about the aboriginals.

Cassandra began her climb again, and once at the

top found Becky peering into the mouth of a cave. The opening was long and low to the ground, and as Cassandra approached, Becky took a candle and matches out of the sack she carried over her shoulder.

"You'll have to bend over to get through the entrance, but once you get inside you can stand upright. I'll light the torches the aboriginals leave inside for their initiations so you can study the artwork better."

"Derek mentioned that there were offshoots of this cave that reach into the hillsides," Cassandra said as Becky lit the candle wick.

Becky nodded. "That's right. The passages intersect and lead all through the cliffs. There's no telling how many years the aboriginals have been coming here. It's one of the most sacred of all their dreaming sites, so we must be careful not to deface anything."

When Becky bent and entered the opening, Cassandra crouched and followed quickly, eager to examine the aboriginal art. Once she had negotiated the slanted sandy floor leading inside, she stood up in a large chamber about thirty feet square with a ceiling of perhaps seven or eight feet high. As Becky walked forward and fired a brush torch attached to the wall, Cassandra picked out two or three other passages leading farther into the darkness of the cavern.

"This picture is my favorite one," Becky said, her voice reverberating hollowly inside the stone chamber.

Cassandra walked over to the wall supporting the torch and found the entire rock painted with aboriginal figures.

"Why, this is wonderful," she murmured in delight, her eyes tracing the figures of men and animals. "One time back in America, Kapi and Rigi demonstrated for me their techniques for cave drawings, then later on the voyage here they explained about the songlines and dreaming sites. I find it all absolutely fascinating."

"I'll light a couple more of the torches so you can see the paintings on the other walls."

"The artist drew this fish so you could see his internal organs," Cassandra marveled. "See, he's painted the skeleton and heart. And they've done the same thing with some of the other animals. I haven't seen this technique before. I wish I could take a photographic image of these drawings to take back to the Smithsonian."

When she felt Becky's presence close behind her, she started to turn around and thank her for bringing her to such an exciting place. She was totally unprepared when she felt a rush of air and a heavy object connect hard against the side of her head. She cried out in pain as she was knocked against the wall. She crumpled to her knees in the sand, her head reeling from the brutal blow. When she was able to recover her confused thoughts, she found Becky standing over her, a pistol clutched in her fist.

"What happened?" Cassandra groaned, stunned

and disoriented. She placed her fingers to her aching temple. When she drew her hand back, she saw blood from her head wound.

"I like you, Cassie," Becky was saying slowly. "I really do, but don't you see that I can't just give up Derek? Not to you or any other woman. I went through too much trouble and planning to get him to come back home for me."

"I don't understand," Cassie mumbled, gritting her teeth against the jabbing pain in her skull. The blow had cut deep. She could feel the blood trickling down her neck. "What are you talking about?"

"You really had no idea what I was going to do, did you, Cassandra? I know you probably thought I was really stupid. A silly little uneducated girl from the outback, while you were so smart and sophisticated. That's all Derek could talk about when he came to see me that first night at Reeati. But I'm smarter than all the rest of you put together. I suppose you'll appreciate my cunning now that you're at my mercy."

Cassandra stared at her, appalled by the feral look glowing in Becky's dark blue eyes. Oh, Lord, they were alone, miles from camp. How could she not have seen this coming?

"Please, Becky, listen, I know how you must feel about Derek and me—"

"No, you don't!" Becky cried viciously. "You don't have any idea how I feel. Derek just up and left me one day. Went to sea without even saying good-bye. Do you realize how I suffered while he was gone?

How long I waited for him to come back for me? Four long, endless years of hoping and watching the road before I gave up on him and married Karl. But I never loved Karl, and I never wanted him. I took one of my bodyguards as my lover just because he resembled Derek. I would pretend he was Derek when he made love to me."

Becky gritted her teeth, and her words seemed to grate and grind with rage. "Then Derek came back again, and I went to him. He made love to me, and it was so good, so right, and I knew I couldn't live without him anymore. Then he found out about Karl and me, and he just sailed away as if we hadn't shared that wonderful night in his cabin." Her voice choked as if she were going to weep, then she got angrier. "That's when I decided I'd have to make him come back to me."

Horrified, Cassandra listened to Becky's insane ravings, thinking that she had to harness her dizziness enough to figure a way out of her predicament. If she wasn't still so woozy, she would try to run for the horses, but her head wound would make her unsteady on her feet. Becky would catch her before she got out the entrance. She had to keep talking or Becky might decide to finish her off with more blows from the gun she wielded.

"What do you mean? How did you get Derek to come back?" she asked, groaning slightly under the effort.

"My plan was brilliant, if I might be allowed to brag a bit. It worked wonderfully from the beginning and would have succeeded without a hitch if Derek hadn't seen fit to bring you back to Malmora with him. You see, I began feeding Derek's father lies about Joey being Derek's son. He wasn't, of course, he was Ray's, but I told Donald Courtland that Karl was abusing the poor baby because he was a bastard."

Becky came closer, and Cassandra could see the anger mottling her face even now as she told the story.

"I expected him to write Derek and tell him he was the father," Becky continued in a tight voice. "But no, Donald Courtland had to be the big hero himself. He told me he was going to the courts in Melbourne and try to get custody of Joey. But I couldn't let him do that because that would rob Joey of the Reeati inheritance. He's going to own all Karl's property someday as well as Malmora, once I get rid of you and can marry Derek."

*Oh, God help me,* Cassandra thought in horror, *Becky's going to kill me, right here, right now.*

"That's why I had Ray shoot the old man, but then after he was dead I realized his threats had been quite a fortuitous development. Derek hates Karl. I knew he would come home for vengeance if he thought Karl had murdered his father. That's when I began to intimate to Lily that Karl had done it. I harassed her at night by shooting her dogs and killing some of her livestock. It didn't take much to drive her off in search of her brother. I knew she would go after Derek, and I knew he would come back to find his father's killer. So I just sat back and waited. But he had to bring you and ruin everything." For a moment, Becky looked undecided. "I don't want to kill you, Cassandra, but don't you see, Derek's left me no other choice."

"I'll leave, Becky. Today. I'll go home to America where I belong, and I won't tell Derek where I'm going—"

"Don't you see? He'll follow you, no matter where you go. He thinks he's in love with you. That's why I can't let you live. He'll never get over you if you're alive and well someplace, but if you're dead, he'll forget you and love me the way he used to. I was going to simply shoot you, but now I'm afraid the aboriginals might hear the shot and come looking for us. Derek can't find out that I killed you. That would ruin everything."

Cassandra tensed with terror when Becky calmly drew the same long, deadly knife out of her knapsack that she had wielded at the corroboree.

"Close your eyes, Cassandra, and it won't be so bad." Becky suggested solicitously. "I don't want you to have to suffer, so I'm going to slit your jugular vein the way they do the sheep in Reeati's slaughtering house. I've watched the butcher do it. I promise you that it'll only take a moment or two for you to die."

"Derek will know it was you, Becky, he'll never forgive you if you kill me!" Her chest heaving with fear, Cassandra dug her fingers into the floor as she spoke and tightly clutched sand in her fist.

"He won't find your body, I assure you, no matter how hard he looks. I'll even join him in the search. I'll say you wandered off down these passages and got lost. There are sinkholes and quicksand all over these caverns. He'll never suspect me, just like you never suspected I was bringing you here today to kill you."

*She is crazy*, Cassandra thought, *and she's actually going to kill me if I don't do something quick.* As Becky came closer, the knife blade glinting, Cassandra hurled the sand into her eyes. Becky cried out but slashed out blindly with the long knife, and Cassandra screamed with pain as a deep gash sliced open behind her shoulder. Terrified, she lunged away and fled blindly into one of the dark passages.

"You're certain that Moolonga said Strassman's going to attack the camp today?"

From where they lay beside him behind the rocks, Kapi and Rigi nodded in affirmation. Derek frowned and peered down into the canyon where his men were hiding among the cliffs and craggy boulders while armed aboriginals manned the higher canyon walls. Everyone had been in place since early that morning when they had received Moolonga's warning.

Fearing an ambush, Derek kept his rifle at hand, his eyes peeled for any sign of movement at the mouth of the canyon. More than anything else, he wanted to know how Karl had discovered the back entrance to the camp. The passage through the complicated series of box canyons was known only to the aboriginals and now a few of the bushrangers, and it was too steep and rocky for easy traveling by horse. For that reason the pass had been left unguarded. If Moolonga hadn't alerted Derek to Strassman's plans, Strassman would have enjoyed complete surprise.

Derek wiped away the sweat beading his forehead, extremely uncomfortable with the whole situation. His intuition was screaming that something was wrong, that danger was lurking close by. His finger itched on the trigger. He had left enough men to guard the aboriginal women and children in the inner canyon, but if there was trouble before he could get back, they knew which caves would be the safest hiding places. He hoped to God that Cassandra and Becky would stay up in the sacred caves where Strassman's men couldn't get to them. Still, Derek was bloody nervous.

Licking sunburned lips, he looked straight up into the noonday sun. Moolonga had said Strassman's raid was to be a morning one. If so, they were late or Moolonga had misunderstood the plans. That idea alarmed Derek but would answer his continued misgivings about the ambush. In the rocks straight across from him he saw a sudden glint which he knew to be Robin's rifle barrel. The metallic flash disappeared when the man shifted position, and Derek returned his attention to the head of the canyon just as the first rider appeared in the rocky crevice.

Derek raised his field glasses and immediately picked out Strassman where he rode near the center of the mounted intruders. There were about twenty men altogether, each armed heavily with six-shooters and rifles. They had come to fight, and thanks to Moolonga, Derek was ready for them. He kept down until they gained the center of the canyon floor so Robin and the other bushrangers could ride through the crevice and close up their only escape route.

When the riders reached the rocks that had to be scaled to approach the back of the camp, Strassman called an order to dismount. Derek could wait no longer. He stood and stepped into sight.

"Hold it right there, Strassman! We've got rifles beaded in on every damn one of you," Derek shouted.

Strassman jerked around in shock. For a moment no one moved, then Strassman ducked low and went for his gun. Derek fired his rifle, but Strassman rolled away, using his horse as a shield. Pandemonium broke out as Strassman's bodyguards began to shoot up at the cliffs where the bushrangers were opening fire. The men trapped below tried to mount their spooked and skittish horses, and several men fell as bullets rained down on them from every side.

As the bodyguards fled back the way they had come, Derek concentrated on keeping Strassman in his sights, determined he wouldn't escape this time. While he scuttled and slid down the loose rocky incline, Strassman finally managed to regain his saddle. He jerked the reins hard, trying to turn his stallion in retreat. Derek raised his pistol, but before he could pull the trigger, a wooden spear came in swift, accurate flight from somewhere high above them in the rocks. The sharpened staff struck Strassman midchest and sliced straight through his heart. For one instant Strassman sat still in the saddle, his face locked with shock, then slowly reeled backward off his horse and lay on his side in the dirt while his men continued to gallop away under sporadic fire.

Derek ran the rest of the way to him, knelt, and pulled him up by his lapels. "Tell me why you killed Father, damn you. He never did a goddamn thing to you. What did you want from him?" Strassman gazed up at him out of pain-glazed eyes.

"I didn't do it," Strassman muttered, blood running from the corner of his mouth. "I didn't kill him—"

"Don't lie to me. Becky told me you killed Father and ran Lily off Malmora."

Strassman reached up and grabbed the front of Derek's shirt. "No, no, you're wrong, don't you see? . . . it's Becky, she's behind everything." He choked on the blood accumulated in his mouth, then grunted hoarsely. "She came back—to Re-eati—last night—she told me how to come through the canyons this way—she said you'd never expect it—"

"I don't believe you," Derek said angrily. "Becky would never betray me like that."

"Don't you see? She's different now—she's gone

crazy with jealousy since you came back with Cassie—she hates Cassie because you love her—" Strassman's eyes rolled back, and Derek stared down at the dying man, trying desperately to make sense of Karl's accusations. But Becky was one of the few whites who knew the route through the canyons. Puzzle pieces he could never quite fit together in his mind began to fly into place. God help them, Becky was the key factor in everything that had happened. She had been the one to tell Lily about Karl's villainy, she had summoned Derek to Reeati the first night, she was behind everything. And oh, God, she had taken Cassie up to the caves!

Disregarding the fighting still going on at the mouth of the canyon, he scrambled his way to where Kapi and Rigi waited with the horses. He swung into the saddle and spurred the horse into a gallop. He had to get to the caves! He had to get to Cassie!

# Chapter 28

Cassandra felt her way blindly along the dank, mildewed stone, trying desperately to see through the oppressive blackness. Her shoulder was nearly numb now, and bleeding so heavily that her sleeve was soaked. Her temple ached so violently she could barely think. When she stopped to listen, she heard scuffing sounds as Becky hesitantly followed her down the passage.

"Cassie, you're wasting your time, you know. You can't get away from me. I have all day to find you because I've arranged for Karl to keep Derek busy in the canyons."

As Becky's voice echoed in the darkness, her threats bouncing eerily off the moldy walls, Cassandra struggled to untie her neckerchief. Biting her lip against the agony of the slash wound, she bound the cloth tightly around her shoulder. She paused and heaved in several deep breaths in an attempt to clear her muddled brain.

The cavern was pitch-black. At least she could hide from Becky, if she didn't make a sound to give herself away. She stumbled farther down into the depths of the cavern, sightlessly sliding her palms along the rough, pitted surface of the rock. When she glanced back again, her heart fell when she saw a faint glimmer in the dark behind her. Lord help her, Becky had a torch!

Cassandra moved faster, continually looking back to gauge the distance between her and her stalker. As she hurried around a slight turn in the tunnel, the floor suddenly dropped from beneath her feet. A short scream tore from her throat as she fell, but the cry ended abruptly when she landed thigh-deep in a pit of soft sand. She tried to wade out and couldn't seem to move her feet, and the terrifying truth hit her like a brick. Oh, God, quicksand!

Her mind cringed and trembled with horror, then quickly plummeted into pure panic. She struggled frantically and found that her violent jerking only made her sink faster. She was waist-deep in the muck now, and she could feel the sand still giving way beneath her weight.

*Oh, God,* she thought wildly, *what had Dr. Henry taught her about the deadly substance when they were in Peru?* All she could remember was that the more she fought the pit, the faster she would go down. Hysteria rose in her throat as the awful mire slowly sucked her into its belly. Fear such as she had never felt before locked around her, overwhelming and immobilizing.

"Help!" she cried shrilly. "Oh, God, please help me!"

Within minutes Becky's face appeared at the edge of the pit. The flickering light of the torch cast grotesque shadows across her face, turning her smile into the grimace of a gargoyle.

"I must say, Cassie, that you're being most cooperative in your own demise. Now I don't even have to worry about disposing of your body."

"Please, Becky, help me, I'm sinking so fast. I'll go away, I'll leave Derek, and I'll make sure he'll never find me, please don't let me die this way—" A sob caught in the back of her throat.

"He would never stay with me as long as you're alive. Once you're out of the way, we'll only have Karl to worry about. Who knows? Maybe Karl's already dead. If Derek kills him today, I'll be a widow." She smiled, as if very pleased with herself. "You see, I showed Karl how he could come through the back canyons and surprise Derek. Then I made sure Moolonga knew about the plan so Derek could be waiting in ambush for him. You see, I'm not the least bit stupid, like you thought. And now I don't even have to kill you. I've never murdered anyone myself because Ray was always willing to do it for me. All I have to do is sit here and wait for you to go under."

Becky hunkered down above the hellish pit, and Cassandra sobbed with despair because she saw no compassion, no human feeling in the other woman's eyes, only the insane light of cold, grim satisfaction.

Derek slowed his horse when he saw Becky's palomino pony still tied at the base of the cliff alongside

Cassandra's horse. They were still in the sacred caves. He leaped from the saddle and glanced back down the rocks to where Kapi and Rigi were following him on foot. They were still a good distance behind, and he didn't wait for them to catch up but scrambled up the steep rocks, his heart thundering with fear.

There was no sign of the women outside the mouth of the cavern, but as soon as he ducked underneath the low-hanging entrance he saw that torches had been lit to illuminate the main chamber. No one was in sight, but Becky's knapsack lay in the sand near the sacred wall of ancient paintings. He pulled his gun.

"Cassie! Where are you?" His cry reverberated in waves down the low tunnels.

Somewhere in the bowels of the cavern Cassandra screamed for help. Oh, God, where was she? How could he ever find her?

"Help me, Derek! Help! Help!"

Her terrified cries led him into the right tunnel. Appalled by the shrill horror in her voice, he ran down the passage toward a dim glow of light. "Cassie! Keep talking so I can find you!"

"Hurry, hurry! Becky's got a gun!"

When Derek rounded the last curve of the passage, he came face-to-face with a scene from his worst nightmare. Becky stood with a pistol leveled directly at his chest while Cassandra struggled neck-deep in quicksand just behind her.

"Get the hell out of my way, Becky," he warned harshly. "Don't make me shoot you."

"No. I'll shoot her if you come any closer!" Becky pressed her back against the wall and swiveled her gun until the barrel pointed straight at Cassandra's head.

"Becky, don't do this. I know what you've done. It's over. Karl's dead. Killing her won't make any difference. Give me the gun now, and the law'll go easier on you."

"No! I'd rather die than go to jail!" Becky choked on a sob. "I'd rather her die right here than to be with you. You're mine—you've always been mine!"

The thick gray muck was creeping up over Cassandra's ears, forcing her to raise her chin to keep her nose and mouth clear.

Becky's revolver was still trained on Cassandra. Becky was an expert shot. If Derek rushed her, the gun would go off. Oh, God, he had to get her gunsights off Cassandra!

"Captain! Miss Cassie!"

As the cries of Kapi and Rigi echoed down to them from the tunnel behind him, Becky turned slightly in surprise and Derek made his move. He rushed her, grabbing the barrel of the gun just as it went off. The bullet grazed his thigh with a thrust of red-hot pain, but he wrested the gun from her, then backhanded her hard enough to send her flying brutally against the wall. She fell heavily, then struggled to her feet and ran back toward the front chamber. Derek let her go, thinking only of getting

Cassandra out of the pit. He groaned with horror when he realized how close she was to disappearing into the quicksand forever.

"Oh, God, God, Cassie, hold on, hold on!" He fumbled desperately with his belt. When the buckle finally gave, he jerked it off and flung the strap out across the mire to Cassandra.

"Grab it, Cassie, you've got to grab it! Get it, dammit, get it!"

"I can't reach it," she cried weakly.

Desperately, Derek jerked back the belt, then leaned out as far as he could, realizing how close he was to losing her. He tossed the belt to her again, then moaned with relief when he saw her fingers pierce the thick gray mire and catch hold of the strap. He forced his voice to sound calm. "Don't let go, Cassie, do you hear me? Get your other hand on it, and hold on!"

Terrified that he might inadvertently jerk the lifeline out of her grasp in his haste to get her out, he forced himself to tow her slowly toward him. He locked his jaw with effort, leaning out farther and farther until the quicksand gave way and she began to move toward solid ground. It seemed an eternity before she was close enough to him to grasp her shirt. He jerked her bodily out of the deadly substance and crushed her in his arms.

"You're all right now, I've got you," he managed hoarsely, sick with the realization of how close she had been to death. She clutched him tightly, and he held her trembling body as she wept uncontrollably against his chest.

Kapi and Rigi sat on their haunches in the main dome of the cave, listening for someone to answer their calls. They were still breathless from their long run.

"We have to help Miss Cassie," Kapi whispered to his brother. "The captain say Miss Becky gonna kill her."

"Cannot go deeper in sacred mountain," Rigi replied, his eyes wide and frightened. "It be forbidden."

"But Miss Cassie in danger."

Kapi looked at his twin for a brief moment, not sure what he should do. There had been no answer to his shout. He jumped up quickly when he heard footsteps running in one of the passages. Seconds later Becky Strassman rushed out of the cave, and Kapi froze, then stared at her in fear. Her long reddish hair was all tangled and dirty, and her mouth was bloody. Kapi took a wary step backward when he saw the long hunting knife in her hand.

His brother was braver. As the white woman tried to dart past them, Rigi grabbed her skirt. "Where Miss Cassie be?" Rigi cried.

To Kapi's sudden horror she swung the knife out wildly, opening a long gash across his brother's bare chest. Rigi stared down at the blood oozing out of his body as if shocked she had actually cut him, then he crumpled weakly to the ground.

As the crazed woman ducked out of the cave, Kapi knelt by his twin. Rigi was crying and holding both palms over the gaping wound. Blood flowed freely between his small fingers, and when Kapi saw his brother's life leaking from his body, rage such as he had never known before leaped like flames in his heart. He jumped to his feet and ran after the evil woman.

By the time Kapi reached the cliff, Becky had mounted her palomino and was galloping down the narrow canyon floor. He couldn't let her get away! Captain Derek had to punish her for what she had done! He had to stop her!

He ran as fast as he could along the edge of the rocks that towered over her escape route. As she slowed her mount to enter the narrow rock fissure which led out of the canyon, he jerked his boomerang from his belt. He stood very still, as he had done so many times before when hunting, then took steady aim and hurled the weapon with every ounce of his strength.

The sharp-edged boomerang curved end over end in graceful, silent flight toward its target, and Kapi gave the tribal yell as his club struck true. The fleeing woman was knocked from her horse, Kapi's boomerang embedded deeply in the back of her head. She lay facedown in the dirt, and Kapi sobered when he realized he had killed her. He had not meant to take her life. He had only wanted to stop her escape. He had never killed a human being. He felt sick inside, even though she was bad and had tried to kill Rigi and Miss Cassie.

When he heard the captain's voice calling to him from the sacred caves, he turned and ran back to where Derek and Miss Cassie were kneeling beside Rigi. Miss Cassie was crying and her clothes were all wet and gray and covered with blood.

"Rigi's going to be all right, Kapi."

Kapi hardly heard the captain's words as he fell to his knees beside his injured brother. Miss Cassie was cradling Rigi's head in her lap and trying to comfort him, but Kapi could see blood dripping off her arm, too. He watched Derek strip off his shirt and tie it around Rigi's chest. "The cut's not too deep, thank God. Did Becky do this to him?"

Kapi nodded, his lips trembling. "She be down there now. She dead. I use boomerang to stop her."

"Oh, God," Derek said, standing up and peering down the canyon. "Are you sure she's dead?"

Kapi nodded, and his eyes filled with tears when he thought how he had snuffed the life out of the woman. Miss Cassie put her arm around him. She was crying.

"She tried to kill me, Kapi," she whispered, "and she hurt Rigi."

"It's all right, Kapi, you had to try to stop her." The captain placed his hands on Kapi's shoulder as he spoke the words, and Kapi felt better. He watched Derek lean down and carefully gather Rigi into his arms. "Kapi, you help Cassie get down to the horses while I carry Rigi. We've got to get them both to a doctor. Come on, we better hurry."

Kapi saw how weak Miss Cassie was and how upset Derek was over what Miss Becky had done to her, and he felt better about killing the white woman. She was surely evil, a *mamu* set free upon the earth to torment his people. She had entered the holy caves and done wickedness in the most sacred of dreaming sites. Tjilkamata and the other elders would be pleased that Kapi had exacted vengeance on an enemy of the Pitjantjatjaras.

# Epilogue

Cassandra stood alone on the veranda of Malmora and gazed out into the dark, quiet night. Although several weeks had passed since Becky Strassman had cold-heartedly stood by and watched her sink into the quicksand, she was still gripped by terror when she remembered how helpless she had felt in those awful moments trapped in the deadly quagmire. Goose bumps rose and rippled over every inch of her flesh, and she was glad when Derek came out onto the porch behind her.

"I brought you a wrap. It's chilly out tonight," he said, draping a warm shawl around her shoulders. He enclosed her in his arms and drew her back against him. "How's your shoulder feel today?"

"It's better, I think, but I'm still sore." Cassandra lifted the sling slightly and felt the familiar tingle of pain. "Did you check on Rigi before you came out?"

"He's asleep, and Kapi and Big Roscoe are playing hide and seek with Joey in the living room."

Cassandra leaned contentedly against her husband's solid frame. Since the trauma of her ordeal, she had kept close to Derek and the children, where she felt safe. She hadn't wanted to go anywhere or do anything.

"I'm so sorry, Cassie," Derek whispered softly. "I got you into all this mess. I should have seen through Becky from the beginning, before she could hurt you."

"It's not your fault. I didn't suspect her motives, either," Cassandra reminded him. He had apologized for Becky countless times, but he had saved her life with literally seconds to spare.

"I was stupid not to have seen the change in her, but she was never cold and calculating like that when I knew her before. I don't know what happened to change her so much. Unless she just couldn't accept my love for you." He heaved a deep sigh. "I've just about gotten my father's business matters taken care of, and I've decided to leave Malmora under the care of John and Robin and some of the others who have nowhere else to go. We can sail for Virginia within the week, if you like."

Cassandra's heart soared at the news of their imminent departure, but she wanted very much for Derek to be happy, too. "Do you want to stay here on Malmora, Derek? Do you want to take over for your father?"

"I don't know. Maybe someday I'll want to return. But I never loved ranching the way he did. I love the sea, and I want us to live wherever you'll be most content. If that's Virginia, that's fine with me, providing we're both not still wanted by the law there."

Cassandra smiled, but her mood remained serious, as it had been since Becky's attempt on her life. "I need to go home and find out what has happened to Twin Pines. If the Yankees have destroyed it, there's nothing left for me there other than my brothers. I want to see Harte especially, and apologize for some of the things I did to him. And I want to find out if Stuart made it through the war. Maybe he'll be home now that the fighting is over."

"We'll find him. I want to see Lily, too. She might want to come home to Malmora to live, but I doubt it. Her place is with Harte, just as mine is with you."

"Isn't it strange, Derek? The way we all went along, living our lives thousands of miles apart, then one day purely by accident Harte and Lily met and fell in love. Then you came along and kidnapped me."

Derek gave a low laugh. "You're never going to let me forget that one little mistake, are you?"

"No," she whispered, her voice catching in her throat, "because I'm so grateful you took me with you."

Derek turned her in his arms and kissed her tenderly, and Cassandra reached up with her good arm and touched his bearded cheek. "There's something else, Derek. I've thought about this for days, but I'm not sure how you'll feel about it. I know he's not your son, but I'd love to take Joey back to America with us. I know how you felt about Karl, and Becky, too, but now they're both gone. He's got no one, Derek, and he's such a sweet little thing. I already love him, and I do so want a child of my own."

Derek cradled her face between his palms and smiled down into her eyes. "Then he'll be the child we can never have, and we'll love him and raise him as if he's our own. He'll never have to know what happened here. I want you to forget it, too, Cassie, because I'll never let anyone hurt you again, I swear it."

His voice was so tender, his words so welcome in her heart, that tears welled in Cassandra's eyes. "Oh, Derek, I do love you so."

Derek pulled her close and stroked her hair. To her surprise he gave a low chuckle. "There's one thing we won't ever have to worry about, luv. Big Roscoe will make a dandy nanny for Joey—a bit unconventional maybe, but he absolutely dotes on that little boy."

Cassandra smiled, thinking of the gentle giant and the way he handled Joey with such kindness. "Now if we could only get Kapi and Rigi to return to America with us, everything would be perfect."

"I don't think they'll agree. They really belong with their people. They'll be happy here, especially now that Karl's men will no longer be hunting the aboriginals. The Pitjantjatjaras will always have sanctuary on Malmora as long as I own it."

When Derek's lips touched her forehead, Cassandra smiled, warm pleasure flooding through her body. Her eyes closed as he kissed her again, and she felt more at peace with herself than she had in a very long time. Even if Twin Pines was gone and her old life back in Virginia destroyed, she had a new life now with a man she adored. Their future promised to be filled with happiness and joy, and who could ever hope for anything more wonderful?

ANNOUNCING THE
# TOPAZ FREQUENT READERS CLUB
## COMMEMORATING TOPAZ'S 1 YEAR ANNIVERSARY!

### THE MORE YOU BUY, THE MORE YOU GET

Redeem coupons found here and in the back of all new Topaz titles for FREE Topaz gifts:

Send in:

 2 coupons for a free TOPAZ novel (choose from the list below);
- ☐ **THE KISSING BANDIT**, Margaret Brownley
- ☐ **BY LOVE UNVEILED**, Deborah Martin
- ☐ **TOUCH THE DAWN**, Chelley Kitzmiller
- ☐ **WILD EMBRACE**, Cassie Edwards

 4 coupons for an "I Love the Topaz Man" on-board sign

 6 coupons for a TOPAZ compact mirror

 8 coupons for a Topaz Man T-shirt

Just fill out this certificate and send with original sales receipts to:

**TOPAZ FREQUENT READERS CLUB-1ST ANNIVERSARY**
Penguin USA • Mass Market Promotion; Dept. H.U.G.
375 Hudson St., NY, NY 10014

Name_____

Address_____

City_____State_____Zip_____

Offer expires 1/31 1995

This certificate must accompany your request. No duplicates accepted. Void where prohibited, taxed or restricted. Allow 4-6 weeks for receipt of merchandise. Offer good only in U.S., its territories, and Canada.